D0249901

New York Times Bestselling Author

MAISEY YATES

Claiming the Rancher's Heir
&
Rancher's Wild Secret

Recycling programs
for this product may
not exist in your area.

ISBN-13: 978-1-335-15400-2

Claiming the Rancher's Heir & Rancher's Wild Secret

Copyright © 2020 by Harlequin Books S.A.

Claiming the Rancher's Heir
Copyright © 2020 by Maisey Yates

Rancher's Wild Secret
First published in 2019. This edition published in 2020.
Copyright © 2019 by Maisey Yates

This edition published by arrangement with Harlequin Books S.A.

For questions and comments about the quality of this book,
please contact us at CustomerService@Harlequin.com.

Harlequin Enterprises ULC
22 Adelaide St. West, 40th Floor
Toronto, Ontario M5H 4E3, Canada
www.Harlequin.com

Printed in U.S.A.

CONTENTS

CLAIMING THE RANCHER'S HEIR

Chapter 1

Creed Cooper was a cowboy. A rich, successful cowboy from one of the most well-regarded families in Logan County. He also happened to be tall, muscular and in possession of the kind of good looks a lot of women liked.

As a result, nearly nothing—or no one—was off-limits to him.

No one except Wren Maxfield.

Maybe that was why every time he looked at her his hands itched.

To unwind that tight bun from her hair. To make that mouth, which was always flattened in disapproval—at least around him—get soft and sexy and get all over his body.

And he had that itch a lot, considering he and Wren were the representatives for their respective families' vineyards. Rivals, in fact.

And she hated him.

She hated him so much that when she saw him her eyes flared with a particular kind of fire.

Fair enough, since he couldn't really stand her either.

But somehow, years ago, a piece of that dislike inside him had twisted and caught hard in his gut and turned into an intensity of another kind entirely.

He was obsessed.

Obsessed with the idea he might be able to use that fire in her eyes to burn up the sheets between them.

Instead, he had to listen to her heels clicking on the floor as she paced around the showroom of Cowboy Wines, looking like a smug cat, making him wait to hear whatever plan it was she'd come to tell him about.

"Are you listening to me?" she asked suddenly, her green cat eyes getting sharp.

She was dressed in a tight-fitting red dress that fell to the top of her knees. It had a high, wide neck, and while it didn't show a lot of skin, it hugged her full breasts so tight it didn't leave a lot to the imagination.

Even if it had, his imagination was damn good. And it was willing to work for Wren. Overtime.

She had on those ridiculous spiked heels, too. Red, like the dress. He wanted to see her in only those heels.

He wasn't into prissy women. Not generally. He liked a more practical girl. A cowgirl who would be at home on his ranch.

Wren looked like she never left her family show-room, all glass walls and wrought iron furniture. Max-field Vineyards was the premier wine brand for people who were up their own asses.

And still, he wanted her.

That might be her greatest sin.

That she tested control he'd had firmly leashed for the last eighteen years and made him want to send it right to hell as he burned in her body.

Of all the reasons to hate Wren Maxfield, wanting her and not being able to do a damn thing to make himself stop was number one on the list.

He looked around the Cowboy Wines showroom, the barrels with glass tabletops on them, the heavy, distressed beams that ran the length of the room.

And then there was him: battered jeans and cowboy boots, a hat for good measure.

Everything a woman like Wren would hate.

A testament to just why there was no reason to carry a burning torch for her fine little body.

Too bad his own body was a dumbass.

"I wasn't listening at all," he said, making sure to drawl it. As slow as possible. He was rewarded with a subtle flare of heat in those eyes. "Make it more interesting next time, Wren. Maybe do a dance."

"The only dancing I'll ever do is on your grave, Creed."

The sparring sent a kick of lust through him. They did this every time they were in a room together. Every damn time. No matter that he knew he shouldn't indulge it.

But hell, he was afraid the alternative was stripping her naked and screwing her against the nearest wall, and that wasn't a real option.

So verbal sparring it was.

"What did I die of?" he asked. "Boredom?"

Those eyes shot sparks at him. "It was tragic. You were found with a high heel protruding out of your chest." Her magic lips curved upward and he felt it like she'd pressed them against his neck.

"Any suspects so far?"

"Your own smart mouth. Are you going to listen to me or not?"

"You're already here. So am I. Might as well."

He leaned back in his chair and, for effect, put his boots up on the table.

Her top lip curled up into a sneer, and that thrilled him just as much as if she'd crossed the room to straddle his lap. Okay, maybe not just as much, but he loved that he got to her.

"Fantastic. As you know, things at Maxfield Vineyards are changing. My father is no longer the owner. Instead, my sister Emerson, her husband, Holden, and our sister Cricket and I now have ownership.

"This plan is Emerson's idea. To be clear. As she is the person who oversees our broader brand." She waved a hand in the air as if to distance herself yet further from whatever she was about to say. "I had to defer to her on the subject. She doesn't think a rivalry is beneficial for any of us. She thinks we should join forces. A large-scale event where both of our wines are represented. As you know, wine tours and the whole wine trail in general have become increasingly popular."

"A rising tide lifts all boats and gets more people drunk?"

"Basically," she said.

"I'm not really sure I see the benefit to me," he said. "Seeing as everything is going well here."

"Everyone wants to expand," she said, looking at him as if he had grown a second head.

"Do they?"

"Yes," she responded. "Everyone."

"Well, the way I see it, our business is running well. We have just the right amount of staff, every family member has a position in the company, and it supports us very well. At a certain point, Wren, more is more. And that's it."

She looked at him, clearly dumbfounded. There were very definite and obvious differences between the Cooper and Maxfield families. The Coopers might be wealthy, but they liked their winery to reflect their roots. Down-home. A Western flare.

In the early days, his father had been told that there was no way he would ever be successful unless he did something to class up his image. He had refused. Digging in deeper to the cowboy theme was ultimately why they had become so successful. There was no point in competing with fancy-pants places like the Maxfields'. It wasn't the Coopers' way.

Joining up with the Maxfields made even less sense than trying to emulate them, in his opinion.

"Come on," she said. "You're ambitious, Creed, don't pretend otherwise."

And that was where she might have him. Because he didn't like to back down from a challenge. In fact, he quite liked a challenge in general. That she was issuing one now made him wonder if she was just baiting him. Taunting him.

He wasn't even sure he cared. All he knew was that he instantly wanted to take her up on it.

There was something incredibly sexy about her commitment to knowing her enemy.

"What exactly are you proposing?"

"I want to have a large event featuring all of the wineries in the area. A wine festival. For Christmas."

"That's ambitious. And it's too early to talk about Christmas."

"All the stores would disagree, Creed. Twinkle lights are out and about."

"Ask me if I care."

"I'd like to do a soft launch, a large party at Maxfield in the next month," she continued as if he hadn't spoken. "We'll invite our best clients. Can you imagine? The buzz we'll make joining forces?"

"Oh, you mean because everybody knows how profoundly our families dislike each other?" He paused for a moment. "How profoundly *we* dislike each other?"

It wasn't a secret. They were never civil to each other. They never tried to be.

"Yes," she said. "That."

"And how exactly do you think we're going to get through this without killing each other?"

She looked all cheerful and innocent. "Look on the bright side. If I do kill you, you'll get that dance you wanted so badly."

"Well. A silver lining to every cloud, I guess."

"I like to think so. Are you in?"

The only thing worse than giving in to the attraction he had for her would be hurting a business opportunity for it. He didn't let other people control him. Not in any way.

Least of all Wren Maxfield.

And that meant he'd do it. No matter how much he'd rather roll in a pit of honey and lie down on an anthill.

"How is this going to work? Logistically. I'm not going to roll up to your event in a suit."

"I didn't think you would. I thought you might be able to bring your rather…rustic charm." The way she said *rustic* and *charm* implied that she felt the former did not go with the latter.

He smiled. "It goes with me wherever I go."

"Do you have to wear a hat?" She wrinkled her nose.

"That is nonnegotiable," he said, reaching up and flicking the cowboy hat's brim with his forefinger.

"I figured as much." She sniffed. "Well. I can accept that."

"You have no choice. We'll provide the food. Barbecue."

"You really don't have to do that."

"I am not standing at a fancy party with nothing but raw fish on a cracker to eat. And anyway, if you want my clients, you better have meat."

"With wine."

"Hey. We work hard to break the stereotype that cowboys only like beer. I myself enjoy a nice red with my burger."

"Unacceptable."

His gaze flickered over her curves. That body. *Damn* what he'd like to do to that body. "Too repressed to handle a little change, Wren?"

Color flooded her cheeks. Rage. "I am not. I just don't like terrible ideas."

"It's not a terrible idea. It's *on brand.*" He said the last bit with no small amount of self-deprecation, and a smirk.

"Whatever. I don't care what you like with what. Really. I just want to know if I can count on you to help me put this together."

"You got it."

"I look forward to this new venture," she said. She smiled, which was strange, and then she extended her hand. He only looked at it for a moment. Then he reached his own out, clasped hers and shook it.

Her skin was soft, like he had known it would be. Wren was the kind of woman who had never done a day's worth of manual labor in her whole life. Not that she didn't work hard, she did. And he knew enough about the inner workings of a job like theirs to be well aware that it took a hell of a lot of mental energy. It was just that he also worked on his own ranch when he wasn't working on the wine part of things, and he knew that his own hands were rough as hell.

She was too soft. Too cosseted. Snobby. Uppity. Repressed—unless she was giving him a dressing-down with that evil tongue of hers.

And damn he liked it all, as much as he hated it.

The thing was, even if he'd been a different man, a man who had the heart it took to be with someone forever, to do the whole marriage-and-kids thing, if he'd been a man who hadn't been destroyed a long time ago, it wouldn't be her.

Couldn't be her.

A kick of lust shot through him, igniting at the point where their hands still touched. Wren dropped her hold on him quickly. "Well. Good. I guess we'll be seeing a lot more of each other, then."

"I guess we will. Looking forward to it."

"Dear reader," Wren muttered as she walked back into the family winery showroom. "She was not looking forward to seeing more of his arrogant, annoying, infuriating, ridiculous…"

"I'm sorry, what?"

Wren stopped muttering when her sister Emerson popped up from where she was sitting.

"I was muttering," Wren replied.

"I know. What exactly were you muttering about?"

"I was muttering," she restated. "Which means it wasn't exactly meant to be understood."

"Well. I'm nosy."

"I just had my meeting with Creed."

"Oh," Emerson said, looking her over. "Huh."

"What?"

"I'm checking you for burn marks."

"Why? Because he's *Satan*?"

"No. Because the two of you generate enough heat to leave scorched earth."

She narrowed her eyes at her sister. "You'd better be talking about anger."

Regrettably, anger was not the only thing that Creed Cooper made her feel.

Oh, Creed Cooper *enraged* her. She typically found herself wanting to punch him in the face within the first thirty seconds of his company.

He was an asshole. He was insufferable.

He was…without a doubt the sexiest man she had ever encountered in her entire life and when she woke up at night in a cold sweat with her pulse pounding between her thighs, it was always because she had been dreaming of him.

"Yeah," Emerson said. "Anger."

"What?" Wren snapped.

"It's just… I don't know. The two of you seem to be building up to some kind of hate-sex situation."

Wren shifted, hating that she felt so seen in the moment. "No."

"Why not?" Emerson asked.

"Several reasons. The first being that he disgusts me." Her cheeks turned pink when the bold-faced lie slipped out of her mouth.

"Is that what the kids are calling it these days?"

"You would know. You're...*on fleek* on the internet. Or whatever."

"That is an incredibly passé bit of pop culture there, Wren. And I think we both know disgust is not what he makes you feel."

She pulled a face. "Can we talk about business?"

"Sure, sure. So, what was your conclusion?"

"He's a dick."

"Yeah. I know. But what about the initiative?"

"Oh. He's on board. So I guess we'll be having a party. But he's insisting on barbecuing."

"Barbecuing?" Emerson asked, her sister's hand rising upward, bent at the wrist, her fingers curled.

"Yes." Wren lifted her nose. "Beef."

"I guess that's what we get for joining forces with cowboys."

"Says the woman who's married to one."

Emerson shrugged. "Sure. But I don't let him plan my parties. He has many uses, the primary one being that he allows me to do good work and save horses."

"Save horses?"

She batted her lashes. "Ride a cowboy?"

"For the love of God, Emerson."

"What? He's hot."

She was not here for her sister's smug married-frequent-sex glow. Emerson had very narrowly escaped an arranged marriage with a man their father had chosen for her. The whole thing with her husband, Holden, had been dramatic, had involved no small amount of blackmail and subterfuge, and had somehow ended in true love.

Wren still didn't quite understand it.

Wren also didn't understand why she felt so beset by her Creed fantasies. Or why she was so jealous of Emerson's glow.

Wren herself wasn't overly sexual.

It wasn't her thing. She'd had a few boyfriends, and she enjoyed the physical closeness that came with sex. That much was true. It had been a while since she'd dated anybody though, because she had been so consumed with her job at Maxfield Vineyards. She enjoyed what she did for work quite a lot more than she enjoyed sex, in point of fact.

Her dreams about illicit sex with Creed were better than any sex she'd ever had, and she found that completely disturbing.

Also, proof that her subconscious didn't know anything. Nothing at all.

"Great," Wren said. "Good for you and your libido. But I'm talking about wine, which is far more important than how hot your husband is."

"To you," Emerson said. "The hotness of my husband is an entirely consuming situation for me."

"Anyway," Wren said, her voice firm. "We get our joint party."

"But with beef."

"Yes," Emerson said. "And then hopefully in a few months we'll have the larger event, which we can presell tickets to. Hopefully we can bring a lot of people into town if we plan it right."

"I do like the way you're thinking," Wren said. "It's going to be great," she added, trying to affirm it for herself.

"It will be," Emerson agreed. "Have you talked to Cricket about it at all?"

Cricket was their youngest sister. She had been... She had been incredibly wounded about the entire scandal with their father.

The situation with their parents had gone from bad to worse. Or maybe it was just that they were all now aware of *how* bad it had always been.

The reason Holden had come to Maxfield Vineyards in the first place had been to get revenge on their father for seducing Holden's younger sister and leaving her emotionally broken after a miscarriage.

After that, Wren and her sisters found out their father had carried on multiple affairs over the years, all with young women who were vulnerable, with so much less power than he had. It was a despicable situation. Holden had blackmailed Emerson into marriage in order to gain a piece of Maxfield Vineyards, but he and Emerson had ultimately fallen in love. They'd ousted their father, who was currently living out of the country. Their mother remained at the estate. Technically, the two of them were still married.

Wren hoped that wouldn't be the case for much longer. Her poor mother had put up with so much. She deserved better.

They all did.

But while most of the changes that had occurred around the winery really were good things, their sister Cricket had taken the new situation hard. She had a different relationship with the place than the rest of them did. Cricket had been a late-in-life baby for their parents. An accident, Wren thought. And it had seemed like no one had the energy to deal with her. She'd been left to her own devices in a way that Emerson and Wren had not been.

As a result, Cricket was ever so slightly feral.

Wren found her mostly charming, but in the current situation, she didn't know how to talk to her. Didn't know what Cricket wanted or needed from them.

"She's been… You know," Emerson said. "Cricket. In that she's not really talking about anything substantial, and she's been quite scarce. She doesn't seem to be interested in any of the winery's new ventures."

"It's a lot of change."

"True," Emerson said. "But she's not a child. She's twenty-one."

"No," Wren said. "She's not a child. But can you imagine how much more difficult this would have been for you ten years ago?"

"I know," Emerson said softly. "It is different for us. It's different to have a little bit more perspective on the world and on yourself. I think she feels very betrayed."

"Hopefully she'll eventually embrace the winery. She can have a role here. I know she's smart. And I know she would do a good job, whatever Dad thought about her."

Emerson shook her head. "I don't think that Dad thought about her at all."

"Well, we will," Wren said.

The Maxfields had never been a close family in the way people might think of a close family. It wasn't like there had been intimate family dinners and game nights and things like that. But they had been in each other's pockets for their entire lives. Working together, deciding which direction to take their business. Their father was a difficult bastard, that was true. But he had entrusted his daughters with an extreme amount of responsibility when it came to the winery. It was weird now, to have the shape of things be so different. To have everything be up to them.

"Everything will be fine," Wren said. "It's already better, even if it is a little difficult."

Emerson nodded. "You're right. It's better. And things will only get even better from here."

"You agreed to do *what*?"

Creed looked at his older brother, Jackson, who had an expression on his face that suggested Creed might've said he planned to get out of the wine business and start raising corgis, rather than just coordinating an event with the Maxfield family.

"You heard me the first time," Creed said.

"What's the point of that? They're a bunch of assholes."

Normally, Creed would not have argued. Or even felt the inclination to argue. But for some reason, he thought back to Wren's determined face, and the way her body had looked in that dress, and he felt a bit defensive.

"You know the girls are running it now," he said. "James Maxfield absolutely was an asshole. I agree with you. But things are different now, and they're running things differently."

"Right. So you suddenly kissed and made up with Wren Maxfield?"

The idea of kissing Wren sent a lightning bolt of pleasure straight down to his cock. And the idea of… making up with her made his gut turn.

"Not a damn chance," Creed responded.

"So, the two of you are going to do this, while at each other's throats the entire time?"

"The logistics aren't exactly your concern. The logistics are my concern, as always. You just…be a silent partner." Creed narrowed his eyes. "You're awfully loud for a silent partner."

"I'm not technically a *full-on* silent partner," Jackson said. "It's just that I would rather invest money than make decisions."

"So then I'm letting you know what the plan is." Creed thought back to the moment he had told Wren that he was going to barbecue. Now he had to barbecue. "We have to bring some grills."

"I'm not even going to ask."

"Fine with me."

"I'm sorry, what are we planning?" Their younger sister, Honey, walked into the room. She was named by their mother, who had been so thrilled to have a daughter after having two sons that she had decided her daughter was sweet and needed a name that suggested so.

Honey had retaliated by growing into a snarky tomboy who had never seen the use for a dress and didn't know which end of a tube of lipstick to use. He had always been particularly fond of his sister.

"An event. With the Maxfields," Jackson said.

Her mouth dropped open. "Are you out of your mind?"

"I asked him that already," Jackson grunted.

"Well, ask again. Then check him for brain damage."

"No more brain damage than I had already," Creed said.

"Then why are we doing this?" Honey asked.

"Because," he said, taking a long moment to chew on the words that were about to come out next, because they hurt. "Wren had a point. She thinks we should join the wineries together. Make this area more of a tourist destination for wine. Wine trails, and things like that. There's no point in being competitive when we can advertise for each other. People like to try all different kinds of wines, and experience all different atmospheres when they're on vacation."

"You sound like a brochure," Jackson said.

He probably did. Mostly because Wren had sounded like one and he was basically repeating her. "Well. That's a good thing," Creed said. "Since we need some new brochures. And somebody has to write them. It isn't going to be either of you."

"True," Honey said cheerfully.

"You do have to help me barbecue. And you have to help set up this party. I need you two there. If for no other reason than to be witnesses."

"Witnesses to what?" Jackson asked.

"Just in case Wren decides to murder me."

"You could take her," Honey said.

Yeah. He could take her. That was for damn sure. But not in the way his sister meant. "You know I would never hurt a lady."

"That's far too gallant if the lady is willing to murder you," Honey said pragmatically.

"You could try to be less annoying," Jackson said.

"Look," Creed said. "She came to me. So, it's up to

her to behave herself. I didn't go to her, and I wouldn't have."

Though, truth be told, he would have to behave himself, too. The prospect of spending extra time with Wren Maxfield was definitely problematic. But he'd spent the last five years *not* touching her. A few weeks of working in close proximity shouldn't be an issue.

Hell. They *wouldn't* be.

Because when Creed Cooper decided something, he stuck to it. Control was what he was all about. He might be a rich cowboy who could have everything he wanted, but that didn't mean he *did* have everything he wanted. Not anymore. Not after he had experienced the disastrous consequences of that kind of behavior.

He had learned his lesson.

And he would never again make the mistakes he'd made as a kid.

That was for damn sure.

Chapter 2

Sometimes it still felt strange and disorienting to walk through the large Italian villa-style home, knowing their father would likely never return. That everything here had been previously certain but now…wasn't.

For as long as Wren could remember, her life had been on a steady course. Everything had been the same. From the time she was a child she had known she would work for Maxfield Vineyards. And the only real question had been in what capacity. Emerson's contribution had been based on her strengths. She was a social media wizard, but that was not something anyone could have anticipated, considering the medium hadn't existed in the same form when they were younger.

But Wren… Wren had always had a talent for hospitality. She had always been able to make people feel at ease. Even when everything had been going well in her parents' marriage, from the outside looking in, there had been an invisible band of tension in the house. The tension had only ever been worse when they were dealing with the Coopers. Whatever the reason, her father hated that family. And he had instilled a hefty dose of that dislike in her. Though, Creed had taken that dislike to a personal level.

Even so, Wren was an expert at managing tension. And making everything seem like it was okay. Delightful, even when it was decidedly less so.

Even when she and Creed wanted to dismember each other, they could both do their jobs. She imagined that was why he was in his position in his family company. The same as she was in hers.

Event planning and liaising with other companies in a personal way to create heightened brand recognition was something she excelled at. But, it had also been the only real surprise in her entire life. Apart from when James Maxfield had been utterly and completely disgraced.

Yes. That was really the first time her life had taken an unexpected turn.

She still wasn't sure how she felt about it. On the one hand, her father was clearly a monster. And, having never been…*emotionally* close with him—not in the way Emerson had been—it didn't devastate Wren. But it did leave her feeling adrift.

Now she was drifting into uncharted territory with this Cowboy Wines partnership, and she truly did not know how she felt about that either. But it was happening. So, there wasn't much to be done about it.

In fact, she was meeting with Creed this morning. The two of them were going to be talking logistics and

deciding which wines to feature. They wanted to show-
case the broad spectrum of what each wine label did
best, while not stepping on each other's toes. Unusual,
since generally they were deliberately going head-to-
head.

But now they weren't. Another unusual thing in a
slew of unusual things.

She got into her shiny little sports car and pulled
out of the grand circular drive that led to the top of
the mountain where the family home sat. She took the
drive all the way down to the road, and as she put distance between herself and the villa, she was surprised
to realize the pressure she hadn't noticed building in
her chest began to get lighter and lighter.

And that shouldn't be what was happening. She
should be feeling more and more stressed the closer
she got to Creed. It didn't track with what she knew to
be true about herself.

That she loved her family and her life and *hated* him.

She mused about that as she maneuvered her car
down the winding two-lane road, through the pictur-
esque main street of Gold Valley, Oregon.

Her family had been based here all her life, but she
had always felt somewhat separate from it. She and her
sisters had gone to boarding school on the East Coast,
coming back to Oregon for summers.

All the men she'd dated had been from back east.
Long-distance relationships that had become inconvenient and annoying over time.

But those men had been like her. Educated in the
same kinds of institutions, from families like her own.
In fact, in those groups, often she was among the poor-
est. Hilarious, all things considered. But that made her

feel…somewhat out of place here. She didn't go out drinking at the Gold Valley Saloon, a favorite watering hole of most people who lived here.

She didn't have occasion to eat at any of the local restaurants, because they had a chef at home. They threw lavish parties at the villa, and ultimately… She just didn't often venture out of the estate. She had never considered herself sheltered. Not in the least. Instead, she had considered herself worldly by comparison with most of the people who lived in Gold Valley.

She had traveled extensively. Been to some of the most lavish resorts in the world. But suddenly it seemed obvious to her that she existed in a very particular kind of bubble—by choice—and there was something about having to face who her father really was that had…well, *disturbed* the bubble she lived in. It hadn't popped it altogether. She remained in it. But as she passed through town, the thoughts about her father passed through her mind, and she focused on getting her armor in place so she could deal with Creed.

Creed's family vineyard was beautiful. The winery facilities themselves were not her style at all, but they were pretty, and she could appreciate them. Rustic barns that had been fashioned into showrooms and event spaces, along with picnic tables that were set up down by the river, live bands often playing during the summer. She knew that food trucks came in during those events and added to the down-home atmosphere.

She could see why it appealed.

Now she really was worried that she had a headache. Wondering about the local bar and appreciating the aesthetic of this place. She snorted, pulling her car into the showroom lot and getting out, immediately scuffing her high heel on the gravel.

Oh, *there it was*.

All the ready irritation that she possessed for this place, and the man she was about to meet.

Her beautiful yellow leather pumps all scuffed…

And then, she nearly fell off her beautiful yellow leather pumps, because suddenly he was standing in the doorway, his arms crossed over his broad chest and his expression as unreadable as ever. He looked cool. His lips flattened into a grim line, his square jaw locked tight. His green eyes were assessing her. And that was the thing she hated the most. He was always doing that. Looking at her as if he could see straight through her dress. As if he could see through her chest. As if he could see things she wasn't sure she had ever examined inside herself.

She didn't like it.

Added to the *long* list of things she didn't like about him. That one went right below his being way too handsome for his—or her—own good.

"Howdy, ma'am."

"Sup, asshole." She crossed her arms, mirroring his own posture.

"I thought you were supposed to be a lady."

"That's the thing. I know how to behave like a lady in the right venue. I also know how to go toe to toe with anyone. A by-product of my private school education. Rich people are mean."

"Well. *You're* certainly mean."

She shifted uncomfortably. "Not always."

She didn't know why she felt compelled to strike at

him. Constantly. Why had they slipped into the space of open hostility with such ease?

You don't know?

Okay. Maybe she had a fair enough idea. But she didn't want to marinate on it. Not at all.

"Just to me?" he asked. "Aren't I special."

He moved away from the door and allowed her entry into the tasting room. There, he had several bottles of wine out on the table. They were already uncorked, glasses sitting next to them.

"Isn't this nice?" she asked.

"You didn't answer my question."

"You're certainly something," she responded. The answer seemed to settle between them, rather than striking immediate sparks. But that left an odd note lingering in the air. They just stared at each other for a long moment. And it was like everything in the air around them went elastic, stretched, then held tight.

"Nice to know."

She had hoped that his voice, his words, might banish that strange threat of tension. But it didn't. No. If anything, it felt worse. Because there was something about that voice that seemed to shiver over her skin, leaving goose bumps behind.

"Don't let it go to your…head." His eyes dipped down, to her lips, then lower.

"Let's drink wine," she said, far too bright and crisp and obviously trying to move them along from whatever was happening now.

"Did you bring some for me to try?"

"Yes. I have a crate in the car…"

"I've got it." He extended his hand.

"What?"

"Keys?"

"Oh." She dug in her purse for her key fob, and clicked it twice. "It's open."

He went outside and returned a moment later with a crate full of wine bottles slung up over his shoulder.

And it was… Well, it was impossible for her not to admire all that raw male beauty. His strength.

He had big hands. The muscles on his forearms shifted as he slung the crate down with ease onto the table, beginning to take the wine bottles out. They looked small in those hands. For some reason, she had an immediate image of those hands on her hips. All that strength, all that…largeness…

That was another thing.

She felt outside a lot of experiences here. And she had never… Well. Not with a man like him.

All of her past relationships had been based on having things in common. Liking each other. Being able to see a potential future, where she served as the appropriate ornament, and they served as the appropriate accessory.

The kinds of people who fit into each other's lives with ease, and because of that decided to make a go at fitting into bed with each other.

As a result, she hadn't had the most exciting sex life. It had been fine.

But she never had a wild…well, a wild anything.

She hadn't gone out to bars and hooked up.

Creed Cooper was a bar-hookup kind of guy. She just had that feeling.

That he was the kind of man women saw from across the room, all warm with whiskey and the promise of bad decisions, and thought… *He looks like a terrible choice.*

Before gleefully climbing on.

She had never done anything like that and there was something about him that made her think of those things. If she was honest, made her yearn for those things. A rough, bad decision like the kind she'd never made before.

"Let's get to pouring," he said.

And so they did. Portioning out samples for each other to try.

Infinitely safer and better than her standing there pondering the potential badness of climbing on top of Creed.

"Should we start here?" He picked up a glass of Max-field Chardonnay.

"It's as good as any as far as I'm concerned," she said. Though, now she was feeling fragile and like maybe she shouldn't be drinking around the man. Her thoughts were doing weird things. But she'd been in a weird space since she had driven away from the house today. Or maybe, since even before then.

She was familiar with this wine, and it was one of her favorites. Citrusy, with notes of white peach and apricot. It was a decent wine for her mood because of the tartness.

"Nice," he said. "Very nice."

"I thought it might pain you to admit that," she said.

"Not at all. Actually, I would be disappointed if I didn't like your wine. Because I would hate to be in competition with somebody who was terrible."

"I suppose that's a fair call," she said.

"Us next."

He offered her Cabernet Sauvignon, and the notes were completely different from the Chardonnay. Smoky oak and rich espresso. It reminded her of him. Full-bodied and rich. Tempting, but a very bad idea to over-indulge in.

"Nice," she said.

"A compliment from you," he said dryly. "What an achievement."

"Not one I would think you'd care about."

"I didn't say I *cared*. I was just remarking."

"You're irritating," she said, taking another sip of the wine. They moved through the wines, and she felt a looseness in her limbs. Relaxation pouring through her. She knew how to taste wine without getting drunk. So she had to assume the feeling had something to do with him. Which was honestly more disturbing than thinking she might have overindulged.

"Why shouldn't I be irritating? You're no better."

The smug male arrogance in those words rankled. He tipped his too handsome face backward and took another sip of wine. "You know, this event might also need a bouncy castle."

"No," she said.

He wasn't serious. She knew that. That was ridiculous. This was not going to be some family Sunday picnic. He knew her well enough to know that, whether he agreed or not.

"A dunk tank."

"Absolutely not," she responded. "It's happening in October."

"This is your problem, Wren. You can't think outside the box. You want to bring two labels together that historically have never had anything to do with each other. You want to bring together two very different types of people."

"The kinds of people that are at my winery do not want bouncy castles. Or children running around anywhere."

"Oh, they want perfect little Stepford children just like all of you were?"

Irritation twisted in her stomach. "You don't know me. You don't know us."

"Don't I? You're proving that I do. You're all worried about appearances here, like you always have been, when this whole thing with your daddy should have taught you appearances don't mean much of anything."

"How dare you?" She was trembling now, irritation turning to total outrage. "How dare you bring my father into this?"

"It was too easy."

"I've been through enough. We've been through enough. I don't need you flinging things at me about my family that I can't control. You want to talk about living in a box… You've never even left here, have you?"

"We both know that's not true. A fair amount of travel is required to do this job."

"Did you even go to college?" she asked.

"No," he responded. "I was too busy working to build the family label. I guess you think attending college makes you smarter than me, but all it means is you were from a different sort of family. You see, we are not from money. Not like you. You think that makes you better, but it doesn't. Because you know what else? My dad never sexually harassed a woman either. Unlike yours."

Raged poured through her and she fought to keep from showing just how mad he'd made her. He was doing it on purpose. He didn't deserve the satisfaction of knowing he'd succeeded in getting to her.

"Where is your damn wine cellar?" she asked. "I want to go look at what else you have."

"You don't want to keep having this conversation?"

"I never wanted to start having it," she said, each word coming out in a monotone. Because if she allowed her voice to amp up, she was going to say something she would regret.

Not that there was much she could say in anger that she would regret having spat out at Creed. It wasn't the anger that scared her. It was everything that hummed underneath it. That it could still hum underneath when she was so infuriated with him. When he was being such a…such an unrepentant asshole.

"Wine cellar's this way," he said.

He led the way to the back of the barn, where there was a staircase that led straight down.

She was reluctantly charmed by it. By the uneven rock walls that gave it the vague feel of a French country home. The thick, uneven slabs of wood that made up the staircase, making it feel old-world and resonant.

She was irritated she didn't hate it. She was irritated that he had homed in on the exact thing about herself that was bothering her at the moment.

That he had managed to poke at her exact point of insecurity. All the things she had been thinking of when she had driven into town. About how there was this whole other life here—a whole other life in general— that she had never even considered living because she was a…a *Stepford child*. It was exactly what she had been.

Going where her father had chosen for her to go, growing into exactly what he had wanted her to grow into. Taking the job he had given her. And she was still doing it all. All of the exact same things she had done before her father had gone away. Before he had stepped down from the company in disgrace.

And it did make her wonder... What creature had she been fashioned into?

And for whom?

She didn't think there was an alternative reality where she would be in favor of a bouncy castle at her event, but she truly didn't know. She could only speculate.

Everyone is a product of their circumstances. Don't be so hard on yourself.

She nearly nodded at the affirmation she gave herself. The problem was, she couldn't agree. Because she wasn't actually ever all that hard on herself.

She never made any mistakes. Not in the way that she thought of mistakes. Because she had always, without fail, done exactly what she had been charged with.

By your father.

And still, her father had never been effusive about his pride in her. But she had lived for that praise. Because who didn't? Who didn't want to make their father happy? And her father was... He was a monster.

All these thoughts had her feeling absolutely and completely off-kilter. And that was only serving to make her even angrier at Creed. How could she handle all of this stuff *and* him? And how dare he cut her so close to the bone?

He didn't know her. He didn't have the right to say the things he'd said. To say things that made her feel more seen than anything anyone in her family had ever said. That was for sure.

"So, the Cooper family is just all rainbows and butterflies?" she asked as they made their way through the aisles of wine.

"And horseshit," he said. "Which wine were you thinking?"

"I don't know. Pick something good."

"The array of wine upstairs is good," he said. "That's why I picked them."

"Something different." She felt difficult and she didn't care.

"Rainbows and butterflies," he reiterated. "And my dad's not a criminal."

"And all of you work here at the family winery because you just love each other so much."

"Is that difficult for you to believe?"

It wasn't. Not really. There was a reason she was choosing to stay at the Maxfield winery, after all.

A reason that went beyond just being afraid to start over, or not knowing what else she would do.

Emerson was her rock, and Cricket needed her.

"I'm close with my sisters," Wren said. "I love them."

"And I love *my* family. You ought to love your family."

"I'm just saying. I'm not in a box. I just know who I am." Those words had never felt less true. Not that she loved her family. She did love her family. It was just that right now she felt like she was wearing a Wren suit and somewhere inside was a different creature. She felt like she was inhabiting the wrong body. The wrong space.

"Honestly, Wren, if you believed that, you wouldn't be so bound and determined to try to convince me."

"You don't know me," she said. "You're not my friend."

"Something we can agree on."

"You don't get to say what I know or don't know. You just don't."

"Too late. I did."

"You're such a… You're ridiculous."

"Just take a bottle of wine so we can get on with this. I will feel a lot better dealing with you if I'm drunker."

"This isn't exactly a picnic for me either," she said. "You are without a doubt the most insufferable man I've ever known."

"You don't like me, Wren?" he asked, taking a step toward her. "However will I survive?"

"The same as you always do, I imagine," she said. "High on an unearned sense of self-confidence and a little testosterone poisoning."

He huffed. "You like it," he said.

"I'm sorry, what?"

"You like it. My testosterone. You'd like to be poisoned by it, admit it."

"There's that sense of unearned self-confidence," she said, her heart hammering steadily against her chest. "Right on time."

"It's not unearned. I watch you. When we fight. Your face gets all flushed."

"That's called anger."

"Why? What is it about me that makes you so damned angry?"

"You… You are just…a useless, base ape."

"Base?" He asked the question with a dangerous sort of softness to his voice, and it made her tremble. "That's what you think? That I'm like an animal who can't control himself?"

"Yes," she spat. "I know all about you and your reputation. You get drunk at the bar, you pick up women every night of the week."

"I don't get drunk," he said. "That's not me."

"Maybe that's how you see yourself, but it's not what I hear. I hear that you're just a big, dumb, blunt instrument. You might go on and on about how you pulled yourself up by your bootstraps, but your daddy made all this happen. You might wear a cowboy hat, but there's a silver spoon in your mouth the same as mine. So don't you dare go acting like you're better than me just because you can't be bothered to put on an ounce of refinement. Because you don't have the manners to leave my dad out of a conversation. Just because you can't be bothered to try to be a…a civilized human being."

"You think I'm an animal, Wren?" he asked again, his voice low and rough. "You think I don't control my baser instincts? I have, Princess. You don't even know. Maybe it's time you saw what it looks like when I don't."

And that was how she found herself being backed up against one of the stone walls in the wine cellar, six-foot-plus of angry man staring down at her, his green eyes blazing. "You want an animal?" He put his hand on her hip, and she nearly combusted. "I've half a mind to give you one."

Her heart was thundering so hard she felt like it might rattle the buttons clean off the front of her blouse. And if it did, it would leave her top open. And then he would be able to…

She was throbbing between her thighs, her throat utterly and completely dry. This couldn't be happening. This had to be some kind of fever dream. The kind of dream she had every other night when she had to deal with Creed.

When anger turned into something much hotter, and much more *naked*.

But it couldn't be real. Anger couldn't really turn into this seething, hot well of need, could it? This couldn't really be what was beneath all of their fighting. That was... That was her being confused.

Her having some kind of fantasy that allowed her to take control of him.

That was just what she told herself whenever she had sex dreams about him.

That sure, he might be hot, but she didn't actually want to *have sex with him*. It was just that the idea of manipulating him with her body appealed to her subconscious, because it was always such a sparring contest in real life.

And the idea that maybe her breasts could reduce him slightly was tempting.

But that wasn't real. People didn't really do this.

She didn't really do this.

You're just trapped in a box...

And suddenly, she wondered what it might be like if she did really do this. If she dared. If she returned his volley right now.

If she let herself be the animal she'd accused him of being.

She'd gotten to him. Really and truly. Something about her accusing him of lacking civility and control clearly irritated him. And she wanted to keep on doing it. She wanted to push him.

She arched her hips forward, and her pelvis came into contact with the evidence of just what he was feeling, there in the front of his jeans. He was hard. He might be mad, but he was hard. For her.

"Oh, I see," she said. "So that's your real problem. Pulling my pigtails on the playground because you like me?" She rolled her hips forward, and she nearly gasped at the sensation. She might be taunting him, but she was on the verge of overheating. Spontaneously combusting. "If you want me to lift up my skirt so you can see my panties, you should've just asked."

"You're infuriating," he bit out.

"No more so than you."

"You know what, I'm tired of that smart mouth of yours. Maybe it's time you found something else to occupy it with."

And before she could say anything else, those lips had crashed down on hers. He was kissing her, hard and deep. And he was so… Hot and strong and male. So far and beyond any man she had ever touched before. She was used to civilized men. And he might be angry that she'd called him uncivilized, but the fact remained that he was. Dangerously so.

She was panting, writhing against him as he cupped the back of her head so he could take the kiss deeper. His tongue was hot and slick against hers, and the friction made a well of need open up between her thighs. She felt hollow, she felt… Like she might die if she didn't have him. Thrusting hard and deep inside her.

"You talk big," she said against his mouth. "I hope you've got the equipment to back that up."

"I've never had any complaints, Princess."

"I'm sure I could find a few."

"No, baby. You're not going to have any. Not after this."

"Are you just going to talk? Or are you going to fuck me?"

She had never spoken to a man like that in her life. Had never even dreamed of saying something so raw and carnal. Because she'd never been this desperate before. And it didn't matter. Because it was Creed Cooper, and he didn't even like her. So it didn't matter what he thought of her. Didn't matter if he thought she was dirty or bad or wrong for talking to him that way. For demanding that he take her up against a wall. For fighting with him with one breath, and demanding he do something about the heat between them with the next.

There were no boxes here. That was the beautiful thing. There was nothing but this.

"My pleasure."

Then her shirt was torn open. Buttons scattered all over the floor, and she didn't care. He pulled her bra down, exposing her breasts, and then those big, rough hands were cupping her tender flesh, his thumbs skimming over her nipples.

She gasped, arching toward him, reveling in the way she filled his palms. She had never been like this.

And suddenly, as he stripped layers of clothes off her skin, she felt like that suit had been removed along with it. That layer that had felt so foreign. So wrong. And even though she had never in all her life behaved like this, the situation suddenly felt more real. Suddenly felt more like who she was. Like the Wren beneath all that she had been created to be.

It was her turn next. She pushed his shirt, shrugged it over his shoulders, and revealed a body that put her wildest fantasies to shame.

She hadn't known. Not really.

She hadn't even begun to guess how beautiful the man was. How much all those muscles would appeal to her. His chest hair, the scar on his side. Everything that made him a rough, uncultured-looking man, the likes of which she had never had before.

And everything after that became a blur.

A fumble born out of desperation.

She worked at his jeans while he pushed her skirt up over her hips, hooking his finger around the elastic on her underwear and shoving it to the side while she freed his cock. It was big and thick, gorgeous. And she had never particularly thought that part of the male anatomy was *gorgeous* before, but that was the only word for it. A thing of actual beauty. She was far too happy for herself to be annoyed with him that his outrageous ego was not in fact misplaced. He had earned the right to be full of himself.

And all she wanted was to be full of him, too.

"Please," she whispered against his mouth.

"That's the first time you've ever asked me nicely for anything," he growled, pressing the head of his arousal to the entrance of her body, teasing her, teasing them both.

She'd never been so wet so fast in her life. So ready. She had never craved penetration like this before. She had never craved another person like this before.

She had never thought much about her sex drive, because it had never really felt like a drive. She had thought of it as something like a sweet tooth. Something people had to varying degrees, and sure, sometimes a piece of cake would be nice. But she just wasn't one of those people who obsessively craved sugar, or sex.

This felt like a drive. An urge. Something that came from deep inside her that she couldn't control or minimize. This was something like insanity.

"Did you still want that fuck, sweetheart?" His voice was a growl, feral and compelling.

"Yes," she said. "Please yes."

And then he was inside her.

He was so big that it stretched at first. Hurt a little bit. But in the best way.

Every time he drew away and then thrust back into her body, he did so with a growl. And she clung to him, the hard drive of him deep inside her everything she had fantasized about and more. She had not truly known that it could be like this. She had thought that people made up stories. She had thought for sure that...

Well, when her sister had lost her mind over Holden, Wren had judged her.

But she hadn't known it could be like this.

Raw and terrifying. Wonderful. Electric.

There had been no more denying this than there was denying herself air.

It seemed to make perfect sense now. This thing that had mystified her only a moment before. This anger turned need that rocked everything she was.

Of course, this was right next to the anger that was always threatening to combust between them. Of course, this was the other side of all that need. Of course.

How had she ever thought it was anything else?

He whispered things in her ear. Dirty things. Shocking things. But he called her beautiful. And he kissed the side of her neck, and it made her feel like she might break apart. She didn't know why.

And then suddenly, everything came to a head, and she couldn't breathe. All she could do was cling to him, to keep herself from collapsing onto the ground, to keep herself from flying into a million pieces. She dug her fingernails into his shoulder and cried out as pleasure took over. He wasn't far behind. On a growl, he found his own release, his body pulsing inside her. And when it was over, they both collapsed there against the wall, sweaty and breathing hard.

"This wine," he said, reaching around her. "This will do." He grabbed the bottle, then bent and picked his shirt up from off the floor. He righted his clothes disturbingly fast, and then left her standing there.

She tucked her blouse as firmly into her skirt as she could, crossing the bottom ends and getting the thing to more or less cover her breasts. And then she just stood there for a moment, shell-shocked.

She'd just had sex with Creed Cooper against the wall.

And he had walked away like they hadn't missed a beat between talking about wine and screwing each other senseless.

She pushed the skirt down over her hips. If it wasn't for the intense throbbing between her legs… If it wasn't for that, she would have thought she had hallucinated it all. Because how… How had that just happened?

She grabbed another bottle of wine, not even reading the label, and walked back upstairs. He was in position, his face like absolute granite.

"Want to finish tasting?"

"Are you… Did you hit your head down there?" she asked.

"Where?"

"Why are you acting like we didn't just have sex?"

"It's done," he said.

There was something bleak in his green eyes, and it disturbed her. She was a woman. Wasn't she the one who was supposed to freak out about this kind of thing? She wasn't particularly worried about how many partners she'd had, but it was one of those things other women often seemed to worry about. But he was the one who looked…well, vaguely ashamed.

"It's just that…"

Those green eyes were hard as emeralds now. "I don't really want to talk about it."

"Why not?"

"It's not going to happen again."

Well, on that they could agree. Because there was no way—absolutely no way—that she would ever do anything like that with him again. It had been stupid to do it the first time.

Even though it had felt amazing. She wanted to tell him that. She wanted to cling to him, for just a little while longer. To make him hold her up, because her knees still felt weak. To tell him it was the best sex she'd ever had, and she didn't know what to do with the knowledge that the man who could make her body do things she hadn't known it could do was the one man she had decided she hated more than any other.

She wanted to ask him why that was, because he had taken pleasure with her, too, so maybe he could understand it. He'd certainly had more partners than she had. Had more experience overall. So surely he should be able to…

And she realized she was being a ridiculous stereotype. A woman who was putting emotions into something that had been purely physical.

She had been caught up in that moment. In being outside herself. Well, she had done something out of character. And that was that. There was no going back. But there was also no need to continue on with it now.

He was still Creed. She was still Wren.

She didn't like him any more now that she'd seen him naked than she had before.

Well. That wasn't true.

The man had given her the most insane orgasm of her life. It would be impossible not to like him slightly more now than she had before.

"I trust you to make your selections," she said. She felt numb and shaky. And maybe he had a point that the two of them should act like nothing had happened, but she couldn't do it while in the same room as him.

"I'll just leave you to it."

"You're leaving?"

"Yes," she said. "We'll be in touch."

It wasn't until she got back in her car, and was safely back on the road, that she started shaking. She had lived out some kind of fantasy she hadn't even fully realized she'd had. She'd had sex with her enemy up against the wall. She didn't intend to have a relationship with him. They couldn't. They couldn't even be in the same room without biting each other's head off.

She didn't like him. He didn't like her.

It had been just… Just to feel good.

And then, in spite of the shaking, in spite of the nerves riding through her body, she felt a smile curve her lips. Maybe what she'd done had been out of character. But it had been her choice. And she had liked it. She had liked it a lot. And what was wrong with that? What was wrong with doing something wild? She hadn't hurt anybody, not like her dad. And she hadn't done it for anyone else. She had done it for her. She had done it because she hadn't been able to make any other choice. Because she had wanted it so damn much.

That was a Wren choice. The real Wren. The Wren who lived somewhere deep inside her. Who didn't just do things for approval, or because it was easy. Because it was the next step on the path.

She couldn't help but be proud of herself for that.

And she couldn't be ashamed of it either.

For the first time in her life, Wren Maxfield had done something truly spontaneous. And she was just going to enjoy it.

Chapter 3

Eighteen years of flawless self-control had been completely destroyed in under an hour. He could throw a whole parade fueled by his guilt and regret. The trouble with guilt and regret, for him, was that it was such a tiresome old standby that his body immediately converted it to anger.

He was currently outside on his ranch trying to burn off the rage that was firing through his veins. She had done this to him. She had made him into something he didn't recognize. Or worse, something he did recognize. Someone he knew from a long time ago. Someone who had made mistakes others had to pay for.

Damn Wren Maxfield.

And damn his libido.

He was thirty-four years old. He was better than that. Better than a quick screw against a wall. Better than ignoring her and what had happened right after.

Dammit. He had not handled that well.

He picked up a large boulder, hefted it upward, then walked about five feet before dropping it down in the spot where he was building a retaining wall near his house.

The ground was soft and slick here, made of clay, and when it rained, it had a bad habit of turning into a flood, and quickly. So he was building a wall to make sure that the water funneled where he wanted it to funnel. He'd already dug a trench, which had helped with a little of his frustration. Lifting boulders would hopefully be the antidote for the rest of it.

"I thought I might find you here."

He turned and saw his brother, Jackson, standing there, leaning against the stone post at the bottom of the driveway.

"What are you doing here?"

"Thought I might ask you the same thing. Since you didn't show up to the winery this morning."

"I had work to do here." He gestured to the stones.

"Looks like it. Except… Normally you let us know when you're not coming in."

"Since when are you so up in all the winery stuff?"

"I always have been. It's just that I don't usually have to come looking for you. So maybe you don't notice."

"Did Dad send you?"

"No. But he did ask after you."

"Well, Dad needs to keep himself busy."

In the two years since their mother had died, their dad had become something of a hermit. The work at the winery had shifted more to Creed, Jackson and Honey. It was difficult for Law Cooper to deal with the loss of his wife. In fact, it could be argued that he hadn't dealt with it at all. He'd simply buried his head in the sand, doing things on the ranch that didn't require him to interact much with people.

"You know, I'm not sure I believe Dad asked after me."

"He did," Jackson said, a strange blankness in his expression. "He worries about you. He worries about all of us. Hell, I think he worries about everything these days."

"Maybe he should start doing winery work again. It might take his mind off things."

"Might."

"Anyway. Now you know where I am. You could have called like a normal person."

"You wouldn't have answered. Because you're avoiding me."

"What makes you think I'm avoiding you? I don't come into work one morning and you immediately think it's about you? Nice ego on you, Jackson."

"All right, not me specifically," Jackson said. "But something."

"It's just this whole thing planning the party." Creed figured he would get close enough to the truth without actually giving his brother all of it, and that would probably be more believable. "That woman is giving me hell."

"Scared of a girl?" Jackson took a swing at him, verbally. He was his older brother, and Creed knew he lived for that.

Creed wasn't in the mood.

He shot his brother a dead-eyed look. "I live for the day a woman gives you hell."

"Not going to happen," Jackson said. "I'm not going

to let myself get tangled up in knots over a woman. Especially not a Maxfield."

"The only other Maxfield is Cricket. And she'd kick your ass if you came near her."

Jackson snorted. "I'd kick my own ass ten ways till Sunday if I ever did anything that stupid. She's... young." He grimaced. "Wren, on the other hand, is perfectly age appropriate. If you want her, just have sex with her and get it over with."

Creed gritted his teeth. "That's not always the answer, Jackson."

"Look," he said. "I know you had a bad experience. But it's not like you're a monk."

"No," Creed responded. "I'm not. It isn't that I quit having sex, but I don't let my body tell me what to do."

Too bad he had. Too bad he had one hundred percent followed his libido and nothing else.

And he knew that he should talk to Wren about the fact that they hadn't used protection. But she was a grown woman. She was probably on birth control, and if she wasn't, she would handle anything she needed to on her own.

"The problem is that you banged her already," Jackson said, his expression suddenly going sly. "And you're pissed about it."

Creed about ground his teeth into powder. "Go away."

"You did. Well, what the hell are you going to do about it now? Is there any point beating yourself up over it?"

His brother's question gave him pause. "I mean, I think there's always a point in beating yourself up about something."

"Yeah, but you're a martyr. So, let that go for a second. You're a grown person, she's a grown person. You don't like her, who cares? You've been with plenty of women you don't even know."

"Sure. But then the *possibility* for liking them exists."

"What does it matter? You're not going to be in a relationship with her."

"No, but it seems…like the wrong thing to do."

"Sometimes the wrong thing to do feels pretty damn good. Maybe you should try it."

"You forget. I did."

"You're not sixteen anymore. Neither is she. You're not going to have your life gutted by some girl and her family intent on keeping her to the straight-and-narrow path they put her on."

And that was the bottom line of it all. Creed had to keep control, because he knew what happened when he didn't. And more to the point, he knew the way that other people could then take control of your life.

"I know that."

"Yeah, but you act like you don't sometimes."

"If I didn't learn from a mistake like that what kind of fool would I be?" Creed asked.

"The normal kind."

"Well, whatever is going on with that now, you don't know what it's like to disappoint him quite in the way that I did."

Jackson only chuckled. "You don't know everything about my life, little brother. And I don't claim to know everything about yours. But quit moping. We have things to do."

"Since when do you care about any of it?"

"I don't. But honestly, talking about this joint venture with the Maxfields is about the only thing that's gotten a reaction out of Dad in way too long. He was interested in it. And… I care about that."

Well, so did Creed. Anything to get their dad out of his depression. They'd already lost their mother. They didn't need to watch him slowly slip away, too, because of his sadness.

"Then it'll get done. Don't worry about it."

And maybe Jackson even had a point about himself and Wren. They were adults. And as long as everything proceeded with a bit more planning and caution than they had yesterday, what was the harm?

Maybe it was possible for Creed to drink his wine and have his beef, too. Or something like that.

"I'll be down at the winery in a couple of hours," he said. "I really do need to finish this wall."

"All right. See you back at the ranch." His brother tipped his hat, and turned and walked back toward his truck. And he took with him Creed's excuses.

Creed supposed he should write his brother a thank-you note for that. He was right. Creed was good at self-flagellation when it came to losing control. But sex with Wren had been incredible.

What was the harm in going back for more?

That was, if she wasn't too angry at him.

A slow smile spread across his face. Of course… Anger, with them, didn't seem to prevent the sex from happening.

Quite the opposite.

He might never have experienced anything like this before, but he was eager to experience it again.

Wren had managed to keep her interactions with Creed confined to text messages for the last couple of weeks. His responses had all been short and on-topic, and that weirded her out more than anything else. There was no teasing. No goading. Of course, she hadn't teased or goaded him either.

It was weird and unsettling. To not be engaged in some kind of sparring match with him. She would have said that she wanted this distant professionalism that didn't leave her feeling hot, bothered or angry. Anyway, it got all of the planning done for the event. And today it was all ready to go. An open house, of sorts, set out on the front lawn of Maxfield Vineyards.

Thankfully the late October weather was playing nicely, and it was sunny and warm. Oregon Octobers were a gamble. They could be infused with all the warmth of spring, with deeper golds infusing the air. Or they could be gray, damp and snarling, with a harsh bite in the wind.

Today was golden, and so was the event.

There was no dunk tank. Neither was there a bouncy castle. But there were barbecues and smokers, coupled with lovely covered seating areas, and some places that had quilts set out like an old-fashioned picnic. She had to admit, the barbecue was a nice touch. It did make everything seem welcoming.

And people from Gold Valley, along with folks from the neighboring town of Copper Ridge, seemed to be pouring in to engage in the event.

It was a success. And she was… Well, she was thrilled.

But she felt like she should be something more.

Maybe that was the problem. She was mentally pleased. But she wasn't as happy as she might have been. Because she knew that Creed was going to be here soon. If he wasn't already.

She had spent a few hours early this morning making sure everything was ready to go, so she could go off and get herself dressed and also maybe so she could avoid him.

Anyway, they had a very good team hired to take care of all the logistics, so it wasn't as if she needed to micromanage anything.

Her stomach twisted, butterflies jittering there. She told herself it was because the event was about to begin, and that always made her feel a little bit nervous.

But she could no longer pretend that was the case when it felt like the crowd parted and the sun shined down upon those who had just arrived. Law Cooper, Jackson Cooper, the family's friend and surrogate son, Jericho Smith, and petite, feisty Honey Cooper.

But it was Creed Wren couldn't look away from.

Creed, with a black cowboy hat on his head, a black suit jacket, white shirt opened at the collar, showing a wedge of chest that she now knew full well was as spectacular as advertised.

He had not shown up in jeans and a T-shirt.

Often, even at formal events, he did wear them, as if he was very intentionally flouting convention. He somehow never looked unprofessional. And she knew that had to do with the fact that his choices were just so damned intentional. He wasn't rolling into places that way on accident. No, he was wearing his country roots like a second skin, and it was provocative in their sorts of circles.

But for this, he had dressed up. For this, he had worn a suit. She wanted to…

Well, there was no use marinating on what she wanted to do.

The things she had wanted to do every day since the last time he had touched her.

She had tried to simply appreciate the triumph of a good rebellion. But it wasn't that easy. Because her body was so greedy and desperate for more of what he had given her. For more sex as it existed for others, more of this realm that had been completely unknown to her prior to Creed's touch.

She was *so* messed up.

She probably did need to see a therapist. What had happened with her dad was no small thing, and now she was climbing on top of men who were mean to her. That had to say something about her mental state.

But her physical state had enjoyed it quite a lot, and it was difficult for her to accept it as a one-off. Especially when she kept having sweaty dreams about it.

"Well," she said, looking him up and down. "Don't you clean up nice."

"You, too," he said.

She was very aware that the eyes of every member of his family were on her.

In fact, she was so certain, it took her a while to absorb it since the fact was vaguely embarrassing. But when she did catch his father's eyes, she did not see the speculation she had expected. Instead, he had a strange, wistful look on his face.

"Wren," he said. "Right?"

"Yes," she said.

"You look very much like your mother."

She blinked, feeling a strange sensation at the comment. Her mother was beautiful. But Wren didn't have a lot in common with her. At least, she'd never felt like she had.

Over the years her mother had become more and more quiet. More withdrawn.

And Wren could understand why now. Because clearly not all had been well in her parents' marriage. Her mother must've had a sense that her husband was unfaithful at the very least. A predator at worst.

"Do you know my mother?" she asked.

"A long time ago," he said.

"Let's go find you a place to sit," Honey said, grabbing hold of her father's arm. "Nice to see you."

The youngest Cooper clearly didn't think it was all that nice to see Wren. Jericho and Jackson, on the other hand, were perfectly pleasant. They were both stunningly handsome men, Jackson as tall as his brother, and a bit broader, his eyes the same green. Jericho was even taller, with darker skin and brown eyes, and wide shoulders that looked capable of carrying any number of burdens upon them.

She found them both aesthetically pleasing. But her reaction wasn't the same as what Creed made her feel.

Which was a shame, really, because Jericho and Jackson were so much more pleasant.

"Good to officially meet you," Jericho said, extending his hand. She shook it, then Jackson's.

"It's a great event," Jackson said. "A great idea."

"Well, it's my sister Emerson's doing. Actually, a whole lot of this new direction is."

"I hear her marriage started the tidal wave."

Wren laughed. "The blackmail did."

"Was the blackmail related to the marriage?" Jericho asked.

"Oh, yes," Wren said. "Well, not now. I mean, in the sense that Emerson and Holden are totally fine and no one is being blackmailed to stay in the marriage. It's complicated."

At least, it had been. But now Holden and Emerson just loved each other.

Jackson and Jericho left, which put Wren and Creed far too close to each other.

"Nice to see you. In fact, I was beginning to think you had vaporized."

"No," he said. "Just getting my head on straight. Figured it would be best to focus on the planning of all of this."

"I suppose so," she said.

"Looks amazing."

"You were right about the barbecue. People love it."

"Now, I'm surprised you didn't burst into flame."

"You know, I might have, but recent events left me somewhat inoculated."

"Good to know. I thought they might have left you…"

"Oh, now you're concerned? You certainly didn't show any concern when you decided to pretend nothing happened."

"Is that what you want to fight about now?"

"I don't know. I haven't decided yet. There's such a huge array of things we could fight about. Considering we haven't seen each other in a couple of weeks and a whole lot has happened. Though, I do think the obvious thing to fight about would be the sex that we had, which you're still trying to pretend didn't happen."

She had not intended to open with that. She hadn't intended to be talking about this with him with guests all around them, and members of their family in close proximity. But it just kind of poured out of her. Maybe it was him. But maybe it was her, too. Maybe it was everything that she was.

Everything that she had become in the last couple of months.

This creature she was trying to remake herself into, in her own image, and not that of her father.

And really… What was the point of watching what she said around Creed? Everything was already as horrifying as it could ever be. Everything was already ruined. There was no dignity left to be had.

She had climbed him like a tree and had an earth-shattering orgasm seconds after he had thrust into her. She was sure she'd left him bleeding from digging her nails into his back. She'd probably caused hearing damage with how loud she'd screamed when she'd come.

There was pretty much no coming back from that.

Her dignity was toast.

He knew how much she wanted him. But the flipside was she knew how much he wanted her. And she suspected the fact that he had pretended that nothing had transpired between them was only evidence of just how much he wanted her.

Something about wanting her bothered him.

But then, he had come to this event all dressed up.

She couldn't figure the man out.

And as much as it pained her to admit it, she sort of liked that about him. That he wasn't easy. That she didn't intimidate him. That he didn't want her money or her influence. Everything about him that was so annoying was simultaneously also compelling, and that was just the whole thing.

"Come here," he said, his voice suddenly hard. "I want to show you something."

There was a big white tent that was still closed, re-served for an evening hors d'oeuvre session for people who had bought premium tickets, and he compelled her inside. It was already set up with tables and tablecloths, everything elegant and dainty, and exceedingly Max-field. Though there were bottles of Cowboy Wines on each table, along with bottles of Maxfield select.

But they were not apparently here to look at the wine, or indeed anything else that was set up. Which she dis-covered when he cupped her chin with firm fingers and looked directly into her eyes.

"I've done nothing but think about you for two weeks. I want you. Not just something hot and quick against a wall. I need you in a bed, Wren. We need some time to explore this. To explore each other."

She blinked. She had not expected that.

He'd been avoiding her and she'd been so sure it was because he didn't want this.

But he was here in a suit.

And he had a look of intent gleaming in those green eyes.

She realized then she'd gotten it all wrong.

"I… I agree."

She also hadn't expected to agree.

But her heart was about to fly out of her chest, and she was achy and wet between her legs already. She sort of wanted to ask him if they could try it up against the wall of the tent. But she had a feeling that would only culminate in the two of them falling through the filmy fabric and embarrassing themselves.

She just didn't have the willpower to resist him.

"I want you now," she whispered, and before she

could stop herself, she was up on her tiptoes and kissing that infuriating mouth.

She wanted to sigh with relief. She had been so angry at him. So angry at the way he had ignored this. Because how dare he? He had never ignored the anger between them. No. He had taken every opportunity to goad and prod her in anger. So why, *why* had he ignored this?

But he hadn't.

They were devouring each other, and neither of them cared that there were people outside. His large hands palmed her ass, pulling her up against his body so she could feel just how hard he was for her. She arched against him, gasping when the center of her need came into contact with his rampant masculinity.

She didn't understand the feelings she had for this man. Where everything about him that she found so disturbing was also the very thing that drove her into his arms.

Too big. Too rough. Crass. Untamable. He was everything she detested, everything she desired.

All that, and he was distracting her from an event that she had planned. Which was a cardinal sin in her book. And she didn't even care.

He set her away from him suddenly, breaking their kiss. "Not now," he said, his voice rough. "Tonight. All night. You. In my bed."

"But can't we just…"

"We are in a tent."

"I don't really care," she said, amazed.

"You don't?"

"Maybe I'm having a nervous breakdown," she said. "It's entirely possible. It has been a very weird few months. And I just… I don't know. I don't know who

I am anymore. I'm not sure I want to know who I am. You're right. I've been in a box. And I didn't want to admit it. I just wanted to be mad at you. I just wanted to yell at you. But then we kissed, and then we did other things, and I've spent the last two weeks being incredibly confused about it. But you know what confuses me most? That I'm not ashamed. But I'm not sorry. I think it was good. Because even if it was the biggest mistake of my life, at least it was my mistake. I've done everything that's ever been asked of me. I've dated only men that were expected. I've never had sex outside of a relationship."

"It's fun," he commented.

"Apparently. I know that now. And…it was just for me."

"I don't know about that. I got something out of it, too."

"Well, good for you." She sighed heavily. "Okay. I'm not baring my soul to you or anything like that. But… Look, it's been weird. The whole thing with my dad. I swear to you, I didn't know how awful he was."

"I'm sorry that I brought your dad up the other day."

"No. It's okay. I mean… It's not. It was painful. But I'm working through things. And, I think I'm getting there. Better. This is part of it."

The left side of his mouth lifted. "Sexual healing?"

"Why not?" she asked. "Nothing else has worked." She took a breath, and then everything just poured out. "I worry about Cricket. Because she's not really talking to anyone. My mom is just kind of… Well, she's doing what she does. She's hiding. Emerson has Holden, and she seems to be coming out of it just fine. I feel like I'm in a weird space. I can't exactly live in denial. I'm too involved in this business. I feel the loss of my father too much. But I don't really feel okay about any of it. Or over it. I'm not sure that I feel okay about me. I need to figure out what I want."

"You're not thinking about leaving the industry, are you?"

"No," she said. "I think I feel like *this*—" she gestured to the interior of the very Maxfield tent "—is mine. But... What I'm saying is a little rebellion is what I need right now."

"Happy to be a part of it."

"Yeah, well." It was unexpected just how easy it was to tell him all of this. Somehow, she couldn't really be embarrassed around this man.

She had yelled all kinds of unflattering things at him over the years. She was not the best version of herself when he was around. It was like he tapped into some unfettered part of her that she didn't normally have access to. And when he was in the room, she just let fly.

It now extended to sex, apparently, and again, she wasn't even embarrassed about it. She had a total and complete lack of inhibition with him.

And right now, that felt like a gift.

Because she'd had nearly thirty years of being inhibited. Of following a very specific path. And Creed represented something wild and free that she'd never thought she could be.

Maybe that was the real reason he made her so angry. That he had been free in about a thousand ways she was sure she never would be.

"Then let's go do our jobs," he said. "The sooner we get finished with all of this..."

The last part was left unspoken, but the promise in

his tone was clear. And her whole body responded to that. Effortlessly. Deeply.

And she knew she had made the right choice. To continue down this path with him.

It might end badly… But there was something in her that didn't fear the consequences. Not really.

She had gone down the expected path before. She had done it all of her life. And look how that ended. With her father…

There were no guarantees.

There were no guarantees. And she would rather live free.

Chapter 4

His body was on fire.

He was burning for her, and he'd decided to jump into the flames. That was control. He'd made a choice and he was resolved in it.

Or he'd just decided to take his hands off the wheel and let the car steer itself. One or the other.

He had to admit that the event was going well. His father even looked like he was enjoying himself. Though, his entire countenance had taken on an odd tone after he had met Wren.

Creed didn't really understand it.

He knew that there was…weird blood between the Maxfield and Cooper families, but he didn't fully know why. He had always assumed it was because they were business rivals, but effectively… They weren't anymore. Maybe it was just old habits dying hard. Except there had been no animosity in his father's bearing. None at all. He'd shown a strange kind of wistfulness. A sadness. But then, everything his father did these days was wistful and sad.

The old man missed his wife, and there wasn't much anyone could do to fix that.

They all missed their mother. It didn't matter that it was the natural order of things to lose a parent. You knew that you would. If everything went according to plan... You did.

But you were never ready for it. It was never time.

It would always feel too soon.

But it *really* had been too soon.

And they'd been suffering the aftereffects of grief, as a family incomplete, ever since.

Incomplete and different. Jackson had been distant. But Jackson had always been closest to their mother. Still, it was just another thing.

Creed hadn't had a drink or a bite to eat all day, mostly because he felt like he was being fueled by desire for Wren, but he was about ready to go and get himself some brisket when everything inside him went still.

He'd experienced this a couple of times in his life. But not for a long while. And it was never for a *good* reason. It was only ever for one reason. He closed his eyes, steeling himself.

Why the hell would she come to this?

He turned slowly, and that was when he saw her.

Louisa Johnson. Her accomplished doctor husband, Calvin Johnson. And as far as all the world was concerned, their four children. Including their oldest son, who was taller and broader than his father.

As a matter of fact, the boy looked a hell of a lot like Creed.

His stomach went acid.

He hadn't seen the kid in... Maybe going on four years.

The boy was eighteen now. Creed knew his birthday. Every year marked itself on his heart. A deep groove. A line in a particular chart that spoke of the hours, weeks, months, years that he'd been father to a son he could never acknowledge.

It was a small town. He couldn't always avoid Louisa. But her actually coming to one of his events was a study in sadism. Even he didn't think she could be quite that evil.

Just self-centered and hell-bent on creating the life she wanted. Never willing to admit she had given her virginity up to somebody other than her longtime boyfriend. And that when she'd gotten pregnant at sixteen it had not been with Cal Johnson's baby. But she'd gone and fixed that uncomfortable fact really quickly, slept with Cal right away and claimed the kid was his.

Creed knew the truth.

Creed had thought they were in love.

A virgin himself, he'd believed that having sex with her meant something. That her climbing into the bed of his truck with him had mattered. And he'd been so overwhelmed by desire that he hadn't stopped to think about anything.

He was sure... He had been so sure that it meant she was going to break up with that college-bound boy for him. Even though he wasn't from a fancy family, wasn't a future doctor. He'd been sure she'd fallen for him all the same.

But no.

And even when she had found out she was pregnant...

He wondered, to this day, if Calvin knew who fathered the kid. Wondered if he didn't especially care, not given the life they had built on the back of that lie.

Creed realized he had been standing there frozen for a full minute, and Louisa hadn't even looked his way.

The kid was harassing a younger sibling, laughing.

And then Calvin reached over and playfully punched his oldest son in the arm, gently telling him to knock it off.

They were a family. Built by years and birthday parties, Christmases and good-night kisses. By fights and celebrations and soccer games and barbecues in the backyard. In the face of all that, genetics didn't matter.

Except they mattered to Creed.

Because he'd had eighteen years of never getting to know that kid, and all the regret that went with it.

But what was he supposed to do? She hadn't put his name on the birth certificate, refused to admit they'd ever had sex. Creed's father had tried, he had damn well tried to get a court-ordered paternity test, but the judge refused to do it. To subject an underage girl to scrutiny, to call her a liar when she said staunchly that the only boy she'd ever slept with was her longtime boyfriend.

There had been nothing Creed could do, and everyone had said that he was just mounting a smear campaign against a girl who had rejected him. A girl who'd already found herself in a *delicate situation*.

They were happy. Clearly. She had Calvin. Their four kids.

What was he?

He didn't even know.

Suddenly, he felt a soft hand on his shoulder. "Is everything all right?"

He turned and saw Wren. Louisa wasn't looking at him, not even with the full force of his anger turned in her direction. But Wren had seen him.

"Fine," he responded.

"You look like you're about to start a fight."

"No," he said, turning away. "I'm not."

"Good."

Suddenly, the feeling inside him went from hungry to ravenous. And he needed this damn thing to be over so he could lose himself in Wren's body.

He lived with the mistakes of his past every day. But having to stare them down was a particular kind of torture he was never quite prepared for.

And he needed something, anything, to find a little oblivion. If it wasn't Wren, it would be the liquor on the table, but he would rather have her.

It was strange, the exchange they'd had back in the tent, and this one. Because it wasn't as sharp and hard-edged as most of their interactions.

But it was still tinged with that same kind of raw grit. Which he recognized now as just desire. Only not desire like he'd ever known it before.

The closest thing that came to it was that sixteen-year-old lust haze he'd found himself in with Louisa. But that had been born out of inexperience. Out of desperation to know what it felt like to be inside a woman.

Well, he knew what it felt like now. That wasn't why Wren created this wildness in him.

It wasn't about knowing what it was like to be inside a woman, but what it was like to be inside *Wren*.

He knew the answer to that now, but a simple answer wasn't enough. He wanted more. He wanted her.

And that want began to eclipse the pain in his chest.

He was desperate for it. Because the promise of it—of her—was so big, so intense, with the capacity to take away this hurt. And he wanted that. He damn well did.

Needed it. Especially now.

He bent down slightly, careful to make it look like they were just having a business exchange, and not like they had shared any kind of intimacy.

If you could call sex against a wall *intimacy*.

"I can't wait until you're naked beneath me," he said.

She arched a brow. "Who says I'll be beneath you? I was kind of thinking I might like to be on top."

"There's time for that," he said. "There's time for a whole hell of a lot."

"So many promises."

"I promise you one thing—you're going to be screaming my name all night."

She looked up at him, her eyes glittering a challenge. "You'll be screaming mine."

"I plan on it."

They parted then, the tension between them so intense it would combust if they didn't release their hold.

So they did, because they both knew they were in a public setting, and a professional one. And whatever the hell he thought of Wren, whatever she thought of him, they were both damn good at their jobs.

He turned away then. From the direction that Wren walked. From the place where Louisa stood with her family.

A piece of his family. A piece of his heart.

He would focus on getting through all of this. And then he would focus on getting Wren into bed.

That was his life.

Work. Sex.

What the hell else did he need?

Everything was done, everything was cleaned up, and Wren was sitting in the driveway of Creed Cooper's house. She had made her excuses to her family about being tired, having a headache and a few other things she couldn't readily remember, and scampered off almost immediately after the last guest left.

She knew Emerson thought she was acting strange, but Wren didn't much care.

Wren was obsessed with Creed.

And if she were honest with herself, she could admit she had been obsessed with him for quite some time.

She might have couched that obsession in irritation, but the fact of the matter was, it had been deeper than that.

He hadn't annoyed her at all today.

No. Quite the opposite. He had been wonderful at his role during the event, and more than that, she had seen humanity in him that she didn't particularly want to see.

She had no idea what had been going through his mind when he had been standing there staring into the crowded party right before she had come up to him. But she had seen that it was something. The intensity that had come off him in waves had been palpable, at least to her.

She wasn't entirely sure whom he had been looking at, but she thought it might have been Louisa Johnson, a woman Wren knew because she and her husband frequented the winery and often had birthday parties and events there. It was common for wealthy families to come to Maxfield for special events. It was a status symbol. And Louisa had always seemed like the kind of woman who enjoyed her status.

Wren quite liked her. Louisa was nice, and she was funny, and a generous tipper to the waitstaff.

If it was Louisa that Creed was staring at, though, Wren had the feeling that he *hated* her.

And there was really only one reason for people to hate each other like that.

Love gone wrong.

Wren screwed up her face.

Well, there were actually a lot of reasons for people to hate each other. She and Creed hated each other, for no real reason.

Except, as she got out of her car and walked toward his front door, she couldn't find any of the hatred that she normally felt. She only felt giddy. Excited to have his hands on her, to have him make good on all those promises he had issued earlier at the event today.

She liked it when their verbal sparring had a bit of an edge, even if it wasn't a fight.

There was something electric and exciting about their exchanges.

She liked the danger that came with talking to him. She just did.

She walked up to the door, prepared to knock, when it opened, and she found herself being dragged inside and pressed against that door, six-foot-plus of muscular man pinning her there as he kissed her. Kissed her with all the pent-up longing she knew had been building in both of them for the entire day.

She kissed him like he might hold all the answers she was so desperately seeking.

"Please let's make it to a bed," she whispered against his mouth. "I like the desperate stuff, but I really just want to see you naked."

"I can oblige," he growled.

He picked her up off the ground and carried her straight to a staircase, taking them two at a time. There was an edge of darkness to all of this that was so different from how it had been before. That first time had been charged by anger, the kind of anger they commonly felt toward each other, reasonable or not.

But this was different.

He seemed fractured, broken in some way, and like he thought perhaps this might put him back together. She was used to him looking at her and being irritated. And that one day down in the wine cellar he had found pleasure. But today, he seemed to be after something altogether deeper, and she wasn't entirely sure she could help him find it.

But she wanted to.

And that was perhaps even more surprising than his looking to her for something deeper in the first place.

He pushed open the door, revealing a large bed made of heavy wooden beams. The bed was the largest thing in the room, a clear indicator of exactly where his priorities were.

His house was Spartan. Everything about it was serviceable, practical. And she knew full well he didn't need that much mattress for sleeping.

No, he was a man who clearly used his bed for more athletic pursuits. And she knew already he was a man who did those pursuits well.

"You said you wanted to see me naked." He set her down lightly on her feet. Then he moved away from her, unbuttoning the crisp white shirt she'd been looking at all day. Exposing that gorgeous chest, those impressive abs. He shrugged the shirt and jacket off, his body a thing of outright beauty the likes of which she had never seen before she'd seen him.

"Trading," he said, gesturing to her.

She reached behind her back and grabbed hold of the zipper tab on her dress, pulling it down slowly, letting her dress pool at her feet. She was wearing only heels and a matching red lace bra and panties.

She wasn't insecure about her body. Men, in her experience, were quite simple about things like that.

But the hunger in his eyes surpassed anything she had ever experienced before from other men. This passion, which seemed to simmer so intensely it was bound to bubble over, was something foreign to her. Something entirely different from all her previous experiences. Sure, she had found sex pleasurable before. But she had not found it to be fire and hunger. She hadn't found it to be the air she needed to breathe. She had never felt like the urge to be touched was so intense it was a physical agony.

And she could see all that she was feeling mirrored in his face as he looked at her.

She hadn't known. Hadn't known that having him, this man—this man who didn't even like her—look at her like she was... Like she was a wonder. Like she was perhaps the most beautiful thing he had ever seen...

Like she was seen.

Her.

Wren Maxfield.

This new version of herself that she was finding, inventing and creating as she went along...

He was captivated by her.

He wanted her.

It was a revelation.

Because she wasn't insecure about her body, but she felt new and fragile in her skin. In all that she was, in all that she was going to be.

Didn't even know what that might be in the end.

But when Creed looked at her, she thought she might be closer to finding it.

And it didn't make sense, how it was somehow more affirming to have it be him who made her feel that way, but it was.

Maybe because her sister Emerson would be supportive of her no matter what. Her mother would say that she loved Wren regardless of what she did.

Creed wouldn't. Creed found her intolerable.

He would never tell her anything just for the hell of it. He wouldn't pretend that he wanted to touch her, kiss her, be inside her. He would only do what he wanted to do.

It was freeing.

And with all the freedom it gave her, she reached behind her back and undid her bra, throwing it to the ground, glorying in the look of absolute need on his face.

She wiggled out of her panties, leaving herself standing there in nothing but her high heels. And then, she leaned backward on the bed, arching her breasts upward, letting her thighs fall slightly apart. She knew she looked like a wanton. And she had never been one, not particularly.

But she wanted to be.

Here. Now. For him.

She wanted to take this thing between them and test it to the breaking point. Wanted to test *herself* to the breaking point.

And whatever dark emotion was rolling beneath the surface of his skin... She wanted to unleash it.

Because she wanted to go as far as she could. She wanted to take them both to the edge.

This felt safe, with him, because it wouldn't be forever.

Because they didn't have a relationship, and they wouldn't. Because it was only this. Only her trying to figure out who she was, and only him trying to contend with whatever demons were clawing at him right now.

She could take it. For now.

And he could take her. Imperfect and new and unsteady.

They could both please themselves.

It was a miracle.

And she badly needed a miracle.

Creed didn't disappoint.

Because then he dropped to his knees, a position of submission she had never expected from him. He was beautiful from this angle, too. The planes of muscle on his shoulders and chest intoxicating. His strength, bowed before her...

Oh, she shivered with it.

Of course, immediately following that submissive posture he revealed that it was not submissive at all. Because he grabbed hold of her ass and pulled her forward, burying his face between her legs and licking her until she screamed.

Until she couldn't breathe.

He had all the control. There was no restraint. No quarter given.

He tortured her with pleasure, and if that wasn't the most Creed Cooper thing on the planet, she didn't know what was.

That he sank to his knees and yet managed to still have all the control.

And she didn't want to fight it. Didn't want to stop it. No. She surrendered to it. To just taking. Everything that he wanted to give. To the slow glide of his fingers inside her, and the wicked friction of his tongue against her. She surrendered to all of it. To the absolute glory of knowing this man needed to taste her.

Because that's what this was.

He *needed* to taste her.

He had no control. His movements didn't have finesse. It was a devouring. He had fallen upon her like a beast, like a man possessed.

Because of her.

Tension coiled inside her, and she just let go. When her orgasm broke over her like a wave, she cried out with her pleasure, completely unembarrassed by the sound that came from her body.

She felt remade, and she wanted him to feel the same. She scooted herself back farther on the bed, her thighs open even wider, an invitation.

"Take what you need," she said.

A shudder wracked his big frame, and he undid his belt buckle, sliding it slowly through the loops and letting the belt fall to the floor. He undid the closure on his pants, and took his shoes, socks, pants and underwear down to the ground. And then she could see him. Fully naked, fully erect.

Hands down the biggest guy she'd ever seen.

He was stunning.

She'd thought so the first time, too. But now she had a moment to really look. And…

Truly, he was beautiful. She couldn't wait to feel him inside her again.

He reached over to the nightstand and grabbed a condom. And something, a small alarm bell, went off in the back of her mind. She dismissed it. Pushed it to the side.

He tore it open, rolling it onto his length before positioning himself at the entrance of her body. Those green eyes, her adversary's eyes, meeting her as he slid inside her, inch by agonizing inch. She felt full, of him, of desire. Of need. She had been so ready for him that she let her head fall back, a deep sigh of pleasure on her lips.

And then he began to move, slow and languid at first, letting her feel each delicious inch of him on his slow glide out, and back in.

And then it all became harder, more frantic, a desperate race to completion. She wrapped her legs around his hips, letting him thrust deeper, harder. And she arched against him each time, meeting his every thrust, chasing a second climax, which before, for her, had been unheard of.

But it was Creed.

It was Creed making her feel these things.

And when their eyes met again, and she saw the hollow bleakness there, she felt him all the way down in her soul.

She kissed him.

She kissed him deep and long and hard, and she tried

to…to give him some of the wonder and pleasure inside her. Because if he could feel her pain, then maybe he could feel her pleasure, too.

She didn't want him to be hurt. And he was. She could see it.

And even if it was over another woman… Well, Wren wasn't his woman. Not really. This was just sex. And she would make it the best ever. She would make sure she took away some of his loneliness. Some of his bleakness.

She got a perverse kind of pleasure out of that. That she, a woman he didn't even like, might give him something that the woman he had once loved denied him.

Wren was making assumptions. But she was pretty sure she was assuming right.

He thrust into her, hitting the spot deep inside that sent sparks shooting off behind her eyes, made her come so hard she could scarcely breathe. And then he followed right along with her, shaking and shuddering his pleasure as he came deep inside her.

And she just held him for a while. Pressed his head against her breasts as they both lay there breathing heavily.

She didn't want it to be over.

"We're just getting started," he mumbled, and she wondered if she had said the words out loud.

She was afraid she might have.

"You wanted to be on top, remember?" he mumbled.

"Yes, but I think you killed me. I'm too weak."

"I have food," he said. "I have cake."

She lifted her head. "How do you have cake?"

"My sister. She makes excellent cakes."

"Well, I could have some cake."

"If you eat my cake, I'm going to expect you to put out."

"I will put out for cake."

"Will you ride me?"

"Only if you promise that later you'll tie me to that headboard."

She was shocked by the words as they came out of her mouth. Because she'd never wanted anything quite like that before. And at first it had just been to dare him, but now she found she really wanted it.

"I think that's a deal I can stick to."

And some of the bleakness from his eyes did seem to be gone, so she supposed she had accomplished her goal.

She wouldn't think about what would happen after tonight.

She didn't want to.

Tonight, she just wanted to be the Wren she was becoming with him. Tonight, she wanted to be new.

Tonight, she wanted to be with Creed.

Chapter 5

It had been two weeks since he'd last had Wren Maxfield in his bed. Two weeks, and she was all he could think about.

It was starting to impact…well, everything. His work, his sleep, his ability to be a halfway decent person and not be an absolute dick anytime someone in his family wanted to talk to him.

He wanted her again, but he didn't know how to justify it. Sure, they were going to be working together on that big cross-winery event, but it wouldn't just be the two of them working on it.

He didn't know if that night after the party had been transformative because he'd been in a really dark place, or if… He just didn't know. All he knew was that he wanted more. And Wren didn't seem to be coming back for it. Which was a damn shame.

And then, as if his thoughts had conjured her up, he looked through the windows of the tasting room and saw her standing outside. She was staring at the door, not moving.

He watched her, without changing his position, until she turned and her eye caught his. There was something bleak and strange in her expression, and he didn't know how to read it. So they just stared at each other through the window.

If she was waiting for him to make the first move, she was out of luck. She was the one who had come here to knock on his door. She was the one who was going to have to close the gap.

Finally, she did.

Finally, she walked through the door, but then she stood there in the entry, her hands clasped in front of her. "We need to talk."

"We do?"

"Yes. We do."

"I've been waiting to see you," he said, "and I have to tell you, it's not talking I want to do."

"Well, it's talking we need to do. Creed…" She closed her eyes and swallowed hard. "Creed, I'm pregnant."

Suddenly, he felt like he was falling into a chasm. A chasm that led to some moment eighteen years ago. A moment he didn't want to relive.

But you knew this might happen. You did. He pushed the thought to the side. *You tried not to think about the fact that you screwed her without a condom, but you know you did.*

No. Wren was the same age as he was. It didn't seem possible that the woman wasn't on birth control. Or that she wouldn't have said something about the condom if she wasn't taking something.

You didn't say anything about it either.

"I didn't even think," she said. "After the time in the wine cellar. I didn't think. It didn't occur to me until we were at your house and you took a condom out of your bedside drawer that I realized…that we didn't."

"You're not on…the Pill or anything?"

"I haven't been in a relationship in like a year and a half. And I… I didn't really like the way I felt on it. It made me gain weight, so I quit taking it after I broke up with my last boyfriend." She grimaced. "I'm not really somebody who hooks up."

"Well," he said, his voice rough, "I am. I am, so I sure as hell should've thought of a condom. Because I use them all the damn time. I… I'm sorry. I should have thought of it. I should've done better."

"No," she said. "That's stupid. I should have, too. I… Creed, I want to keep the baby."

Cold fear infused itself into his veins. "You want to keep the baby?"

"Yes. I understand that it might surprise you. But I… I'm thirty-two years old. I would like to have a baby. And I'm at a point in my life where I don't really know what's coming next, what I want to do. And this pregnancy feels like… Well, it feels like a pretty clear sign of something that I could do to change my life. Because it's happening. And I… I want it. When I found out a couple of days ago, I cried. I spent the entire day crying. I've been avoiding my family. Because I knew that I needed to tell you first. But I also knew… I knew immediately that I wanted the baby. I… I just *do*. And I don't need anything from you. I'm completely fine and taken care of. I have a house, I have a business, and I don't need you to be involved at all."

"I will be fucking involved," he said, his voice hard.

"I didn't mean you *couldn't* be," she said. "I just didn't want you to think I was making demands of you, or your money…"

"This baby is mine," he said.

"Of course it is," she said.

"No," he said. "You misunderstand me. That wasn't a question. It was a statement. This baby is mine, and that means I will be involved. I am this baby's father."

Echoes of everything that he had lost were shouting inside him. Because he knew how easy it was for a woman to take a child from a man.

A *girl* to take a baby from a *boy*.

That was the thing. They'd been kids. And everything about it had been messed up. All of it.

But he was not a child anymore, and he would be damned if anybody took anything from him.

His child.

For his son, it was too late. He couldn't have his son. Not now.

He had just seen that boy with his…with the man he thought was his father, with his siblings. They were a family. Creed never could be. He was just a man who had donated the material that had created the boy.

That wasn't being a *father*. He could never have that back. That boy was grown.

Even if he found out about Creed someday… He could never be the boy's dad.

No, he had lost that chance. But he would never lose that again. Never again.

"You're going to marry me," he said.

"I… I most certainly am not," she said. "That is… It is not a good reason for people to get married."

"It is the only damn reason for people to get married. It's legal protection, Wren. For both parties involved."

"That's not how the world works anymore."

"It is damn well how the world works. What's to keep you from taking my name off the birth certificate?"

"I won't."

"What's to keep you from preventing me from seeing my baby?"

"I won't," she repeated. "I won't do that. We were both involved in this and…"

"You say that, but you don't know. You don't know how it will go. You're marrying me. You're marrying me, and we're going to live in the same house. I am not missing a moment of my child's life."

"Creed, I didn't say that you would. But we are not in a relationship. We don't even like each other, let alone love each other."

"That doesn't have anything to do with this. This isn't about us."

"Be reasonable. I didn't even think you would want this baby."

"Because you don't know me," he said. "Not at all. We were naked together, that's it. But you don't know me well enough to think that you know whether or not I want this child. I do."

He did. With every breath in his body.

And the resoluteness he felt over what needed to be done was as intense as it was real.

"I am not letting you take this baby from me."

"Creed, I won't. But I don't have to marry you to…"

"We are getting married."

"Or what?"

Everything in him turned to ice. If she wanted an ultimatum, he would give it to her.

"Or I'll do what I have to do to make sure that most of the custody is with me."

"What?"

"Do you think it's fair? For one parent to only be with the child on weekends? Do you think it's fair for one of us to miss that much of the child's life? Because I don't. But if you think it's fair, then you won't mind if it gets flipped on you. Do you think it'll be fair to miss a week of the baby's life?"

"I'm the mother," she said.

"And I am the father," he said, the conviction in his voice shocking even him. "I'm the father," he repeated. "I'm not missing this."

"Creed…"

"You listen to me," he said, speaking with all the firmness he could when his life had just been turned completely upside down. "You listen to me, Wren Maxfield. Either you become my wife, or I'm going to have to make this difficult."

"You listen to me," she said. "You might be used to issuing edicts, but you don't get to tell me what to do. Because I've lived my entire life walking on another path that was set out for me by someone else. By a man. I will not be dictated to. If you want to fight, I will give you a fight, Creed. You can bet on it."

And then, she turned on her heel, walking out of the room.

And he could see that she was certain that she could get her way.

All he could see was another woman walking off with his child.

It wouldn't happen. It wouldn't.

It wasn't for another hour that the shock wore off.

And that was when he clutched his chest like he might be having a heart attack and leaned against the wall of the tasting room.

He was going to be a father again.

And Wren Maxfield was the mother.

And he had no idea how in hell they were going to survive this.

Chapter 6

She was a coward. She had run away from him, and she could see that whatever was driving him to be unreasonable, and make actual threats, came from a place she didn't understand.

She could see that, and still, she had run away from him rather than sticking out the conversation to see where it might go. And wasn't that basically what he was saying? That he assumed she would be a coward when push came to shove? That she would keep their child from him because it was easier or less challenging, because she didn't want to deal with him?

And maybe... Just maybe it had been easier for her to assume he wouldn't want anything to do with the baby. Maybe that's why she'd been able to come here and tell him about the pregnancy.

Before that, she had spent two days in agony.

She hadn't been lying to him when she'd said she cried. She cried enough to make a flood. It just wasn't good timing. At least, that was what she told herself in the beginning.

Wrong time.

Wrong man.

And then she thought… Maybe he was the right man. Because he wouldn't want anything from her. Because he was not a paternal type, and there was no way he was secretly yearning for a wife and family.

She had never considered herself particularly maternal, either, but when she looked at the situation objectively, she could see that, well, this was an opportunity.

Because she had everything she needed to raise a child, including the assumed support of her family. She had job security. Money. A place to live. A great many things that people took for granted. From that standpoint, she was in a spectacularly great place to raise a child. And the more she thought about it, the more she had wanted to grab hold of this major life change and see where it took her. The more she thought about it, the more she had felt…a sense of excitement, rather than one of despair.

But her revelation had been selfish. Utterly and completely.

It had never included him.

She didn't know how to include him in that.

And then he demanded that she did.

Honestly, he'd demanded it in the most extreme way she could have imagined. Even if she had let herself truly think about a scenario in which he wanted the baby, wanted to be in the baby's life, she had not imagined that he would…demand marriage and issue threats.

But that's what he'd done. And it became clear that she really didn't know all that much about him, and that lack of knowledge actually mattered.

Having sex didn't mean they knew each other.

Oh, they knew things *about* each other. Creed knew things about her that no one else did. She had done things with him she hadn't done with any other man.

Including that moment of absolute loss of control. The lack of protection.

But that didn't mean they knew each other.

And so she was now looking for the person she should have gone to in the first place.

Emerson was at the house she shared with Holden, working from home today, which was something Wren could never have imagined Emerson doing before. Given that Emerson had been wholly and completely tied to the family home.

But not only had she moved away from the estate, she seemed to prize the separate life she and Holden had built.

Wren would be fascinated by it if she didn't find it so annoying.

She parked her car and got out, walking to the door. It took a couple of minutes, but her sister opened it, wearing a large, elaborate-looking robe, her hair piled on her head, her fingernails manicured to perfection, a giant wedding ring that she'd gotten from Holden glittering on her finger.

"Well," Wren said. "Good afternoon to you, too."

"I was taking pictures," she said.

She swung the door open wider, and Wren saw that the couch and coffee table were set just so, a glass of rosé in her sister's glass, and a book sitting next to it.

"Are you reading?"

"I was taking pictures," Emerson said dryly. "It's a great afternoon to indulge in a little Maxfield luxury and *hashtag self-care*, don't you think?"

"I think that I'm glad you run the internet properties and not me. Since I don't understand any of this."

"Luckily, you don't have to. Because I'm a savant."

"An influencer savant." But Wren smiled, because she really did find her sister to be a wondrous magical creature.

Emerson should be annoying. She wasn't.

"Where's Holden today?"

"He's gone to visit his sister. She's getting settled in her new house after getting out of the rehab facility. We are hopeful that she's going to keep doing better and better."

"I'm glad to hear it."

Holden loved his sister, and Wren and Emerson's father had caused her immense distress. Wren was rooting for her.

"So what brings you by? Because you look like an absolute disaster."

Wren stepped into her sister's house and craned her neck so she could see her reflection in the mirror on the wall. Emerson wasn't kidding. Her makeup was smeared, in spite of the fact that she hadn't been crying. She assumed that maybe she had wiped her fingers firmly across her eyes to try to keep the tears back. But she hadn't even been conscious of doing it.

Her hair was in disarray, and there was just something…shocked looking about her expression. Her skin was pale, and her cheeks seemed especially hollow.

"Well, I feel terrible," she said. "So that's fair." She sighed heavily. "I have to tell you something."

Emerson looked bemused. "Am I hiding a body? Should I get a shovel? Because you know I will."

"I do know you will." Wren sighed heavily again. "I don't think I'll need your help with that. Though, I guess we'll see how all this goes. I'm pregnant."

Her sister's schooled expression became very serene. Wren could tell that Emerson was covering shock, because there was no way she was that serene about such an announcement.

"Congratulations," she said. "I didn't expect that."

"Well. Just wait until you hear the next part. Creed Cooper is the father."

A bubble of sound escaped Emerson that was almost a laugh, but not quite. "That doesn't surprise me at all. I actually figured you were here to tell me that you slept with him. But obviously that ship sailed a while ago."

"Multiple times," she muttered.

"I mean, I can't exactly lecture you."

"Why not?"

"Well, I jumped into bed with our father's enemy while I was still engaged to somebody else. So, when it comes to making good sex choices… I mean look, luckily, I married him. It all worked out in the end. But, I get how men can make you really stupid. And I didn't get that before Holden."

"Well, Creed doesn't make any sense to me. I don't like him," Wren said helplessly. "I don't like him and yet… I want him. I want him so much. And the sex is so good. It's the best sex I've ever had. I mean, that's weak. It seems like just the thing you say. But sex with him is like a whole other thing."

"I get it," Emerson said. "I mean, I profoundly get it."

"I guess you managed to use condoms, though."

"Yeah," Emerson said. "That we did."

"We forgot. And…"

"What are you going to do?"

"Well, I was all resolute. I'm not a kid. I'm in a great place to raise a child, and everything has been so out of whack I just… I kind of *want* to. I mean, I really want to. I was shocked by the realization, but it's true. I want to have a baby. I want to have *his* baby. It'll be… so cute. But I didn't think he would want me to have a baby. And I didn't think he would care. I thought this would be just my decision, but he told me today that I have to marry him."

That successfully shook Emerson's composure. *"He what?"*

"He demanded that I marry him. Like, demanded. *With threats.*"

"I mean…" Emerson blinked. "Okay, that's shocking."

"I know."

Emerson's expression turned thoughtful. "Well, obviously something happened to him."

"You think?"

"If I know one thing about hardheaded, alpha cowboys, it's that usually demands like that spring from an emotional wound."

"With all the experience you have with them?"

"I may not have experience across a vast section of them, but the one I married was basically a giant walking open wound."

"Gross."

"I know. But everything he did, seducing me, forcing me into marriage, tearing my dress off…tying me to the bed… What was the point I was making?"

Wren narrowed her eyes. "This isn't helping me, Emerson."

"Right. My point. *My point* is everything he did that was awful came from a place of being so angry on behalf of his sister. And a lot of things got twisted up inside him, but he couldn't quite deal with all that anger. It took time for him to sort it out. But ultimately he did. Ultimately, *we* did. But he wasn't being an asshole just to be an asshole. My experience is they're all just lions with big thorns in their paws."

Wren's mouth flattened into a line. "And you want me to… What?"

"I mean, find the thorn. Identify it. Pull it out."

"I'm not going to end up like you," Wren said. "I… I can't say that I hate him anymore, but I also don't really want to marry him."

She imagined the bleakness that had been on his face that last time they were together. She had cared about that. About the pain he was experiencing.

"He *is* hurting," Wren said. "I just don't really know why."

"That's what you have to find out."

"I don't know how to talk to him. Every time we do talk, it… Well, it's exactly what just happened—we fight. Or we have sex. Fighting or sex. Those are the two options."

"Would either one be so bad in this situation?"

"I probably shouldn't have sex with him again."

"Honey, the horse has bolted from the barn, and is in the pasture with the stallion, and is already knocked up."

"I meant emotionally, for *emotional reasons*."

"Right, right," Emerson said, waving her hand.

"You still think I should have sex with him?"

"You seem to want to. And it sure makes men act nicer," Emerson said. "Anyway. As established, I make bad decisions on that score." An impish grin crossed her face. "But I don't regret them."

"I don't know if I regret this. I don't know what I regret."

Wren wanted the baby. She was sure of that. It was all the other things she couldn't quite figure out, including how she felt about Creed. *That* she couldn't quite navigate.

But if Emerson was right, if there was a thorn in Creed's paw, so to speak, then Wren was going to have to approach him differently.

She might not know all she needed to know about him, but she knew him well enough to know she was going to have to come in with a plan. A counteroffer. He wasn't simply going to accept her *no*. She was going to have to come up with an arrangement that would make him happy.

And in order to do that, she was going to have to identify that thorn.

And she couldn't identify the thorn without talking to him.

That was the problem.

She didn't especially know how to talk to Creed.

She knew how to fight with him. She knew how to fuck him.

She wasn't sure she knew how to do anything else.

But they were going to have to figure it out.

For the sake of the baby, if for nothing else.

She realized that for the first time in a very long

time, her thoughts weren't consumed with the winery. The winery was something she loved, but not something she had built with her own hands.

She found herself suddenly much more concerned with her life, her future.

And even in the midst of all the turmoil, that was an interesting development indeed.

Chapter 7

Creed knew he had basically lost his mind earlier, but he didn't regret it.

In fact, he was making plans to call his lawyer. He was going to do whatever he had to do to get his way. That was when Wren showed up on his doorstep.

She looked strange. Because she was wearing jeans and a T-shirt, and she looked smaller somehow, and yet resolute.

It was the resoluteness that concerned him.

"I'm sorry I left things the way they were earlier," she said, breezing into his house without an invitation.

She wandered into his living room, sat on his couch.

When she had come before, she had been in his bedroom, his bathroom and his kitchen for a cup of coffee before she had run out in the early hours of the morning.

Not his living room. But there she was, sitting on

the couch like a satisfied, domesticated feline. Except he had the feeling that nothing about Wren was particularly domestic.

"What exactly are you here for?"

"Not to agree to your demands. Sorry. But it's ridiculous to think that we have to get married just because we're having a baby."

"Is it?"

"It is to me. I'm pretty much one hundred percent *not here for it*."

"That's a shame. Because I'm one hundred percent..." He frowned. "Here for it? What the hell does that even mean?"

"Why?"

She was glaring at him with jewel-bright eyes, and it was the determination there that worried him.

"What do you mean 'why'? I told you earlier. It's because I'm not going to take a back seat to raising my child."

"Why? I mean, you don't even know the kid."

"Neither do you, and you're sure that you want it."

"Sure. But I'm...you know, carrying it. I sense the miracle of life and whatever," she said, some of the wind taken out of her sails.

"No, if you can be certain then *I* can be certain."

"You have to be honest with me," she said. "Because when I left here earlier what I realized was that I don't actually know anything about you. We have worked in proximity to each other for the last five years. And we fight. We... We create some kind of insane electrical surge when we are together, and I can't explain it. And somehow in all of that, I convinced myself that I knew you. But that night that we were here together after the party, there was something wrong. I knew it, even though I didn't know what it was. And when I told you I was pregnant... Look, I didn't expect you to be thrilled about it. But I didn't expect you to demand that I marry you. And I think the problem is, we just don't know each other."

"We know each other well enough. I'd be good to you. I wouldn't cheat."

She didn't look convinced. Not by his offer, not at all. And she should be. What the hell more could she possibly want? Love, he supposed. But here they both were in their thirties, not anywhere near close to settling down, and they were having a kid. Neither of them was young enough or starry-eyed enough to think there was some mystical connection out there waiting for them.

He'd lost his belief in that a long time ago.

Maybe Wren hadn't.

But he didn't see Wren as a romantic. Particularly not after the way things had worked out in her parents' marriage.

"What?" he asked.

"There are other reasons to get married. I just... You would really be faithful to me?"

"Wren, I can't even think about other women when I'm with you. I can't imagine taking vows to be true to you and then betraying them."

"That's nice," she said. "But a lot of men can. You know, my father, for one."

"So that would matter to you," he said.

"Yes," she said. "If I was going to do it... I don't share."

"So now you're considering it."

"I need to know *why*."

"It's not important."

"I have a feeling that it is."

Why not tell her? After all, his family knew. Well, Jackson did. And so did his father. Creed had never talked to Honey about it, but she had been a baby. A kid.

But anyway, it wasn't like no one knew. And he had never agreed to keep it quiet.

Wren looked at him directly. "Does it have something to do with Louisa Johnson?"

The name hit him square in the chest. "How do you..."

"I saw you looking at her. At the barbecue. And afterward..."

"It's not what you think," he said.

"Look. If you needed to be with me to deal with seeing an ex, it's fine. I knew what was happening."

"I wasn't thinking of her. I wasn't using you. Not in the way you mean." He was surprised how much it mattered to him for her to know that.

She looked at him, bemused. "Then what is it?"

"Do you know her at all?"

"They do birthday parties and things at the winery sometimes. That's it. I know her in a vaguely professional capacity."

"So you know her husband, then, and her kids."

"I've seen them. Yes."

He shook his head. "Her oldest son is mine."

For the second time in a couple of days, Wren felt like the ground had tilted beneath her feet.

Her thoughts were coming in too fast for her to grab hold of them.

He had a son.

Creed had a son.

"He... He..."

"You may not remember this, seeing as you didn't go to school here. But Louisa got pregnant in high school."

"I always got the impression that…"

"Yes. By design. That Cal is the father of all her children. She and Cal were dating at the time. She and I started… We were in a study group together, and I developed some pretty strong feelings for her. I knew she was with Cal, but you know how it is when you're young. And you think things will work out just because you want them to. That your feelings have to be good and true and right. Well, I thought mine were. I was a virgin, and what we got up to in the back of my truck sure felt like love to me. I thought it was the same for her. We made a mistake. So, now that you're pregnant… This isn't the first damn time I've made this mistake, Wren. I swore that I never would again. Twice is just… It's damn careless. Especially when you've got eighteen years between who you were and who you are now. I ought to know better."

"I mean… Yeah, I can't really argue with you there. I'd like to reassure you, but that does seem…"

"She didn't put my name on the birth certificate. She wouldn't even look at me at school. She acted like she didn't know me. And when I confronted her about it, she said we never slept together. She told everybody that the baby was Cal's. She was a virgin when we slept together. I knew the baby was mine. But she must have gone and slept with him right after to make sure he believed her. I doubted myself sometimes over the years. I thought maybe… Maybe I was the crazy one. Maybe she hadn't been a virgin. Maybe the timing was all off."

"He looks like you, though, doesn't he?" She felt sick to her stomach. "I don't know him that well, but I remember seeing them all together, and I wouldn't have looked at him and thought he was your doppelgänger or anything, but now that I know…"

"I don't doubt it either," he said. "I haven't ever spoken a word to him. Never been close to him. And the fact of the matter is, he's not really my son now, is he? I didn't raise him. I'm not the one who taught him what he knows. I'm not the one who's been there for everything and paid for his upbringing and… I'm just a guy who had sex with a girl once a long time ago, and got left with a scar that's never going to heal. I can't do that again, Wren. I lost a child already. And I was never going to… I was never going to try to become a father again. I couldn't see any reason to. After all, I never had my first kid. But now it's happening. And I can't go through a loss like that. Not ever again."

"And you think I would do that to you?"

"I thought I was in love once, and I thought the woman loved me back. *We* don't even like each other."

Her heart felt bruised, sore.

He'd been so young to go through something like that. And she could see that it still affected him profoundly. How could it not? But she couldn't go paying for the sins of another person. It wasn't fair.

"We are going to have to get to know each other," she said, resolutely.

"No," he said. "I'm sorry. I'm not budging on it. You're going to marry me. One year. I want us to get married, I want legal acknowledgment of the kid, and I want us to try for one year. And then if you want to divorce, God bless you, but we're going to have to work out a real custody arrangement."

"Creed, it doesn't make any sense," she said. "We can't just get married."

"I won't accept anything less," he said. "I won't accept anything less than marriage."

She looked at him, and she could see that he was absolutely serious. More than that, she could see that what her sister had said was absolutely right. His demand was coming from a place of pain. Unimaginable pain. And it wasn't about simply pulling out a thorn. He wasn't even going to let her get close enough to touch it, never mind remove it.

It was going to require trust. A hell of a lot of trust, and she could see that he was fresh out.

This was his vulnerability. His weakness. The situation they were in, it was the man's worst nightmare. And she couldn't make it work with him if she was continually trying to hold her position, fighting him just for the sake of it.

She wanted her freedom. Her life. The chance to make a future for herself the way that she wanted it made. But not at the expense of their child having the best life he or she possibly could.

Creed might irritate her, but he was a good man. She knew it.

He could be the kind of father her own had never been.

Right now, they had the freedom to make whatever future they wanted. Whatever future they thought was best. She wasn't under the tyranny of her father, and she didn't have to pass any of her pain, any of her issues, on to her children.

Something her own parents hadn't managed.

But it all needed to start here. It had to start with this.

She took a breath, and then she sat down at one of the tables. "Okay. Get a notebook."

"What?"

"Get a notebook. We're going to write out what we both need. What we both expect. Creed, we are not going to make it through this if we don't trust each other. I can understand that you want marriage in a legal sense. If you need that, I can give it to you. But, during the pregnancy, that doesn't have to mean anything. It's not like we need to live with each other or be in any kind of relationship until the baby is born."

"You think that, huh?"

"I do," she said. "I think we need to focus on putting our child first. And we need to build some trust between each other. I would not take your baby from you, Creed. But I understand why you don't just take my words at face value. And, I'm not going to suffer for it either. I just found my life. I just found my purpose. Everything in my world got turned upside down when my dad… I've had to rethink everything. Everything I believe in. Everything I am. I'm not giving everything up to you. Sorry."

He looked hollow. Almost helpless, and that made her stomach drop into her feet.

"I can't bend on this," he said.

She looked at him. And she knew he was telling the truth. His face was drawn and haggard, his tone was tortured.

"I know you can't. I'm going to bend as much as I can right now so we can find someplace where we can meet."

He stood, left the room for a moment, then returned

with a pen and a notebook. He thrust it into her hand. "All right. Start listing your demands."

"First of all, if you want to be involved, you need to be involved. It's really important to me that you're either hands-on or hands-off with our child. All in, or all out." She looked at him, her jaw set, her posture determined.

"Why is that?"

"Because I won't have any of this lukewarm BS. That's how my dad was. He was there just enough to make us…try to perform for him. To make us try to do the very best we could to please him. But he never gave us anything back. Not really. I'm not going to put my kid through that. I want more for them."

"I want *everything*," he said, his voice rough. "I lost eighteen years with my son. I'm not losing any more time. I'm not losing that ever again."

"I won't ask you to. I promise. And that's why…my next thing. No more sex."

"Are you out of your damn mind?"

"No. I'm absolutely *in* my mind. We need to be able to deal with each other, and with this. I need to be able to have you at my house. You need to be able to be around for whatever you want, whenever you feel you need to have time with our child. If we have our own feelings in the way, our own situation, then this isn't going to work. We have to be able to be in the same room and not fight. And not… Well, you know that other *F* word that we seem to be so fond of."

He snorted. "If we had that kind of control, we wouldn't be in this situation."

"But you know as well as I do that getting out of control isn't going to work. It just wouldn't. It couldn't. We have to make this list and stick to it so we can give each other what we need. And I don't think we can do that if we get…all that emotion involved."

"Is that what you think?"

"Well, don't you? Don't you think it's too big a risk?"

His face went hard. Neutral. And then finally, "You're right. And really, it's all just a little control. Which, I had plenty of until you."

"Well, that's flattering. But, I don't doubt you can find it again."

"Sure. What else?"

"Holidays?" she asked.

"Together. Obviously. At my family place," he said.

Always with his family. Was he kidding? But the child was currently a zygote so as pressing matters went, that wasn't a huge one. "Okay, I think we can actually wait on that."

"Marriage," he said. "For the first year."

"Until the baby is born," she said. "I'll give you that. Marriage until the baby is born so you can be sure you have your legal protection. And then we can work out whatever custody agreement you want. We can cohabitate, whatever. But, if the primary concern is custody, and you making sure that you have all your parental rights… I'll go that far."

"I can deal with that. For now. Let's go get a marriage license, then," Creed said, fully and completely matter-of-factly, as if they'd worked out everything.

"What, *right now*?"

"Do you have a better time frame?"

"I don't… I wasn't exactly thinking of a time frame. But… I'm like six weeks pregnant, Creed. We can chill out."

"Nope," he said. "It may have escaped your notice, Wren, but I don't have any chill."

"It didn't escape my notice at all. Nothing about you suggests that you have chill."

But he was already gathering his things, and he was ushering them both out the door and toward his truck.

"I can't… We're just going to go get a marriage license?"

"This isn't Vegas. We can't get married the same day. We need to figure out all the specifics."

She made an exasperated sound and got into the truck behind him. As they drove to town, she was completely and utterly overwhelmed by an out-of-body sensation.

Because *surely* this wasn't actually happening to *her*. She wasn't really going down to the courthouse to get a marriage license with the man who irritated her more than…

"You don't even like me," she said.

"I'm not pretending to *like* you."

That shut her up, because it was true.

He wasn't pretending to like her. He wasn't pretending that there was anything to this other than a legal practicality.

And that was how she found herself standing in front of a clerk's desk in the old brick courthouse, filling out forms.

They could get married three days after the license was purchased.

"Then we'll get married in three days," Creed said.

She didn't reply, or say anything while they finished signing off on all the papers. But when they were back outside the courthouse, and walking on the sidewalk down Main Street, heading back to where they had parked the truck, she gave him the evil eye.

"You have to be joking," she said. "Three days?"

He lifted a shoulder. "Do you want a hamburger?"

"Do I look like I want a hamburger?" Her stomach growled. She frowned furiously at it. She did in fact want a hamburger.

"I think you do," he said. "Let's go to Mustard Seed."

"You don't know what I want more than I do, Creed Cooper," she groused, trailing along after him as he abruptly reversed course and headed to the small, unassuming diner that was just off the main drag.

"I believe I'm pretty good at anticipating what it is you want, Wren Maxfield."

"In bed," she muttered as he pushed open the door, holding it for her.

She stepped inside and looked around. She couldn't remember the last time she had been here. Maybe once. When she was a kid, and she had tried to hang out with some of the local teenagers during the summer. The floor was made of pennies, all glossed over with epoxy, making a coppery, shimmering surface. There was quirky local art everywhere. Little creatures made out of spoons and forks.

The tables were small, and there was a bucket of dry-erase markers on each one, everyone encouraged to create their own removable art on the surfaces.

"Do you come here often?" she asked him.

"Yes," he answered. "My favorite burger place."

"Oh."

A waitress who looked like she was probably the same age Wren had been the last time she had come into this place approached the table. "Chocolate milkshake," Creed said. "Cheeseburger, extra onions, French fries."

"I'll have a Diet Coke. And a cheeseburger. And sweet potato fries."

Then they sat staring at each other across the small table.

He was her fiancé.

A hysterical bubble of laughter welled up in her throat.

"What?" he asked.

"Well, of all the ways that I imagined getting engaged, it wasn't being dragged down to a courthouse to sign papers, then being taken out to a diner for a burger."

"Oh, right. I imagine you figured it would come with something fancy."

"And a diamond."

"Do you *want* a diamond?"

She had a sudden image of him getting down on one knee. Sliding a ring on her finger. And that felt…

That felt too close to real.

And the feeling in her chest was far too tender.

"No," she said. "A diamond won't be necessary."

"So what is it you think this is going to be?"

"In name only," she responded. "You want legal protection, and while I'm sure we could manage that without a marriage, I can appreciate the fact that this is maybe the simplest route. And… It's fine with me. We're having a baby together. I'm not going to act like this is somehow…going to bond us together in a way that it isn't." She sighed heavily. "It's weird, though. Because I certainly never expected to be starting a family without being *really* married. I never expected I'd do it with you."

"My brother seems to think it was inevitable."

"The baby?"

"No. The events leading up to the baby."

"My sister seemed to think that, as well."

"What do they know?" he asked, smiling ruefully.

A few moments later their food appeared, and Wren realized how hungry she was. The food was amazing, and she mentally castigated herself for any snobbery that had kept her away from a burger of this caliber.

"Okay, good suggestion," she said.

She tucked into the burger, and between bites, he looked at her. Hard. "So, you think this is going to be an in-name-only marriage. Does that mean you've changed your mind? You think it's all right if we sleep with other people?"

"Well, we can't sleep with each other," she pointed out.

"Right. Because you seem to think that's unreasonable."

"I do. It will only cause problems. I don't know what kind of marriage your parents had. My parents' marriage is a disaster, and it's only gotten worse as time has gone on. You know, for obvious reasons. I just… You and I don't have a great relationship. It's a weird relationship, but all the fighting… It's not personal. I think we can be okay. I think we can make something out of this and be good parents. And I have a lot more confidence in our ability to do that if we keep it simple."

"So, again, you now think it's all right for us to sleep with other people during this yearlong marriage?"

Discomfort rolled through her, and something like sadness. "Well, I'm not going to be sleeping with anyone."

"Why not?"

She stared at him. "I'm pregnant. Not exactly going to go out and find a new lover while I'm gestating a human being. I can't imagine anything less sexy."

He lifted a shoulder. "A lot of men like that sort of thing. I think you could find someone if you had a mind to."

"Do you *want* me to go find someone else to sleep with?"

"Just checking."

"For your information, I was celibate for eighteen months before we had sex." She dipped her French fry into the pink sauce so hard it bent. "I'll be fine for the next nine."

He leaned back in his chair and fixed her with a bold stare. "I don't do celibacy."

She was surprised at the zip of emotion that shot through her. Possession. Anger. She didn't like that. She didn't like the idea of him sleeping with other women. She stared at him. And she had to wonder if that reaction was what he was pushing for. If he was pushing to see if she was actually okay with all of this.

"Maybe I *will* find someone, then," she said. "How about this, I'm probably not going to be actively looking for a lover, but if one presents himself... Who am I to say no?"

"Hey, you have needs, I'm sure."

Now he was just making fun of her.

"Do you have to be such a pain in the ass? What is it you want? Why can't you just say it?"

His gaze went sharp, intense. And everything inside her...shivered.

She wished she hadn't asked for honesty, because

she was sure she was about to get it. Now she wasn't entirely certain she wanted it.

"Here's what I want," he said. "I want for no man but me to ever touch you again. How about that? But that's not reasonable, is it? Because this is just a temporary marriage and you want it to be in name only. And we need to have a *relationship* for the sake of our child, not based on *F* words that involve nudity — your words, not mine."

"Oh," she said.

She was equally surprised by how satisfying this was, that he was showing he was possessive. It went right along with the possession she had felt a moment before.

This was all very weird.

"That's it?" he asked.

"Well, what do you want me to say?" she asked. "You're right, it is unreasonable."

"And you're totally fine with other women touching me while we live together? While we have a marriage license?"

"No." She bit into her French fry fiercely and chewed it with much more force than was necessary. "I hate the idea about as much as I hate you. Which is *a lot*."

"What are we going to do about that? Because it seems to me that it's going to be pretty difficult for the two of us to find neutral ground. We're never neutral. You want to prevent hard feelings by us not sleeping together, but we've got hard feelings already. If there's another lover in play neither of us are going to be nice, and you know it."

"We can't make it worse," she said, feeling desperate and a little bleak. "And we would. We could. It seems obvious to me. I mean, look at us now, after just a couple of… I don't know. Just after a few times. It's already an issue. We can't… We can't do that to our child."

"We could," he said, his tone horrendously pragmatic. She wanted to punch him. "Plenty of people do."

"I…"

"I know," he said. Something in his gaze shifted. "This is my only chance to do it right. I didn't intend to ever have the opportunity to do it again."

"I can't imagine," she said, her heart squeezing. "I can't really explain how it felt to find out I was pregnant. Because I was terrified. And it wasn't like I had completely positive emotions. I didn't. But I feel conviction. I know having this baby is what I want."

He shook his head. "I didn't know. When she told me she was pregnant I was terrified, too. I was sixteen. I wasn't ready to be a father. But I knew what I would do. I knew I'd be there for her. That I'd be there for the baby. Even if it felt scary. And then suddenly… The whole story changed. She acted like she didn't know me. She acted like we never slept together. It was losing the opportunity to be a father that made me realize how much I wanted it. But even then, I didn't really know. I was a kid. There was part of me that was relieved. Relieved that I didn't have to change my life at all. And damn, there's a lot of guilt that goes with that."

She nodded slowly. "I can imagine there is."

"But I've seen him, over the years. So there's never been an opportunity to really forget what I'm missing, what I don't have." His voice went rough. "I can't get over feeling like a piece of myself got stolen. It's just out there in the world, walking around. And sometimes I ask myself if it can't just be enough that he's happy.

Because all the rest of it is selfish, I guess. He's got a dad. He's got a family. He's not missing anything because I'm not in his life."

"That's not true," Wren said. "He doesn't have you."

She was treated to a rueful, lopsided smile. "That's weird that you think not having me is a deficit, Wren."

"Well, what I mean is… Creed, if I didn't think that you would be a good father I wouldn't have bothered to try to include you in our baby's life."

"Maybe that's the thing," he said. "Maybe she just didn't think I would be a good father."

"She was sixteen. I imagine it's more that she didn't think. At least, not about anything much deeper than herself."

"Well, that probably is true."

"We'll do this right," Wren said.

He nodded. "So what do we do about the two of us?"

"We have nine months to figure it out. To figure out how we navigate sharing…a life. Because that's what we're doing. It's going to be complicated, and we don't need added complications. I'll tell you what… No relationships for either of us. For nine months."

He grimaced. "All right."

"Sorry. Get used to cozying up with your right hand."

He snorted. "In more ways than one, it's like being sixteen again."

"The fact of the matter is, we have got to find a better way to deal with each other than we have been. And I mean, we really do. So, we certainly don't have room for anyone else in this whole… situation."

"Fair enough."

"All right," she said. She extended her hand.

He looked at it. "I'm not shaking your hand."

"Why not?"

"Because it's not business, Wren. And it isn't going to be. You and me can't ever be business, sweetheart."

She lowered her hand, her heart fluttering. "I approach everything that way. Because of my dad."

"It's okay," he said. "We just… We are who we are. Can't do much about it."

"I want to do something about it, I guess. This whole figuring myself out thing is going to weave together with figuring out how we can be a family."

She would never have thought she would become family with Creed Cooper. But here she was.

"I guess so."

"Well." She looked down at her cleared plate. "I guess that's it. For now."

"For now. The wedding will be in three days."

"Are you going to invite your family?"

"Hell no," he said. "Just you and me."

"Don't we have to have a witness?"

"Bring your sister."

"Okay."

Then she stood up, and the two of them walked to the counter. Creed paid the bill.

"You didn't have to do that," she said.

"You're feeding my baby."

She looked around, feeling a little embarrassed. It wasn't like they would be able to hide it in the upcoming months. "I guess it can't really be a secret, can it?"

"Why does it have to be?"

"It doesn't," she said.

He had been treated like a secret before. And Wren wasn't about to do to him what Louisa had done.

Wren couldn't hate Louisa for it, though. She'd been

sixteen. Who hadn't done a host of stupid things when they were sixteen? It was just that when Wren had done stupid things, they hadn't affected someone else for the rest of their life.

"It really doesn't," she affirmed.

Then the two of them walked out of the restaurant together, engaged.

It was so strange, because just a few weeks ago Wren had the sense of being on a different path from the one she had been on before. But she hadn't imagined that the path would lead here.

But this was one of those moments where she had to change.

It was actually a good thing. Because she needed a change anyway.

The only way to handle all of this change was to keep on going.

So that was what she would do.

The fact that she had to keep going with Creed... Well, they would figure it out.

They had no other choice.

Chapter 8

It was his wedding day.

He hadn't ever imagined a wedding day. Hadn't figured he would ever get hitched. But then, what he'd said to Wren at the diner had been true. He had never planned to be in a situation where he got a do-over on the biggest regret of his life.

A slug of something hard hit him in the gut. It wasn't really a do-over. Because it wouldn't give him time back with his son. His son whose name he couldn't even think.

Because it wasn't a name he would've given to his kid. And it served as a reminder of the ways in which Creed wasn't part of his son's life.

But that didn't matter.

Today Creed was going to make sure he never missed out again. And the more he'd thought about it over the last few days, the firmer a conclusion he'd come to.

Sure. He could understand where Wren was coming from—she had the idea that they might be able to exist in a middle ground. And that the middle ground would be better than trying and failing at having a marriage.

But what she didn't understand about him was that he didn't do middle ground. He was all in. Or not in at all.

If he decided to make a marriage, then he was going to make it. And there would be no living separately. No other relationships.

No amicable divorce when the year was up.

He wanted to be in his child's life. He didn't want to have regrets. A real marriage was the simplest way to that path he could think of.

He would talk to her later.

After their wedding night.

As it was, he'd gone and dressed up for the occasion. Because she had liked it so much when he had dressed up for their winery event, so he was sure she would like it for this.

She'd said she would meet him at the courthouse. He assumed she was driving there with her sister.

And when he arrived, Wren was standing in front of the red brick building, wearing a simple white dress that fell just past her knees. On either side of her were her sisters. And her mother was there too, looking pale and drawn.

"Well, I didn't realize the whole family would be joining us," he said.

Wren grinned at him, then took hold of his arm, leading them ahead of her sisters and mother. "I had to bring them all," she said. "And they don't know the whole situation."

"Meaning?"

"They don't know that it's temporary."

He nearly said right then that she didn't seem to realize that temporary was off the table. But he decided to save that for after the vows. Instead, he bent down and brushed a kiss across her cheek. The action sent a slug of lust straight down to his gut.

She turned to face him, her eyes wide.

"You look beautiful," he said.

He heard a rustle of whispers behind him. And he gave her a knowing look.

"Thank you. So do you."

He knew she wasn't lying. She *did* think he looked good.

The heat between them was real.

It was all way too real.

Her mother looked between them. "I do wish we could've had a real wedding."

"You know why we have to do it quickly," Wren said.

"Nobody cares anymore if a woman is pregnant at her wedding, or if they have a baby in attendance," her mother replied.

"I care," Wren said.

"I was impatient," he said. "I just couldn't wait."

"Indeed," her older sister, Emerson, said, looking him in the eye with coolness.

"You don't approve of me?" he asked.

"I'm deeply suspicious of you. But then, I would be deeply suspicious of anyone marrying my sister."

"I hear tell that your husband is a pretty suspicious character, too."

"And Wren did her sworn sisterly duty by being skeptical of him."

Well, that was fair enough.

It was the youngest sister, Cricket, who gave him the kind of open, assessing look that made him feel actual guilt.

"You had better be good to her. Our father was terrible, and Wren deserves to be happy."

"I'll be good to her," he said.

He would be. Her happiness mattered. He told himself it mattered only because of their baby.

But somehow, he suspected it was more.

"Good," Cricket said. "Because if you aren't, I'll hunt you down and I'll kill you."

She said it cheerfully enough that he suspected she wasn't being hyperbolic.

They all filed into the courtroom, and he and Wren took their position up near the judge's bench. They exchanged brief pleasantries with the woman before getting down to business.

It was surprisingly quick. Pledging his life to another person. When the ceremony was stripped away, a wedding was just a business deal where you held hands.

Wren's voice trembled on the part about staying together until death separated them.

His own didn't. But maybe that was because he didn't feel like he was lying. He felt as committed as he could be to this. To her.

Maybe it was that simple for him because he didn't have other dreams of love, marriage or anything of the kind. He imagined that Wren, on some level, dreamed of romance. Most women did, he assumed.

He wondered what his sister would say if he leveled this theory at her. She would probably bite him. Honey didn't like to be what anyone expected.

And she would also be annoyed at him for having a

wedding and not inviting her. Probably, she would be irritated at him for not telling her that he was going to be a father.

But Honey was a problem that would have to wait.

"You may kiss the bride," the judge said.

And this... Well, this was the part Creed had been waiting for.

He wrapped his arms around Wren and pulled her against him. The look in her eyes was one of shock, as if she hadn't realized they would be expected to do this. As if she hadn't realized that whether a wedding was permanent or not, in a courthouse or not, if you were trying to pass it off as something real to your family, you were going to have to kiss.

And so they did.

It was everything he remembered. Her mouth so soft and sweet. She was a revelation, Wren Maxfield.

And he tried to remember what it had been like when he wanted to punish her with his passion.

That wasn't what he wanted now. No.

Now what he wanted was something else altogether.

A strange need had twisted and turned inside him, upside down and inside out, until he couldn't recognize it or himself. He might not know exactly what was happening in him, but he knew desire. And desire flared between them whenever they touched. No question about it.

When they parted, her family was staring at them, openmouthed.

He shrugged. "There's a reason we had to get married so quickly."

That earned him a slug on the shoulder. Wren looked disheveled, and furious. And he wondered if he had set a record for husband who got punched soonest after the vows were spoken.

When it was over, they went to his truck, and sat there. Silence ballooned between them.

"I thought you weren't going to involve your family?" he asked.

"I… I didn't know what to tell them. I didn't want to tell them I was getting married to you just because of a legal thing. It felt stupid. And then it snowballed."

"Wren…"

"So, can I come to your house? Just for a while?"

She was making his whole seduction plan a hell of a lot easier than he had expected it to be. He had thought he would have to contrive a way to get her to spend their wedding night together, but it turned out she had walked herself into a situation where she was going to have to do it anyway.

"Gee, I think I can think of something for us to do."

"Creed…"

"You can't deny that it's real between us, Wren. Whatever else—the desire between us is real."

Wren stared at her new husband.

She had to wonder if all this time she had simply been lying to herself. By increments, stages and degrees. Lying to herself that they could be together and *not* be together, that they could somehow have a platonic relationship that wouldn't be affected if the other one ended up with a different partner. That they could be friends, and keep everything easy for their child.

But she realized now that perhaps the real issue in her parents' marriage had been honesty. And maybe it wasn't even honesty with each other, but honesty with themselves.

Wren didn't really know how to be honest with herself, that was the thing.

The realization shocked her about as much as anything else had since she'd started this thing with Creed. About as much as their kiss at the altar, and as much as how real the vows had felt.

It was just so different from how she had imagined. He was different from how she had imagined.

They were different together.

"Take me home," she said softly.

And he did.

The truck moved quickly around the curves as he maneuvered it expertly along the rural road.

"Did you ever want to do anything but work at the family winery?" she asked.

His eyes were glued to the road as he drove. "I have my ranch. Not a huge operation, because, of course, I'm tied up a lot of the time with Cowboy Wines. But I've found a way to do what I want, and what I feel like my responsibility is."

"So it feels like a responsibility to you?"

"Yes. It does. And more so in the years since my mother died."

Her heart went tight. "I'm so sorry. About your mother."

"I'm sorry about your dad," he said. "I know I wasn't very nice about it before. I'm not proud of what I said, Wren. But sometimes I get my head buried in the sand. I turned your family into an enemy, because you were competition, and because I was pouring myself into making our winery better. Since my mother died, I felt like I was on some crusade to make my dad interested in life. I lost sight of some things. But I'm good at that. I'm good at losing sight of things. Sometimes intentionally."

"Does that have to do with…"

"My son?"

"Yes."

"Trying to ignore that pain certainly didn't improve my disposition, let's put it that way. And it's a wound that hurts worse the older I get. The more I realize what I missed. What I can't get back. Kids always make you aware of how time passes, as I understand it. Mine comes with accompanying grief and regret."

She could see that. How that would work. At sixteen, everyone was short on perspective and long on time. But at their age… That's when a person realized how precious it all was, and that feeling only increased with the years. The desire to hang on to what was important.

Of course, she wasn't sure it was age that had given her that perspective.

"You know, losing my relationship with my father the way I did is what forced me to look at my life more critically," Wren said. "It's what forced me to ask myself why I was doing anything. And I think it's what made me feel ready for the baby. But even with those changes, there are so many things I still don't know how to navigate. So many things I'm not sure about. Because all these revelations are so very new and I…" She looked at him. "People like to be comfortable, don't we? We don't want to change. And usually, life doesn't ask us if we want to go through the things that most define us. We just have to go through them."

"I'm sure losing your dad the way you did is a lot like losing my mom."

She shook her head. "No. You can't see your mom

anymore. I don't want to see my dad. It's a loss, Creed, but I wouldn't compare the two. My dad was never who I thought he was."

His truck pulled up to the long gravel driveway that led to the ranch. His house was so different from any she would have imagined herself living in before. Her place at Maxfield Vineyards was styled after the vineyard house itself, which was her parents' taste. Or maybe just her father's taste. Maybe what her mother wanted didn't come into it at all. Wren didn't know.

It bothered her, going from a house that had been decided on by her parents, straight to a man's house.

He stopped the car and looked at her. "What's wrong?"

"I've never had my own place. Not really. I don't know what I like. I don't know…who I am. I try to think of what kind of house I would choose and it's just a blank in my head."

"What *do* you know, Wren?" he asked.

"I know that I want you," she said, meeting his gaze.

Because that was one choice she had made in the middle of all of this, the one choice that had been down to her—kissing Creed Cooper in the first place.

They'd made a deal. A deal to not do this. But she didn't think she could stick to the deal. Didn't think she could be near him, with him like this, and not have him.

So maybe just once?

Maybe just for their wedding night.

Whether it made sense or not, it was what she'd chosen.

That desire for him hadn't come from anywhere but inside herself. And there was something empowering about that.

Maybe the wedding had been his idea, but wanting him… She knew that was all her. Nothing anyone would have asked her to do. Nothing her family was even all that supportive of. Some might have argued it was a bad thing to have given in to, on some level, but it had been her own choice. And right now, sitting in a truck that wasn't hers, in front of the house that wasn't hers, having taken vows that weren't her idea, the desire between them at least seemed honest.

And wasn't honest what she really needed?

Yes, she was trying to be smart, whatever that meant in this situation. Yes, she was trying to do the right thing for her child, but if she didn't know what the right thing was for herself... How could she be a good mother?

She thought about her own mother. Soft but distant, somebody Wren had never connected with.

Because she didn't *know* her. She didn't know her mother, and Wren had to wonder if the other woman knew herself.

"Yes," she repeated now. "I want you. I want you, because I know that's real."

He threw the truck into Park and shut off the engine. Then he got out, rounded to her side and opened the door. He pulled her out and into his arms, carrying her up the front steps and through the door. Then he carried her up the stairs, set her down in his bed.

And when they kissed, she felt like she might know something.

Something deep and real inside herself.

She didn't have a name for it. But it didn't matter.

Because all she wanted to do was feel.

This was different from the other times they had been together. It wasn't fast or frantic. And when it was over, she drifted off to sleep. She had the oddest sensation that in his bed, without her clothes, without any of the trappings that normally made her feel like her… She was the closest to real that she had ever been.

Chapter 9

Wren began stirring in the late evening. They had skipped straight to the wedding night before the sun had gone down, and Creed was certain he would never get enough of her.

Then she had fallen asleep, all soft and warm and satisfied against him, and he would've thought that he'd find it…irritating. That he still wanted sex and the woman had fallen asleep.

But he didn't. Instead, he just enjoyed holding her.

It was amazing how much less of a termagant she was when she was asleep.

As soon as she began making sleepy little noises, he hauled himself down to the kitchen and put together a plate of cheese and crackers, and grabbed a bottle of sparkling cider, which he had bought a couple of days earlier.

How funny for Wren not to be able to drink wine. Wine was their business. It was what they were. But, of course, it wouldn't be part of her life for the next few months.

That meant it wouldn't be part of his either. No wine, but she got him as a consolation prize.

He imagined it was all a very strange turn of events for her.

He brought the food upstairs just as Wren was sitting up, scrubbing her eyes with the backs of her hands, the covers fallen down around her waist, exposing her perfect, gorgeous breasts.

"Happy wedding night," he said, holding up his offerings as he made his way toward the bed.

Her eyes took a leisurely tour of his body, and he could tell she enjoyed the view.

That she had ever thought the two of them could keep their hands off each other was almost funny.

Almost.

The problem was, he didn't find much funny about the way he wanted her. It flew in the face of everything that he was. Everything he knew about himself.

Everything he knew about keeping himself separate.

All the decisions that he'd made about his life eighteen years ago seemed... They didn't seem quite so clear when he was staring at Wren. The woman carrying his child.

The woman who was now his wife.

"Well, this is nice," she said.

"I can be nice."

She chuckled, and pushed herself up so she was sitting a little taller. The covers fell down even farther, and he set the food and drink down on the nightstand next to her, then yanked them off the rest of the way.

"Hey," she said.

But he was too busy admiring her thighs, and that sweet spot between them, to care.

"It's my payment," he said.

"I retract what I said about you being nice."

"If you keep showing me all this glory, I might go ahead and drop dead. And then you can do a little dance on my grave. I really would like to see you dance."

She smirked, then shook her hips slightly as she got up onto her knees, leaning over and taking a piece of cheese off the tray.

"Honestly, I would have married you a lot sooner if I'd known you came with room service."

"Room service and multiple orgasms," he said.

"You know, if you have to be the one to say it…"

"You know you're sleeping with a woman who has more pride than sense?"

"Nothing wrong with that," she said. "A little bit of pride never hurt anybody."

"Neither did a little bit of submission."

"That's where you're wrong," she said. "It hurts unless you want to give it."

"You say that as an expert?"

She shook her head. "Definitely not. Being totally honest, I've had a few *very* underwhelming boyfriends. And none of them have enticed me to do the kinds of things that you entice me to do. So there you have it."

"I haven't had girlfriends. None." He got into bed with her and stretched out alongside her, running his knuckles along the line of her waist. "I hook up. It's never about any one woman in particular so much as about my desire to get laid. That's actually vastly unsatisfying."

"Tell me more." She narrowed her eyes. "And this better end in a way that compliments me and makes me feel singular, magical and like a sex goddess."

"I can't keep my hands off you," he growled. "More to the point, I can't keep my mind off you. When I'm not with you, I want to be with you. And when you said you didn't want our relationship to be physical… I didn't know what I was going to do with that. I think about you, and I burn, Wren. Even if we weren't having the baby, even if we weren't together tonight because it was our wedding night, I think we would still be in my bed."

The frown on her face made his chest feel strange.

"We don't like each other," she said.

"I think we're both going to have to let go of that idea. Because obviously it's more complicated than that."

"We don't mesh," she said.

"We seem to mesh pretty well."

She poured herself a glass of the sparkling cider and took another slice of cheese, leaning back against the headboard, sighing heavily. "My parents' marriage has always mystified me. They don't really talk. It was very civil, but very distant, and I think I always imagined that's what marriage was. I tried to find a similar thing with the men I dated. This kind of external compatibility. We never fought. And anytime I ever broke up with someone… It just sort of fizzled out. Like I would notice it had been a while since we'd seen each other and I didn't really care. Or we were still going to events together, but not even bothering to have sex after. Or worse, we did have sex and I basically spent the whole time thinking about which canapés I liked best at the party, and not about what we were doing. I knew I didn't want that in a long-term relationship. Boredom before we got to forever, you know?"

"Sure."

"But there was never *this*. There was never any fighting, there was never any passion. I just thought passion was for other people."

"Why did you think that?"

She sighed. "It's stupid."

"Look, Wren, you know all about the worst thing that's ever happened to me. You tell me why you can't have passion."

"I never think about it. It's one of those things usually buried in my memory. You know when you're a kid you think you're going to be all kinds of different things. From a unicorn on down the list. For a while, I even fantasized about being a police officer. Chasing bad guys, solving mysteries. And then I realized that I don't like to run, and I never want to be shot at, so that kind of takes being a cop off the table."

He snorted. "Yeah, I can see how that would be an issue."

"But when I was a little bit older, I thought... I got really good grades in math. I really liked it. I also really liked art, and a teacher at school, at the boarding school I went to, told me that combination was sort of rare. She said it made me special, that I could think creatively and wield numbers the way that I did. She talked to me about the kinds of things I could do with a talent like that. One of the things we spoke about was architectural engineering. I was really fascinated by it. By the way you could put different materials together. Marrying form and function. Art with practicality. My father said it just wasn't what he saw me doing. He said my brain would be useful for the brand, and that I needed to remember the school that I went to, the clothes that I wore, everything that I was, came from the winery. Which meant I needed to invest back into the winery. I understood that. I really did. And I just didn't think about architectural engineering anymore after that. I got my degree in hospitality and marketing. And I've found that I really love my job. But I've just been asking myself a lot of questions lately. About who I might've been if my whole life hadn't felt so rigidly *decided*."

"Do you want to go back to school?"

"I have to take care of the winery. Cricket doesn't have any interest in it. Emerson is awesome, but she does a very particular thing, this kind of global brand ambassador stuff that requires lots of computer savvy. She's brilliant. It's actually a very similar kind of skill set as the one I have. She's so good with algorithms, but she's also great at finessing public branding. Doing posts that are visually appealing and that have a result. I mean, I get to use my gifts in my job. It's just every so often I wonder if I had known who my father was back then, would I have worked so hard to make him happy?"

"I don't think you can know that. The same way I can't actually know what kind of father I would've been. The honest truth is, Wren, I can get myself really angry about what was taken from me, and when I do that... Well, in my head I'm the best damn teenage father ever. I give up everything for my kid. Women and drinking and partying and being carefree." He paused, working hard to speak around the weight that settled over his heart. "But I didn't do any of that, I didn't have to.

Louisa did. So did Cal. *They* are the ones who ended up sacrificing. They're the ones who gave my son a family. They're the ones who gave him his life. Yeah, in hindsight I can make myself a hero. But I don't know that I would've been. We can't actually know what we would have done. We can just do something different now."

As soon as he said those words, he realized how true they were. And they made his chest feel bruised.

He looked at Wren, and he felt a sense of deep certainty. "From this day on, Wren Maxfield, you can be whoever you want. You've chosen to be the mother of my child, and I appreciate that. Whatever else you want to be, I would never hold you back from it. I'd support you. If you wanted to quit working and just take care of the baby, I'd be fine with that. If you wanted to go back to school, I'd be fine with that, too. Whatever it is you need, I will help make that a reality."

"Why?" she asked.

"Because I've had more what-ifs in my life than I care to. And this… This gives me the chance to answer a lot of my greatest ones. Getting to be the father that I've wondered if I could be… I want to be a father. Everything else… Everything else doesn't matter as much."

"You don't expect to hear that from men," she said.

"Maybe not. But most men didn't lose out on the chance of fatherhood the way that I did. So for me… If you're going to get a second chance, you gotta be willing to pour everything into it. And that includes caring about your happiness, Wren. I want you to stay my wife."

"Creed…"

"Like I said, be whatever you want along with that. I'll support you. I swear it."

He had assumed so many things about her. He had looked at her and seen the glitter and polish, had associated her with her father and the kinds of things her father had done, and Creed had imagined her to be avaricious and shallow, because it was so much easier to reduce people to stereotypes. Because it was easier to do that than to see her as a person.

Because now that he saw her as a person, he had to contend with the complicated feelings she created inside him. And he knew he had been avoiding that. Avoiding it because something in him had recognized a connection to Wren the moment they first met.

He had no doubt about that.

And he had been running from complicated since the first time emotional entanglements had bit him in the ass when he was sixteen.

But he hadn't known anything then. And he hadn't known anything for a lot of years after because he had simply clung to his anger at Louisa and used it as a shield.

But age forced him to see everything with a hell of a lot more nuance, and being in this situation again demanded the same thing.

He was having to contend with the fact that Louisa didn't seem like such a villain anymore. And that the fact didn't make the past hurt any less for him.

Having to contend with the fact that there was a lot of mileage between just sex and whatever this was between him and Wren.

And whatever their feelings were, whatever they

could be, they were having a baby. And he wanted this child to have the benefit of everything his son had.

If there was one good thing about Creed never busting into his son's life, it was that he'd given him a family. He'd honored and respected that.

But now, Creed wanted the same kind of family for this child.

So he would give Wren anything. Absolutely anything.

"I don't know what I want yet," she said, looking almost helpless. "I'm not sure that I can make that decision while I'm still in the middle of this big…change."

"It's okay," he said. "I understand. Maybe it's not the best time, but my offer stands no matter when you take it."

"Thank you." She looked at him again. "For now, can we just focus on cheese and sex? Because those are decisions I feel like I can make. I would like both."

"And I can accommodate."

And that was when he pulled her into his arms again, and they quit talking about the future, about anything serious.

Because there was a whole lot of uncertainty out there, and in the future. But there was no uncertainty of any kind between them when it came to their mutual desire. It was certain, and it was real. And it made everything else seem manageable. Like it might be the easiest thing in the world for them to find some way to make this marriage and parenthood work.

Creed was determined in that.

If sheer stubbornness could will something into being possible, then he knew he and Wren would succeed.

Because they were two of the most stubborn people on the planet.

He just had to hope they could do it without deciding they wanted different things. Because in the end, that would end up tearing both of them apart.

She and Creed had been living together for two months. She'd wanted a wedding night… She was getting a full-on honeymoon.

She'd wanted to do all this with a clear head. Had wanted to make plans for the baby, for how they would conduct themselves…

She'd wanted to do it all in a lab-like environment. As if they were talking heads who could divorce feeling and desire from everything else.

But they couldn't do that.

He'd set something free inside her and she didn't want to deny it. Didn't want to put it back. He'd asked for permanent and she didn't feel like she could answer him.

Was afraid to.

But she'd be lying if she said she wasn't fantasizing about it.

They had been sleeping together, talking to each other, eating cheese in bed. They'd talked about Christmas, and not just in the context of the event they were planning.

Their memories of it. The way they liked to decorate.

She liked it sparkly. He liked it homespun.

She liked a full turkey dinner. His mom had always made spaghetti, lasagna and bread.

They opened a present on Christmas Eve. He was scandalized by the idea. Christmas morning only.

She liked fake trees because they were perfect and didn't shed.

If he'd had pearls, he'd have clutched them. He'd been subjected to the virtues and tradition inherent in going to the woods and getting your own tree.

Another discussion they'd tabled for later, in terms of how they'd raise their child.

It was so difficult for her to reconcile the man that she was involved with now with the one she had first kissed all that time ago.

She could hardly remember hating him. She didn't hate him now. Not even close. She *couldn't* hate him. Her feelings were starting to get jumbled up, and it was frightening, to be honest.

But no more frightening than when she came home and saw that a real estate sign had been put up at his ranch.

"What is this?" she asked.

"I'm selling this place. Because I want us to pick out our own place."

"What?"

"You heard me. Wren, you told me you didn't know who you were. And that you were going from a house designed to your father's taste to one better suited to mine. I don't want you to feel that way. I don't want that for you. I don't want that for us."

"So you put your house up for sale without talking to me about it?"

"I didn't go out and buy a house without talking to you. That would have defeated the purpose."

She looked at him, and boggled. Because as much as she was coming to feel affection for him, he was still a big, stubborn, hardheaded fool.

And she cared about him an awful lot.

"I can't believe you would do this for me. This is your place. Your ranch."

"That's the only requirement I have," he said. "I do need to have property, or I need to be close enough to property I can lease."

"Don't be silly. That would be inconvenient."

"I don't care about the house," he said. "It can be whatever you want it to be. We could build too if you want, but that would take a lot of time."

"We need a place sooner than that."

They didn't waste any time. They started to house hunt after that. They went overboard looking at places, and Wren felt giddy with the independence of it.

That she was choosing a place. A place to call her own. One that would be shaped around this life she was sharing with Creed and...

She wondered when she had accepted it. That they were going to make a try at this together.

That she wasn't going to leave him after a year. Or when the baby was born, or whatever she had told him all those weeks ago.

Because she knew now that she wasn't going to do that. That there was no way. Because she knew now there would be no separating the two of them. They were forming a unit, as strange as it was.

And somehow, Wren found that their unit didn't compromise her desire for independence. Rather, it supported it.

He supported it.

There was a strange sort of freedom, having this giant brick wall on her team. She couldn't fully explain it. But there it was. True as anything.

The house that stole her heart surprised her.

It was a white farmhouse with red shutters, new, but styled in a classic way. She could see how their Christmas styles might even meet here. A little glitter, a little rustic.

The kitchen had gorgeous granite countertops and white cabinets. Light and airy, but not too modern. Perfect for Christmas Eve lasagna, and Christmas turkey.

She loved the layout of it, the great big living room that she could imagine being filled with baby toys, and a big old Christmas tree.

Fake or real, it suddenly didn't matter.

The way the bedrooms were configured, with one just down the hall from the master bedroom that she knew would make the ideal nursery, was perfect. More than she had ever dreamed. For a life she hadn't been able to imagine before, but could now, so vividly that it hurt.

"What do you think?" he asked.

"This is it," she said.

A life that was theirs. A life that didn't belong to anyone else.

"Yes," she said. "I think this is going to work."

Let it never be said that Creed Cooper was a coward, but he had been avoiding having meaningful conversation with his family for far too long. They were all dancing around the issue of his marriage, and his impending fatherhood. And it was obvious that whatever leash had been holding Honey back had just broken.

He was in his office, finalizing details for the upcoming joint winery event, when Jackson, Jericho, Honey and their father walked in. Or rather, Honey burst in, and the others came in behind her.

"Are we just not talking about this? About the fact that you got married?"

"I mean, there's not much to say."

"You married a Maxfield."

"I did," Creed said.

"She's pregnant."

"Honey, do I have to walk you through how that happens, or did you get sex ed in school?"

"I'm good," Honey said, her tone dry. "Thanks, though. My point is, what exactly is going on?"

"I got her pregnant. I married her. That's what a gentleman does."

Honey rolled her eyes. "I was under the impression a gentleman waited until he was married." She looked like she was deciding something. Then, decision made, her lips turned up into a smirk. "Or at the very least used a damn condom."

"Can you not say the word *condom*?" Creed asked.

"Why? I would assume you'd prefer to think that I was using them rather than not."

"I would prefer not to think about it at all."

"You've given *me* no such luxury. Since you clearly had *unprotected sex*. Like a…horny goat."

"Are you just here to lecture me on protocol or…?"

"Do you love her?"

"What does love have to do with anything?" And the words sat uncomfortably in his gut. Because he felt something for Wren, sure as hell. He was selling his ranch for her, moving into another house.

As if she could read his mind, Honey's gaze sharpened. "Is she *making* you leave your ranch?"

"No," he said. "I suggested we get a place that's more about the two of us."

"You...*did*?"

"It was the least I could do. Considering I basically forced her to marry me."

"You didn't," Honey said.

"I did," he responded.

His sister stared at him, and he could feel his older brother mounting a protective posture. At him? That was ridiculous.

"Honey," Jackson said. "Maybe just leave it alone. Like we told you to when you were ranting a few minutes ago."

"You guys are terrible bouncers," Creed said, addressing his brother and Jericho. "You let her come right through the front door."

"I just don't get it," she said. "Why you would marry somebody you're not in love with."

"There's a lot of reasons to get married, sweetheart," he said. "And they often don't have anything to do with love."

"Then what?"

"Well, lust comes to mind."

"You don't marry somebody just because you lust after them. That's silly."

"Fine. The pregnancy."

"I still don't understand how you could be so stupid. You're not a kid."

"Honey, I pray that you always keep your head when it comes to situations of physical desire."

She tossed her pale brown hair over her shoulder. "I would never get that stupid over a man."

The three of them laughed at her. Well, chuckles, really, but Honey looked infuriated.

"Spoken like a woman who's never wanted anyone," Jericho said.

Honey's face went up in flames. "You don't know *anything*," she said, planting her hand on his chest and shoving him slightly.

"I know plenty enough," he responded.

"Did you guys just come to my office to bicker? To yell at me about something I can't change?"

"They're our rivals," Honey said. "That's what I don't get. Now you're married, and did you do anything to protect the winery when you made that deal?"

No. They hadn't signed a prenup of any kind. And in hindsight that probably wasn't the best decision. But all he'd been thinking of was making sure he was protecting his rights as a father.

He hadn't thought to protect his monetary assets at all.

"Everything will be fine," he said.

"How could you be so shortsighted?"

"I was only thinking about one thing," he said, his patience snapping. "I'm really glad that you can sit there on your high horse. But virgins don't get to talk about what it's like to be carried away by desire. I've made this mistake before." That made his sister look shamefaced, shocked. "And the woman took the kid from me, okay? I missed out on eighteen years of raising my son because I didn't make sure my rights were protected, and I wasn't going to do it again. I did what I had to do. My kid was more important than the winery."

Finally, his father spoke. "You compromised the winery for this marriage?"

"There are things that are more important than a winery, Dad. I would think you would know that."

He couldn't read the expression on his old man's face. "I protected the winery all this time," he said. "It was my…new dream after it became clear I wasn't going to get the first thing I wanted. And I never compromised for it."

"No," Creed agreed. "You didn't. Down to not wanting to make too big of an incident out of me getting a girl pregnant when I was sixteen. Yeah, Dad, you protected the winery. But I protected my son. Can you say you did the same?"

Suddenly, Creed was done. Done with all of it. Done with all of them.

It was easy for them to pass judgment, but they didn't know what they were talking about.

His father had gotten everything he wanted in his life. He'd had a wife, had his children.

And then the old man had withdrawn into himself when his wife had died and let his children take over the running of the winery.

Yeah, he'd used them to protect the winery. At the expense of everything else. His father had asked endless sacrifices of Creed.

Creed was out of damn patience for his family.

"All of you spare me your lectures," he said. "A virgin and an old man who don't know what the hell they're talking about." He shook his head and walked out of the building, breathing in the sharp early-morning air.

He wasn't going to justify his decision to marry Wren. His course was set.

And whatever Honey thought, love did come into it. The love for his child. Nothing else mattered.

Chapter 10

The big cross-vineyard event was tonight, and Wren could hardly keep the nerves from overtaking her.

She got tired much more quickly than usual these days, and her midsection was beginning to get a bit thicker, which made the dresses she normally wore to things like this slightly tighter. She had spent countless hours trying on gowns in hers and Creed's bedroom, until he had grabbed hold of her and said very firmly that he loved her body like it was, and that absolutely everything looked good on her, or off her.

That had ended in him nearly destroying her makeup with his kisses, and she had scolded him roundly about the fact that they didn't have any time to get busy.

She had been filled with regret about that decision, however. And the fact that making love to him seemed a whole lot more interesting than readying herself for something she was supposed to be excited about irritated her.

As she slipped into the formfitting green dress she'd decided on, she tried to tell herself she was irritated simply because having a baby was such a big deal.

It was harder and harder to care about other things right now. She was consumed with the fact that in six and a half months she and Creed were going to be parents.

And for some reason, it kept sticking in her mind even more that they were still going to be husband and wife, for six more months and longer.

The baby was supposed to be what mattered.

And first, this event.

Her family was acclimating to the fact that she and Creed weren't rivals anymore. That they had to be friendly, to an extent, with Cowboy Wines. But it wasn't smooth sailing.

Not entirely. For some reason, Cricket was being difficult about playing nice. And while Wren had a lot of patience for what they were all going through under the circumstances, her sympathy still didn't make it easy to accept Cricket's behavior.

All dressed and ready, Wren kissed Creed goodbye and told him she needed to get to Maxfield Vineyards early.

He grumbled about being reluctant to let her go, but she pointed out that she hadn't been back home since they'd moved. Not to the house, anyway. She'd gone to the winery itself, to the public areas, the tasting rooms. There had been weddings and dinners and other things since she and Creed had gotten married. But she hadn't actually been in the house.

For some reason, she felt like she needed to do that today. And she felt like she needed to do it alone.

Nerves overtook her when she realized part of the reason she felt an urgency to visit was that she hadn't actually been alone with her mother, Cricket and Emerson altogether since the wedding.

When Wren arrived at the house, her mother looked impeccable, but stone-faced, and Emerson looked as radiant as ever. Cricket was wearing jeans and a T-shirt.

"What are you doing, Cricket?" Wren asked.

"Oh, I'm not going," Cricket said.

"Why aren't you going?"

"Because I don't want to," she said defiantly.

"But it's a family event."

"No, it isn't," Cricket said. "It's an event for the winery, and I don't have to be there. There's absolutely no reason for me to get dressed up and parade myself around. I'm not really part of anything that happens with the winery. It's never been me."

Wren was shocked, but she had to wonder if she would feel the same way had she been Cricket's age when their family had fallen apart.

"I'm divorcing your father," her mother said.

"What?" Wren asked.

"I'm divorcing him," she said. "I haven't seen him in months. What's the point of staying married? What was the point of any of it?" Her mother, who was often so quiet, sad even, seemed…not herself.

"More and more I question the point of any of this. I have this beautiful house, but your father never loved me. I have you girls. The only good to have come out of my life in the last thirty years. Everything else is shallow. Pointless. I thought this winery mattered. This house. The money. It doesn't."

"And if it doesn't matter to her," Cricket said, "why should I pretend that it matters to me?"

"I'm all for bids of independence," Wren said. "And I'm not going to say I haven't been on a soul-searching mission myself these last few months. But save your breakdowns so they're not right before my big event?"

"Sorry it's not convenient for you," Cricket said. "You getting married and abandoning me wasn't great timing either."

Wren had a feeling that was directed at both her and Emerson.

"Cricket," Emerson said. "You don't have to go if you don't want. But if you're upset, maybe we should talk."

"We should talk now," Cricket said. "Because this family is a mess, and Wren is just making the same mistakes Mom did. Marrying Creed because she's having a baby, when they don't even love each other. You can pretend all you want but I don't believe you magically fell in love with him. It's going to end like this. Big house, lots of money. Maybe a winery conglomerate. Sad adult children and divorce."

"That's enough," her mother said. "I judge myself for the decisions I made for money. For comfort. For... for turning away from somebody who did love me for somebody who never could." Wren stared at her mother for a moment, not fully understanding what she was talking about. "But the one thing that I'm at peace with is anything I did for the sake of you girls. Wren made a decision for the sake of her child's future. And Creed Cooper isn't your father."

"No," Wren said, her tone firm. "Creed is a good man. He loves this baby. So much. You have no idea."

"Well, I don't have to participate in any of this."

Cricket turned and walked out of the room. Emerson put her hand on Wren's shoulder. "Don't worry about her. She doesn't know what she's talking about. She doesn't know what it's like."

There was something in Emerson's gaze that scared Wren, and she couldn't pinpoint why.

Didn't know what *what* was like? Relationships?

That she would believe. Her sister had led a cloistered life on the vineyard, and hadn't gone away to school the way Wren and Emerson had. In many ways, it had felt like their parents had given up by the time they'd gotten to Cricket. For all that the expectations of their father had been hard on Emerson and Wren, Wren suspected there had been no expectations at all of Cricket.

And that the low bar hadn't done her any favors.

But Wren didn't think that's what Emerson was talking about. And the alternative possibility made her stomach feel tight.

"Mom," Wren said, turning to her mother, deciding to reject any thoughts she was having about herself and deal with her mother instead. "What did you mean about 'someone who could love you'?"

"The Coopers are good men," her mother said. "If Creed is anything like his father, he has a lot more honor than James Maxfield ever did."

Wren's whole world felt shaky, and she decided not to press the issue, because she didn't think she could take on any more right then.

Instead, Wren and Emerson went down to the grand event hall, which was decorated and lit up, overlook-

ing the valley below. It was all pristine glass, floor-
to-ceiling windows and honey-colored wood beams.
A huge fake Christmas tree was at the center, lit up,
merry and bright.

It looked elegant and perfect, and stations for each
winery were beginning to come together. Lindy Dodge,
from another local winery, was there, setting out samples and arranging small plates of food, her big, cowboy
husband, Wyatt, helping with everything. The sight of
those two people, so very different from each other —
Lindy, petite and polished, and Wyatt, big, rough and
ready—did something strange to Wren's insides. Made
her long for something she didn't think was even possible.

She turned away from the couple, and made a show
of looking at some of the displays put up by the other
wineries before busying herself with the fine details
of their own.

And when Creed arrived, her world spun to a halt.
Just looking at him made her mouth run dry. Made everything in her go still, and her sister's words echoed
inside her.

She doesn't know what it's like.

Not a relationship. No, nothing quite that simple. Not
attraction either. Because that was not deep enough.

No, what Cricket didn't understand was what happened when a man entered a woman's life, who was
wrong in every way, but fit so beautifully.

Who seemed to take all the jagged pieces and press
them together, turning something ordinary into something new. Making each fractured line seem a beautiful detail rather than a fatal flaw.

What Cricket didn't understand was the miracle involved in loving someone she shouldn't.

Loving someone who made no sense. And the way that it rearranged one's life into something unrecognizable.

What Cricket didn't understand was that love was a storm.

Wren had always imagined that loving somebody was civil. That it was something she could pick out, like selecting the perfect wine in a refined cellar.

But no. That wasn't how it was with Creed.

He was a brilliant and glorious streak of lightning, shooting across the sky, a low, resonating boom of thunder that echoed in her heart. He was nothing she would have ever looked for, and everything she was beginning to suspect she needed.

And that need wasn't comfortable.

Because just like a storm, she couldn't control it, didn't know how much damage it might cause, didn't know what the landscape would look like after it was finished raging.

Feelings like this, they could uproot trees. Reorder the slopes of mountains.

Damage her heart irrevocably.

She didn't know what to do, because she couldn't unthink all these things. Couldn't unknow the feeling that made her heart squeeze tight when she looked at the man. That made her want to mess up her hair and makeup and make love to him on the floor before an important event.

That made her want to test all his rough against her soft. That made her feel enamored of their differences, rather than disdainful of them.

The reason she had fought with him from the beginning was because she had been desperate to keep him at bay. She could see that now, with stunning clarity.

It was the wrong time to be realizing all of this. Any of this. Because she had to focus on this event. It mattered. It was the reason they were together in the first place, these initiatives.

Is it?

Or had she been unable to see a way forward without Creed because she had been desperate to spend more time with him?

Desperate to make him a part of her life and part of her business.

Honesty.

Hadn't she dedicated herself to finding honesty in who she was and what she wanted?

Her heart felt tender as she gazed at the tall, striking figure of her husband across the room, at a different winery station from her.

She didn't even know how that was going to work. They were separate. Though they were married.

And it wasn't just because they worked at different places. But because there was a very deliberate barrier between them when it came to emotion.

Creed had made it plain he wanted the marriage to last, but she knew that he was motivated by a deep, feral need to keep his child close to him.

It had nothing to do with her, and he'd never pretended it did.

It does, a little bit. He doesn't want anyone else to have you.

It was true. But was that the same as wanting her? Really wanting her?

She didn't know.

And she didn't even know why it mattered.

Why it suddenly felt imperative that there be love between them.

Because other than your sisters, have you ever felt like anyone really loved you?

The question bit into her, and she tried hard to keep on doing her job while it gnawed at all she was.

Eventually, she was unable to keep herself away from Creed any longer.

"This is looking good," she said.

"It is," he responded. "It's good."

She wanted him to say that he was proud of her.

But wanting his praise made her feel small and sad.

Because was she ever really going to be different? How could she ever be new? When she was still just simpering after the approval, the love, of a man who wasn't going to give it back?

Maybe he will. Maybe you just need to ask him.

She looked at his square jaw, at his striking features that seemed as if they were carved from stone.

He had been hurt. Badly. But did that mean he couldn't feel anything for anyone anymore? She knew that he loved their unborn baby. That he was intensely motivated by that love in everything he did.

Although, he had never said those words exactly. He didn't talk about love. He talked about opportunities, responsibility. He talked about not wanting to miss anything. But he had never said the word *love*. That didn't mean he didn't feel it, but it did give her questions about just how much he knew his own emotions.

Considering her own were a big giant news flash to

her, she didn't think it was outrageous to suspect that he might not be fully in touch with his own.

He held himself at a distance. She looked down at his left hand, at the ring he wore there.

He was her husband. And it wasn't a secret. She closed the distance between them, kissing him on the cheek. "I'm glad that we did this."

The look in his eyes was unreadable.

"Me, too."

She didn't know if she had meant the event. The pregnancy. The marriage.

How could she feel something so deep for this man? This man she had thought she felt only antagonistic things for a few months ago. Well, she felt chemistry with him, but she hadn't known him. Hadn't known that deep wound that he carried around. The intensity with which he cared about things.

And whether or not he knew it was love, she did.

He had been ready to set everything aside at sixteen and become a father.

He bled responsibility. He was everything her father wasn't.

And then he had let her choose their house, had sold a place that meant something to him. His own house, so they could build a life together. He'd asked her about her dreams, and he'd said that what she wanted was important.

No one had ever said those things to her. No one had ever offered the things to her that Creed had.

All that, and it came with the kind of intense passion she hadn't even known existed.

How could she not fall in love with him? How could she have ever not loved him?

She swallowed hard and leaned against him, pressing her face against his suit jacket and inhaling his scent. "Thank you for dressing up for me again."

"It was appropriate," he responded, his voice hard.

She could feel him pulling away, not physically, but emotionally. And perversely it only made her want to cling to him even more tightly.

She couldn't help herself.

She was supposed to be focusing on the triumph of the evening. A few months ago, she would have been. It would have been all-important to her. Because she would have gotten approval out of it. Approval from her father.

It was such a different thing to be doing something for herself. She still cared about the winery. It was just that she already knew she approved of the job she'd done. She wasn't waiting for recognition. She was good at what she did, and she didn't question whether or not she could execute something like this.

It freed up her mind to worry about other things. It made all of this less all-consuming. Less important. Because it wasn't an essential part of her happiness. Wasn't an essential part of who she was.

She did this job for the winery. But she was also a sister. A daughter. A wife. Soon to be a mother.

She was interested in other things, and Creed had reminded her of that.

This event, and what happened at the winery, was no longer the highest-stakes thing happening in her world.

She wondered what kind of mother she would be. And she was worried about being a good wife.

About her husband's feelings for her.

This was satisfying. And it mattered.

But it didn't feel half so important or potentially fatal as it would have only a few short months ago.

And suddenly she thought maybe the transformation she'd been going through wasn't so much about becoming a different version of herself, but expanding what it meant to be Wren Maxfield.

Wren *Cooper.*

A woman who could want more than one thing, care about more than just her father's good opinion and this winery.

A woman whose definition of love could expand to accommodate a storm.

A woman who could be proud of what she had done all by herself.

It was a relief.

Because she had been worried. Worried that she might have to break all that she was into pieces and scatter them over the sea, bury them there, so she could become something completely and entirely new and foreign to herself.

But she didn't have to do that. She didn't.

She could just be.

She didn't have to worry about whether or not Cricket approved, or if it made any sense to anyone else that she had married her business rival.

That she loved him.

Her life belonged to her now. And she imagined it would change shape a great many more times before it was over.

But they would be shapes formed by her hands, her heart.

And the people she loved.

No, she couldn't anticipate the landscape and how it would look in the end.

But whatever it was, she knew she would find a way to navigate it, and if necessary, find ways to change it again.

Because she wasn't easily broken.

She was strong.

And she was trying to find a way to make her bravery match that strength. Her instinct was to continue to protect herself, but she didn't think the answers lay there. After all, it had been the strangest choices, the bravest choices, that had brought her here to begin with.

From deciding to join forces with her enemy, to kissing him. Deciding to raise her baby. Agreeing to marry him.

There was that honesty again.

Honesty took so much bravery.

Not fearlessness, but bravery indeed.

The party was packed full of people, and everything went wonderfully. She could feel the bonds she was building between her family business and these other wonderful family-run operations here in Gold Valley. She felt connected. In the same way she had felt disconnected that day she'd driven to town and realized all the things she had missed here, she could feel herself growing roots in the place that she had been planted from the beginning.

A place she had always felt might not be for her.

She had anticipated this cross-promotion being a boon for her business, but she had never expected all of this could matter so much to her personally.

Emerson was standing at the station for Maxfield,

with her extremely handsome husband, Holden, at her side. Lindy was still standing with her husband.

And Wren made a decision, then and there.

Rather than going over to the station for Maxfield Vineyards, she went to the one that had been designated for Cowboy Wines. And she took her spot next to Creed.

She had no loyalty to a label.

She had a loyalty to this man. To all that he was, and more than that, all that they were together.

Yes, Maxfield would always be her family winery.

But Creed was her family now.

Creed was her heart.

Such an easy decision to make. Because now, she knew exactly who she was.

Chapter 11

Creed didn't know what the hell had gotten into Wren tonight, but it was as unsettling as it was arousing. She had been glued to his side the entire evening, tormenting him in that emerald dress that clung to her expanding curves. He loved the way her body was changing. The way her waist was getting thicker, the slight roundness low on her stomach speaking to the life growing inside her.

And, of course, he was enjoying the fullness in other parts of her curves.

She was beautiful in every way, but he was especially enjoying her current beauty because he was responsible for the changes. There was something intensely sexy and satisfying about that. But there was also a look in her eye that he was afraid he couldn't answer, and he didn't know what to make of it.

She had driven over to the winery on her own, but she left with him.

There was a determined sort of gleam in her eye, and it made his heart thunder, low and heavy.

Echoing like thunder inside him.

Like a storm.

She gave him a little half smile as they got into the house. And then she took his hand and led him over to the couch. He sat down, his legs relaxed, his palms rested on his knees.

Her eyes met his, and she reached behind her, unzipping that dress that had been torturing him so, and letting it fall from her curves.

His heart stopped. Stilled.

Everything in him went quiet. He couldn't breathe.

They'd made love countless times. Hadn't been able to keep their hands off each other these last few months. It was a storm of sensation and desire that had been building between them for years, and now that they lived together, now that they shared a bed every night, neither of them ever bothered to resist. But there was something different about tonight. There was an intent to her expression, a dare glimmering in her eyes.

Wren was never shy about sex. She was bold, and she was adventurous, but this was something else altogether. Still wearing her high heels, she unclipped her bra, removed it from her shoulders and let it fall to the floor. She did the same with her panties, standing there looking like a heavenly, dirty pinup that, thank God, was within arm's reach.

He didn't have to confine himself to just looking. He could touch.

He didn't know why he held himself back. Except

that it was her show, and part of him was desperate to see exactly what she was going to make of it.

She pressed her hands to her stomach, slid them up her midsection and cupped her own breasts, teasing her nipples with her thumbs. Her eyes never left his.

"You know," she whispered, "you were my most forbidden fantasy. I tried to pretend that I didn't dream about you. About your hands on my body. But sometimes I would wake up from dreaming about you, wetter than I ever was from being with one of my other lovers."

"You have no idea," he ground out. "The dirty dreams I used to have about you."

"Is that why sometimes you were so mad at me when you would come and see me at work? Because you'd been dreaming about me naked, on my knees in front of you?"

And then she did just that.

Dropped to her knees in front of him, her dark hair cascading over her shoulders, the look of a predator etched into her beautiful face.

She pressed her hand over his clothed arousal, stroking him before opening up the closure on his pants. And then she leaned in, licking him, slowly, from base to tip, before making a supremely feline sound of satisfaction.

"I want you to know, I've never fantasized about doing this. But with you... I used to think about getting on my knees and sucking you to make you shut up. I could get off thinking about putting you in my mouth. That's not normal. Not for me."

And then she licked him again, and his world went dark. There was nothing but streaks of white-hot pleasure behind his eyes. Nothing but need. Nothing but desire.

She was a wicked tease, her mouth hot and slick and necessary.

How had she become *this*? He had thought her spoiled. Silly. Insubstantial.

You never really believed any of those things.

He closed his eyes and let his head fall back as she continued to pleasure him with that clever mouth that he had loved all the times it was cutting him to shreds, and now as it sent him to heaven.

No, he'd told himself those things. Because it was easy to disdain her, but much, much harder to have the guts to give in to a connection like this. A need like this.

Because this had nothing to do with the right thing, the good thing. With a pregnancy, or being a good father. It had everything to do with Wren. With his deep desire to wrap her in his arms and never let her go. With the intense possessiveness he felt every time he looked at her. And now, every time he looked at her and thought *wife*.

His wife.

His woman.

He hadn't asked for this. Hadn't wanted it. Had worked as hard as he could to avoid it, but all that work had been for nothing. Because here he was, and the inevitability of Wren, and his desire for her, suddenly seemed too big to ignore, too great to combat. And he was struck by his own cowardice. He had told himself so many stories about this woman that he had now seen weren't true, so many different things about the way he felt for her, that he could have easily examined and found to be lies.

He could tell himself he hadn't wanted this.

Because intensity had led to ruin all those years ago, and because he had failed.

Had failed as a father. Had failed as a man.

All because of desire. All because of wanting. The wrong woman. The wrong time.

But this was the *right* woman. The *right* time.

He gritted his teeth, rebelling against that thought as Wren's hand wrapped tight around the base of his arousal, squeezing him, sending his thoughts up to the stars and making it impossible for him to concentrate on anything else.

Impossible to do anything but feel.

She was a study in contradictions, so delicate and feminine as she destroyed his resistance with a kind of filthy poise he'd never imagined might exist.

He'd had sexual partners in the past. But he hadn't had a lover. Not really. Wren had become his lover. She'd learned his body, learned where to touch him and how, though he wondered if all these paths had been blazed by her hands, by what she wanted, by what she liked, because she seemed to conjure up sexual necessity out of thin air, make it so he couldn't breathe.

Couldn't think.

Wren had a spell cast on him that was unlike anything he'd ever experienced.

He had been smart to avoid it. Smart to try to turn away from it.

But he couldn't anymore. Not now.

Because she was here, and she was his wife. And everything she did was dark velvet perfection that took his control and ground it into stardust, glittering over the blank, night sky of his mind until she was all there was.

And without her, there would be only darkness.

And then what would he be?

Pleasure built low inside him, and he could feel his control fraying to an end.

"I need to be inside you," he ground out, lifting her up and away from his body, pulling her into his lap. Her knees rested on either side of his thighs, that slick, hot heart of her brushing his arousal. He brought her down onto him, over him, the welcome of his body into hers like a baptism.

Like something that might be able to make him new. Make him clean.

Even as he lost himself in a hedonistic rhythm, he knew many wouldn't call this salvation. But he did. Because the shattered glory he felt was the closest thing to pure he'd ever had.

And he reveled in it. Needed it.

She flexed her hips and rode him like an expert, and he was enrapt as he watched her. Watched her take her pleasure, watched her give pleasure to him. Her head thrown back, her breasts arched forward, the burgeoning evidence of her pregnancy echoing with deep, primal satisfaction inside him.

And when she came apart in his arms, her orgasm making her shiver and shake, he couldn't hold back anymore. He gripped her hips, pounding his need into a body that felt created for it. Created for him. Until the rush of release roared through him.

Then she collapsed over him, her hair falling over them like a curtain, her heart pounding fast against his.

"Creed," she whispered. "I love you."

She could feel it, the tightening of his muscles, the resistance in his body. What she'd said was the last thing he wanted to hear.

He wasn't happy to hear her say the words at all.

It was what she had been afraid of, except worse.

Because she had hoped... She had hoped that even if he wasn't going to say them back right away, he wouldn't resist them, or reject them.

That he would at least accept what she was offering freely, that he would let the words reach him, let the emotion touch him.

But the way those muscles went taut, it was like he had built a brick wall between the two of them.

A shouted rejection could not have been any louder.

With a firm grip, he set her away from him, putting her naked on his couch, the chill in the air feeling pronounced after she had been cradled so close to the warmth of his body only a moment before.

"It was a nice evening," he said. "Please don't spoil it."

"Oh," she said, feeling mutinous and angry. "Me being in love with you spoils the entire evening? Because I have news for you. I've been in love with you for longer than just tonight. It's only that tonight I realized just how deeply I felt about you."

"Wren, it's not the time."

"Why not? Why isn't it the time? We're married. We're having a baby."

"And I have a suspicion that you're trying to make a fairy tale out of all of this. And I get the appeal. Because you've been Rapunzel, locked away in a tower, and you seem to think I might be able to save you, or that I *did* save you. But that's not true. We're just two people who had unprotected sex. We have chemistry, or we wouldn't have done what we did in the first place. The first time I did it, I had the excuse of youth. But this time? You and I have something explosive. We both know that. We're not kids. We're not inexperienced. But because of our age, you should know that chemistry isn't love."

"Why would I know that?" she asked. "Why would I know that chemistry isn't love? I've been in a lot of relationships, and there was nothing like what we have. Shouldn't you want this? With the person you're going to spend the rest of your life with? Shouldn't chemistry be part of it? Maybe it's not love all on its own, but I think it definitely indicates we are the kind of people who could fall in love with each other. And I did. I don't need you to say you love me, I really don't. But I'd like it if you could take my words and at least…at least accept them. Let them sit inside you. See what they could heal. Creed, loving you has fixed so many things inside me. It's amazing. It's more than I ever expected. If you let it, love could heal you, too."

But she already knew he wasn't going to allow it to happen. Not here. Not now. She already knew he was going to say no, because refusal was written in every line of his body. And she knew him.

Knew him like she'd never known another person, and to an extent she had to wonder if she knew him so well because now she knew herself. Because of all that honesty.

She was really beginning to dislike honesty.

She was really beginning to resent this journey she'd gone on to peel back the layers of herself and expose everything she was. Not just to the world, but to herself.

Because one thing she hadn't appreciated about the life she'd had before all this was the protection she'd had. Because she had been able to hide in plain sight, and tell herself she was doing everything she needed to do, when in reality, following that prescribed path presented little to no risk at all.

And now, here she was, on the path she was blazing for herself, standing in front of a man and exposing the very deepest parts of herself.

It hurt.

It was hard.

And this was why Wren understood—without knowing any of the details—that her mother had chosen a safer life. The one with borders and boundaries and limits.

Because these feelings didn't have limits. And there was no guide for how to proceed.

Because Wren felt simultaneously the most and least like herself in this moment that she ever had.

This was bravery.

And she was leaning into it while he was running scared.

"I love you," she repeated. "Isn't that a good thing?"

"I don't want to hurt you," he said, his voice low. "God knows you've been through enough. But that's not what I was in this for. It's not."

"Me either. I didn't kiss you that day down in the wine cellar so I could fall in love with you. So I could marry you and have your baby. But here we are. This has been the strangest journey, and it was the one I needed. Because it *was* a journey to me, a journey to us. Because it was somehow absolutely everything we were ever going to be. It's all right here. You're the only person who has ever looked at me and asked what I wanted to be. And said that no matter what that turned out to be, you would support me…"

"That's not love," he said. "It's convenience. I want

access to my child, and I want the marriage to be mutually beneficial so you don't leave it."

"Well, your generosity created love in me. Love for myself and my life, and for you. I didn't know that I could love you. I *hated* you. And I realize now the reason I hated you so much was that you called to something in me I wasn't ready to reveal. I didn't want my life to change. And something in me knew that you could change it. Just by existing, you could change everything that I was. Everything that I am. That you would drag me out of my comfort zone. Out of my safety. I wasn't ready. So I fought you. I pushed back against you. Until I couldn't anymore. My life was at a crossroads that day. I felt like an alien in my hometown, an alien in my skin, and it wasn't until I gave in to you that things started to feel right."

"That's good," he said. "And that has to be enough."

"That's the problem," she said softly "It's not. Because I realized something tonight when we were at the party. When everybody was at their stations with their husbands, and I had to make a choice. What family was I going to join? I realized that my place was beside you. But it's not because of a piece of paper, and it's not simply because I'm carrying your baby. It's because of love. And it's… I've been chasing that my whole life, Creed. I tried to be the best that I could be, but I was looking for love and acceptance from a man who could never give it. I made myself acceptable for my father, and I lost myself. And I can't hide what I am anymore. Who I am. What I feel. Least of all with you. Please don't ask me to go back to hiding."

"Wren," he said. "I can't love you."

"Can't? Or won't?"

"Something broke in me a long time ago," he said. "I failed. I failed at the most important thing a man can fail at. I'm not a father to my son. And I created an enemy to take the blame. I wanted to blame Louisa. But now I realize… I can't."

"Why not? Why can't you blame her, but you can blame yourself?"

"She must have known. She must've known that I wasn't going to do the job that Cal did. And she did what she had to do to protect her life, her child. But it was my responsibility to be better, to do more, and I couldn't. I didn't."

"Because of that you can't love me now?"

"I…"

"Will you love our baby? Or is what you feel for him or her all tied up in the boy you can't have? Because it seems to me that's awfully convenient. To have put all your emotions into something that you lost eighteen years ago. Of course you love your son. I understand that. It makes sense to me, even though you don't know him. I get it. I do. But at a certain point, you're just self-fulfilling a prophecy. You've decided that you'll fail the people who love you, and you've gone ahead and made sure you will by deciding you're not able to give again. You let that first loss decide how the rest of your life is going to go. Not just for you, but for me, for our baby."

"I want to be there," he said. "I want to take care of you both…"

"I grew up in a house that was quiet. That was half-muted with secrets and emotional distance. I have my sisters, and I love them dearly. But our parents… They didn't love each other. My father couldn't love anyone but himself. My mother is just defeated. I won't put our child in that place."

"I'm not your father," he said. "I would never hurt you. I would never hurt our child. I would never hurt another woman…"

"I know you aren't our father. But I still can't face a life without love. A house without love for me and for my baby. That kind of home was my whole existence before. You can't ask me to make it my life again. I finally found myself. All of myself. But I did that through loving you. And this woman I've become isn't going to accept less than I know that we can have. If I didn't think you could love me, then maybe I would take this. But the problem is… If I accept what you're offering now, then I'm going to be robbing us both, robbing our child. Of the life we can have, of the home we can have. Of everything we can build together."

"I gave you a house," he said. "I gave you vows. What more do you want from me?"

"Only everything," she said quietly. "Just everything that you are, everything that you ever will be. Your entire heart. That's all. And I'll give the same back, but you have to be willing to give to me. And if you can't, then… We'll share custody of the baby. I would never take this child from you." She paused, considering. "And you know what, if at this point you can't believe that I will keep my word about custody, then we really shouldn't be together."

"Wren," he growled.

He reached out and grabbed hold of her arm, pulled her to him, pressing her naked body against his. And then he kissed her. Deep and wild and hard.

But with fury.

Not love.

And she so desperately wanted his love.

Because she had come through the clearing, come through the fire, come through the storm. And she was willing to stand through it, whatever the risk.

And because she'd found a way to be brave and honest, she wanted him to do the same.

Because she loved him more than she had ever thought she hated him, and she desperately needed to know that he loved her, too.

She pulled away from him, even though it hurt. Pulled away from him, even though it felt like dying.

It would be easier to stay. Whether he ever said he loved her or not. It would be easier to just stay. But then he would still be in hiding.

And she would be out in the storm alone.

And he would never know...

He would never find this freedom that she'd found. The sharp, painful, beautiful freedom that made her all she was.

Love meant demanding more from him.

Love meant she had to push them both to be the best they could be. She could not allow him to hide, not allow him to remain damaged but protected.

She wanted him to feel whole in the same way that she felt now. Glued back together, those cracks glowing bright because they were pressed together by love.

"I need you to love me," she said. "I need you to find a way. And if it takes years, I'll still be here waiting for you. But I won't live halfway. I won't live in a house with you without love. I won't share your bed without love. I won't take your name without love."

"You're ruining us," he ground out. "Over nothing."

"No, over everything. And as long as you think it's nothing, that difference is not something we can ignore."

Her dreams started to crack in front of her like a sheet of ice. Dreams of a shared life. A shared Christmas. Those Christmases she thought they might have here in this house, starting with this one.

But it was gone now.

Hope.

She whispered that word to herself.

Just keep your hope.

Wren collected her clothes and dressed slowly.

"Your car isn't even here," he said.

"No," she said. "I know. But my sister will come and get me." She stopped. "If you can't fight me now as hard as you did over the winery business, then... I don't know, Creed. I just don't know."

She went outside then. And it wasn't Emerson who ultimately came to get her, but Cricket.

"What happened?" Cricket asked.

"Oh, my heart is only broken," Wren said, pressing her face against the glass in the car.

"Why did you marry a man you hate?"

"Because I never really hated him. I was just afraid of loving him." She sighed heavily. "Because loving him hurts. Really badly."

"That's stupid," Cricket said. "Love isn't supposed to feel like that. It's not supposed to be that close to... this. All these bad feelings."

"The problem is," Wren said slowly, "when someone has been hurt, it's not that simple. And he's been hurt really badly."

"Well, now he's passed it on to you. And I don't think I can forgive him for that."

"I can," Wren said. "If he wants me to."

Cricket scoffed. "Why would you?"

"Because some people are like Dad," Wren said. "They're toxic. They don't love people because they are too busy loving themselves. But some people are wounded. Creed is wounded. What he has to decide is if he wants to stay that way. Or if he's going to let himself be whole."

"It all sounds overrated to me."

Wren thought back to the last few months, the journey that she'd been on, the one that had ultimately led here, which was so very painful. And she realized she would do it all again. Every time. Exactly the same.

Because however it came out in the end, it had led her to this place, where she had decided to be brave and honest. Where she had decided to heal regardless of what he chose to do.

"Someday you'll understand."

"No. I'm not interested in that kind of thing. And when I am, I'm going to choose a nice man who has nothing to do with any of this."

"With any of what?"

"I want to leave the vineyard," Cricket said. "I realize this isn't the best timing. But I want to tell you… I want my own life. One that's totally different from this. I never wanted to be here. Mom and Dad never cared about what I did and…"

"I think Mom does care," Wren said softly. "But I think, like Creed, she's wounded. And sometimes she doesn't know how to show it."

"I'm not wounded," Cricket said, defiant. "I'm going

to find a place with people who aren't. Present company excluded. It has nothing to do with you and Emerson. I might want a ranch. I want you to buy out my share."

Disappointment churned in Wren's chest. The idea of Cricket leaving the winery was painful. Another loss, but…

Her sister needed her chance. Her chance to find herself, like Wren had found herself.

"It's okay, Cricket. You have to find a place that makes you happy. You have to find your path."

Privately, Wren knew that it wouldn't be as smooth as her sister was imagining. But she also knew Cricket would have to find it for herself. And maybe… Maybe Cricket would find a nice, simple relationship. An easy kind of love. But somehow Wren doubted it. Because Cricket was too tough and spiky to accept anyone soft. To accept anything less than the kind of love that moved mountains inside her.

And that kind of love didn't come easy.

But if Cricket needed to believe she could find a love that *did* come easy, then Wren wasn't going to disabuse her of the notion.

Because just like Wren's own situation, no one could do it for Cricket. She would have to fight her way through on her own.

"And what's your ideal man?"

"One who isn't half as much cowboy drama as yours and Emerson's dudes. I'm going to get a job at Sugar Cup. I've already decided. I'm going to serve coffee while I build my ranching empire. And I'll meet a nice guy."

"I didn't think you were interested in meeting anybody."

"I'm not," Cricket said.

"So there's nobody in particular that you like?"

"We shouldn't be talking about me."

"I prefer it to thinking about myself," Wren said.

"No," Cricket said. And she sounded so resolute that Wren wondered if she was lying. "I think love should make you feel sweet and floaty. I don't think that crushes should make you angry."

"Oh," Wren said. "Sure."

Sweet summer child.

But again, her sister was going to have to figure all this out for herself. Just like Wren had.

And honestly, even though Wren felt like she had figured a lot out in the last few months, she also didn't know how her story was going to end.

But she supposed that was the real gift. She had learned, through this series of changes, that while chapters of one's life would come to a close, there was always a chance to make herself new. To make her life into the best version that she could.

And she would carry that hope with her.

As long as she was here, she would have a chance to change for the better. The hope of better was what made one brave. It was what made everything worth it. And so, she would continue to hope, no matter how dark it seemed.

If that realization and her baby were the only gifts she could ever get from Creed, then she supposed they would have to be enough.

Chapter 12

"All right," his brother's voice came behind him. Creed braced himself for what would come next. "What the hell is the matter with you?"

He turned toward Jackson and scowled. "What's it to you?"

"Plenty. Because it's beginning to impact on my life, and I don't like that. You've been scowling around here for more than a week. It's a pain in my ass. Does it have something to do with your wife?"

He gritted his teeth. "She left me."

"What the hell did you do?"

"It's complicated."

"Try me."

"She said she loved me."

Jackson made a choking sound. "What a travesty. Your wife is in love with you. However will you survive?"

"That's not what this was supposed to be about."

"Oh, your marriage isn't supposed to be about love? What the hell is it supposed to be about, then?"

"I told you. It's complicated."

"I'm all ears."

"And why exactly do you think you're an authority on any of this? It's not like you've ever been in a real relationship."

"Maybe I'm not an authority on relationships, but I'm an authority on you. And you're miserable. Which means you need to sort it out."

"There's nothing to sort out. Nothing changed on my end. I offered her everything that was always on the table. I bought her the house she wanted, I told her she could do whatever she wanted when it came to work, and we set fire to the sheets. I don't know why the hell she thinks she needs more."

"It's this weird thing where people tend to want to be loved. Weird, I know. Especially since it's never been a major priority for either of us. But I think maybe it's not astonishingly strange."

"I don't understand why she needs it."

"I don't understand why it's a problem for you. Hell, you seem like you're in love with her."

"It's impossible. I can't do that. I already… Look, I wasted all my emotion. I can't love her."

"You can't? Or you won't?"

"She asked me the same question. But it amounts to the same thing."

"What's the real problem here? Because I don't get your resistance to this."

"The problem is that I didn't… I didn't get to love my son the way that I was supposed to. So now I'm just supposed to move on? Just make a new family, make a new life? I thought I could. For a little while, I thought I could. But I can't. It's wrong. I can't just decide to get a do-over. I wanted to, but it's killing me. The guilt of it."

His brother just stared at him. "What do you mean you didn't love your son? It wasn't your choice not to be with him. Not to be around him. Louisa chose that for you."

"I could've fought harder. I've seen him around."

"Yeah. And you loved him enough that you didn't go crashing into his life and make it about you. You loved him enough that you let him have the family that he knows. Loving somebody doesn't just mean being in their lives every day. And I never would've thought of that if it weren't for you. But I've never doubted that you love that kid. Because I saw what it did to you all those years ago. It tore you up. But you had to make a choice not to make his life a war zone, and you made that choice. And every time you've ever seen him at an event, including the one a few months ago, you've made the choice to put his happiness above your own. That is love, Creed."

"It hurts," Creed growled.

"No one ever said love didn't hurt. Hurt makes sense. But not guilt. You've got nothing to feel guilty for."

The problem was, his brother's words rang true.

And if there was no guilt… Then there was nothing standing in his way. It was all a matter of being brave enough to step forward. Brave enough to allow Wren to have all of him.

Even though his emotions had been savaged, his heart torn to pieces.

He didn't know if he was brave enough.

But what's the alternative?

Another life spent with so much distance between himself and the people who held his heart.

No, he'd never gotten a chance to be a father before. Not in the way he wanted to be.

But he had the chance now. And not just to be a father, but to be a husband.

It was all well and good to fantasize about how well he'd do those things, but entirely different to take the steps toward *being* those things.

"It's terrifying," he said. "I've been so certain all these years that I would've been great at this, but… What if I'm not?"

"Well, then you're not. That's just part of life. Sometimes you're bad at something, and then you learn to be better at it. Was Dad perfect?"

"Hell no," Creed said. "He's still not."

"Do you love him?"

"Of course I do."

"Well, there's your answer. Did you need perfect, or did you need a father?"

"I'm going to be there for my kid, it's just…"

"Remember what Dad said? That he loved a woman who chose easy over him? That leaves scars. Are you going to leave Wren with those kinds of scars? Are you gonna leave yourself with them?"

"There's no easy answer, is there? There's no pain-proof way to do this."

"No. Life is tough. Nobody gets out alive."

Creed didn't like that reasoning. At all. He also couldn't argue with it.

Because that was just it. There were no guarantees. He just had to be brave.

And with sudden, stark clarity, he saw Wren as she

had been. Standing there open and vulnerable and naked. Beautiful, demanding that he love her. And he realized that he'd failed her. He'd been a coward. An absolute, complete coward.

She had been so brave, after the betrayals she had experienced in her life. And he was… He was hiding behind his own hurt. Using his pain to shield him from more pain.

But it wasn't going to work. And in the end, it wasn't worth it. How could he choose safety at the cost of what could be the greatest joy he would ever experience?

He was hit with a blinding flash of truth.

If you wanted to have everything life could offer, you also had to risk your heart.

Just like Wren had said.

She wanted only everything.

And nothing else would do.

He understood that now.

Everything was the only answer. Everything was the least he could offer.

"I have to go talk to her," he said, his voice rough.

"Yeah," Jackson replied. "You do."

"I'll return the favor when you're in the same position."

"I won't be," Jackson said, chuckling, the sound sharpened by an edge that surprised Creed. "I'm happy for you. It's plain to anyone looking at you that you love her. And that you ought to be with her."

"I hope so."

She'd said she would wait. She'd said he could change his heart.

But he wondered. And he almost wouldn't blame her

if she wasn't waiting. Because she had stripped herself bare, and he had offered her nothing.

He had rejected her.

"I just have to hope that she'll still have me."

Wren was wretched, and no amount of trying to ensure herself that standing in her truth, standing strong in what she needed, was making her feel any better.

Emerson was deeply sympathetic, having been through something similar with Holden. Cricket seemed like she didn't know what to do with her.

And a surprising source of support and sympathy came from her mother.

"I know it's hard to believe," she said, "but I know what it's like to have a broken heart."

"You're going through a divorce," Wren said. "I don't think it's hard to believe."

"Not your father. My heart broke slowly over the choices I made, but he didn't break it. I was in love once. And I'm the one who walked away from it. It makes such a deep scar. I hope Creed realizes it before it's too late. Because you can't protect yourself by turning away from love. You just sign yourself up for a life of…less."

"That's why I left… I wanted him to love me. To find it in himself to admit that he does. Because if he can't find it in himself to admit it, then the alternative would be something terribly sad."

"It is," her mother said. "Believe me. And it's taken me years to get to a place I could have been in a long time ago if I had just done the work on myself back then. But instead I hid. I hid in a marriage that didn't have love. I hid behind money. I hid here in this house, because it was what I chose. Status. Wealth."

"Mom," Wren said slowly. "Were you in love with Law Cooper?"

But she didn't get a chance to hear the answer because Cricket came running into the room. "I told him to go away," she said fiercely.

"What?"

"Your husband," her sister said, her lip curled. "I told him to go away. But he's still here."

"Oh," Wren said, springing out of her chair and bounding toward the door.

"Forget about him," Cricket said. "He's not worth it."

"He is," Wren said. "And when you're in love you'll understand."

And there he was, standing in the entry of their grand home, looking out of place in his blue jeans, T-shirt and cowboy hat, his face bearing the marks of exhaustion, of sadness.

"You look like I feel," Wren said, staring at him.

"I feel like hell," he said. "It's been…the worst week of my life."

"Mine, too."

"Wren," he said. "I'm so sorry. I thought… I was so comfortable punishing myself for what happened with… Lucas. My son's name is Lucas. And I don't know him. And I've used that pain to drive me. I told myself all the things I would have done differently for him. And I made myself feel confident in this hypothetical version of me. And at the same time, I used the guilt to keep me safe. To convince myself that I never had to love again, because I had already loved and lost it. But I was just using that guilt to protect myself. Because it was easier than maybe being hurt again.

"I never loved Louisa," he said. "But what she told

me was that I might not be good enough, and I let that sit inside me. But I want to be good enough. For you. I want to be everything for you."

"Creed," she said. "What you did for me... You brought me on a journey to myself. And it was the thing I needed most, when I needed it most. I spent my life protecting myself, so I understand how compelling that is. I know what it is to live your life feeling like you might not be enough. But we were just trying to be enough for the wrong people. When we're already more than perfect for each other."

"Wren," he said, his voice rough. "I love you."

"I love you, too," she said, flinging herself into his arms and kissing him with everything in her heart. "I love you so much."

"This isn't just a second chance," he said, putting his hand on her stomach. "It's our chance. And I'm so damn grateful."

"Me, too."

Wren Maxfield loved Creed Cooper more than anything. He was a cocky, arrogant pain in the butt, and he was hers. And suddenly, even with all the twists and turns in the road to get here, Wren knew she was living her life, the best life.

She knew who she was.

She was Creed's and he was hers.

And nothing could ever be better than that.

Epilogue

Creed was the proudest father around. Matched only by how proud of a husband he was.

He loved watching his son grow, and he loved watching Wren learn, as she went through the process of getting her degree so she could become an architectural engineer.

The people he was blessed to love astounded him in every way.

He astounded himself, because he never really imagined he would enjoy a one-year-old's birthday party. But he did. It had been the best day, down to watching his son's pudgy little fingers smash the cake they'd had made especially for that purpose.

His fascination a few months earlier with their Christmas tree—fake because Wren wanted a very particular spectacle, and Mac would eat fallen pine needles—had been just as cute. Though they'd had to anchor it to a wall so he didn't pull it down on himself.

But it was the knock on the door after the birthday party that led to the most unexpected thing of all.

Wren was the one who answered it. And she came running to him, where he was sitting on the floor with Mac, only a few moments later.

"Creed. You need to come here." Wren swooped down and picked up Mac, and then stepped back as Creed made his way to the door.

Standing there, outside, was his oldest son.

"You don't know me," the kid said. "But… My mom told me the whole story. Everything, a few months ago. And she said what I did with it was up to me, but… I thought it was time I came to meet you."

Creed's heart slowed as Lucas looked past him. The color drained from the kid's face. "Oh, I hope I didn't cause any problems."

"No," Creed said. "You didn't. I just… I never wanted to go crashing into your life and cause any problems for you. But there's always been a place for you in my life. And there always will be."

"I guess my dad always knew," Lucas said. "You know. My…"

"He's your dad," Creed said. "He's the one who raised you. But I'd like the chance to be something to you."

Because that's what love did. It grew, it expanded, it changed. And it left no room for resentment.

And Creed was damned thankful that he had a woman who understood that. Because Wren accepted Lucas into their lives with as much ease as he could have asked from her.

And sometime down the road he realized it wasn't love that caused hurt. It was fear.

And his family made a rule not to operate from fear. But just to grow from love.

And that was what they did. From then, until forever. They just loved.

And they were happy.

* * * * *

In Gold Valley, Oregon, lasting love is only a happily-ever-after away. Don't miss any of Maisey Yates's Gold Valley tales, available now!

Gold Valley Vineyards
Rancher's Wild Secret

Gold Valley
A Tall, Dark Cowboy Christmas
Unbroken Cowboy
Cowboy to the Core
Untamed Cowboy
Smooth-Talking Cowboy
Cowboy Christmas Redemption

RANCHER'S WILD SECRET

Chapter 1

The launch party for Maxfield Vineyards' brand-new select label was going off without a hitch, and Emerson Maxfield was bored.

Not the right feeling for the brand ambassador of Maxfield Vineyards, but definitely the feeling she was battling now.

She imagined many people in attendance would pin the look of disinterest on her face on the fact that her fiancé wasn't present.

She looked down at her hand, currently wrapped around a glass of blush wine, her fourth finger glittering with the large, pear-shaped diamond that she was wearing.

She wasn't bored because Donovan wasn't here.

Frankly, *Donovan* was starting to bore her, and that reality caused her no small amount of concern.

But what else could she do?

Her father had arranged the relationship, the engagement, two years earlier, and she had agreed. She'd been sure that things would progress, that she and Donovan could make it work because on paper they *should* work.

But their relationship wasn't…changing.

They worked and lived in different states and they didn't have enough heat between them to light a campfire.

All things considered, the party was much less boring than her engagement.

But all of it—the party and the engagement—was linked. Linked to the fact that her father's empire was the most important thing in his world.

And Emerson was a part of that empire.

In fairness, she cared about her father. And she cared about his empire, deeply. The winery was her life's work. Helping build it, grow it, was something she excelled at.

She had managed to get Maxfield wines into Hollywood awards' baskets. She'd gotten them recommended on prominent websites by former talk show hosts.

She had made their vineyard label something *better* than local.

Maxfield Vineyards was the leading reason parts of Oregon were beginning to be known as the new Napa.

And her work, and her siblings' work, was the reason Maxfield Vineyards had grown as much as it had.

She should be feeling triumphant about this party.

But instead she felt nothing but malaise.

The same malaise that had infected so much of what she had done recently.

This used to be enough.

Standing in the middle of a beautiful party, wearing a dress that had been hand tailored to conform perfectly to her body—it used to be a thrill. Wearing lipstick like this—the perfect shade of red to go with her scarlet dress—it used to make her feel…

Important.

Like she mattered.

Like everything was put together and polished. Like she was a success. Whatever her mother thought.

Maybe Emerson's problem was the impending wedding.

Because the closer that got, the more doubts she had.

If she could possibly dedicate herself to her job *so much* that she would marry the son of one of the world's most premier advertising executives.

That she would go along with what her father asked, even in this.

But Emerson loved her father. And she loved the winery.

And as for romantic love…

Well, she'd never been in love. It was a hypothetical. But all these other loves were not. And as far as sex and passion went…

She hadn't slept with Donovan yet. But she'd been with two other men. One boyfriend in college, one out of college. And it just hadn't been anything worth upending her life over.

She and Donovan shared goals and values. Surely they could mesh those things together and create a life.

Why not marry for the sake of the vineyard? To make her father happy?

Why not?

Emerson sighed and surveyed the room.

Everything was beautiful. Of course it was. The party was set in her family's gorgeous mountaintop tasting room, the view of the vineyards stretching out below, illuminated by the full moon.

Emerson walked out onto the balcony. There were a few people out there, on the far end, but they didn't approach her. Keeping people at a distance was one of her gifts. With one smile she could attract everyone in the room if she chose. But she could also affect a blank face that invited no conversation at all.

She looked out over the vineyards and sighed yet again.

"What are you doing out here?"

A smile tugged at the corner of Emerson's mouth. Because of course, she could keep everyone but her baby sister Cricket from speaking to her when she didn't want to be spoken to. Cricket basically did what she wanted.

"I just needed some fresh air. What are *you* doing here? Weren't you carded at the door?"

"I'm twenty-one, thank you," Cricket sniffed, looking…well, not twenty-one, at least not to Emerson.

Emerson smirked. "Oh. How could I forget?"

Truly, she *couldn't* forget, as she had thrown an absolutely spectacular party for Cricket, which had made Cricket look wide-eyed and uncomfortable, particularly in the fitted dress Emerson had chosen for her. Cricket did not enjoy being the center of attention.

Emerson *did* like it. But only on her terms.

Cricket looked mildly incensed in the moonlight. "I didn't come out here to be teased."

"I'm sorry," Emerson responded, sincere because she didn't want to hurt her sister. She only wanted to mildly goad her, because Cricket was incredibly goadable.

Emerson looked out across the vast expanse of fields and frowned when she saw a figure moving among the vines.

It was a man. She could tell even from the balcony that he had a lean, rangy body, and the long strides of a man who was quite tall.

"Who's that?" she asked.

"I don't know," Cricket said, peering down below. "Should I get Dad?"

"No," Emerson said. "I can go down."

She knew exactly who was supposed to be at the party, and who wasn't.

And if this man was one of the Coopers from Cowboy Wines, then she would have reason to feel concerned that he was down there sniffing around to get trade secrets.

Not that their top rival had ever stooped to that kind of espionage before, but she didn't trust anyone. Not really.

Wine-making was a competitive industry, and it was only becoming more so.

Emerson's sister Wren always became livid at the mere mention of the Cooper name, and was constantly muttering about all manner of dirty tricks they would employ to get ahead. So really, anything was possible.

"I'll just run down and check it out."

"You're going to go down and investigate by yourself?"

"I'm fine." Emerson waved a hand. "I have a cell phone, and the place is heavily populated right now. I don't think I'm going to have any issues."

"Emerson…"

Emerson slipped back inside, and out a side door, moving quickly down the stairs, not listening to her sister at all. She didn't know why, but she felt compelled to see who the man was for herself.

Maybe because his arrival was the first truly interesting thing to happen all evening. She went in the direction where she'd last seen the figure, stepping out of the golden pool of light spilling from the party and into the grapevines. The moonlight illuminated her steps, though it was pale and left her hands looking waxen.

She rounded one row of grapevines into the next, then stopped, frozen.

She had known he was tall, even from a distance. But he was...very tall. And broad.

Broad shoulders, broad chest. He was wearing a cowboy hat, which seemed ridiculous at night, because it wasn't keeping the sun off him. He had on a tight black T-shirt and a pair of jeans.

And he was not a Cooper.

She had never seen the man before in her life. He saw her and stopped walking. He lifted his head up, and the moonlight caught his features. His face was sculpted, beautiful. So much so that it immobilized her. That square jaw was visible in even this dim light.

"I... Have you lost your way?" she asked. "The party is that way. Though... I'm fairly certain you're not on the guest list."

"I wasn't invited to any party," he said, his voice rough and raspy, made for sin.

Made for sin?

She didn't know where such a thought had come from.

Except, it was easy to imagine that voice saying all kinds of sinful things, and she couldn't credit why.

"Then... Forgive me, but what are you doing here?"

"I work here," he said. "I'm the new ranch hand."

Damn if she wasn't Little Red Riding Hood delivered right to the Big Bad Wolf.

Except, she wasn't wearing a scarlet cloak. It was

a scarlet dress that clung to her generous curves like wrapping paper around a tempting present.

Her dark hair was lined silver by the moonbeams and tumbling around naked shoulders.

He could picture her in his bed, just like that. Naked and rumpled in the sheets, that hair spread everywhere.

It was a shame he wasn't here for pleasure.

He was here for revenge.

And if he had guessed correctly based on what he knew about the Maxfield family, this was Emerson Maxfield. Who often had her beautiful face splashed across magazine covers for food and wine features, and who had become something of an It Girl for clothing brands as well. She was gorgeous, recognizable... and engaged.

But none of that would have deterred him, if he really wanted her.

What the hell did he care if a man had put a ring on a woman's finger? In his opinion, if an engaged or married woman was looking elsewhere, then the man who'd put the ring on her finger should've done a better job of keeping her satisfied.

If Holden could seduce a woman, then the bastard he seduced her away from deserved it.

Indiscretion didn't cause him any concern.

But there were a whole lot of women and a whole lot of ways for him to get laid, and he wasn't about to sully himself inside a Maxfield.

No matter how gorgeous.

"I didn't realize my father had hired someone new," she said.

It was funny, given what he knew about her family, the way that she talked like a little private school princess. But he knew she'd gone to elite schools on the East Coast, coming back home to Oregon for summer vacations, at least when her family wasn't jet-setting off somewhere else.

They were the wealthiest family in Logan County, with a wine label that competed on the world stage.

Her father, James Maxfield, was a world-class visionary, a world-class winemaker...and a world-class bastard.

Holden had few morals, but there were some scruples he held dear. At the very top of that list was that when he was with a woman, there was no coercion involved. And he would never leave one hopeless, blackmailed and depressed. No.

But James Maxfield had no such moral code.

And, sadly for James, when it came to dealing out justice to men who had harmed someone Holden cared about very much, he didn't have a limit on how far he was willing to go. He wondered what Emerson would think if she knew what her father had done to a woman who was barely her age.

What he'd done to Holden's younger sister.

But then, Emerson probably wouldn't care at all.

He couldn't see how she would *not* know the way her father behaved, given that the whole family seemed to run the enterprise together.

He had a feeling the Maxfield children looked the other way, as did James's wife. All of them ignoring his bad behavior so they could continue to have access to his bank account.

"I just got here today," he said. "Staying in one of the cabins on the property."

There was staff lodging, which he had found quaint as hell.

Holden had worked his way up from nothing, though his success in real estate development was not anywhere near as splashed over the media as the Maxfield's success was. Which, in the end, was what allowed him to engage in this revenge mission, this quest to destroy the life and reputation of James Maxfield.

And the really wonderful thing was, James wouldn't even see it coming.

Because he wouldn't believe a man of such low status could possibly bring him down. He would overlook Holden. Because James would believe that Holden was nothing more than a hired hand, a lackey.

James would have no idea that Holden was a man with a massive spread of land in the eastern part of the state, in Jackson Creek.

Because James Maxfield thought of no one but himself. He didn't think anyone was as smart as he was, didn't think anyone was anywhere near as important.

And that pride would be his downfall in the end.

Holden would make sure of it.

"Oh," she said. She met his eyes and bit her lip.

The little vixen was flirting with him.

"Aren't you meant to be in there hosting the party?"

She lifted a shoulder. "I guess so." She didn't seem at all surprised that he recognized who she was. But then, he imagined Emerson was used to being recognized.

"People will probably be noticing that you're gone."

"I suppose they might be," she said. She wrinkled her nose. "Between you and me, I'm getting a little tired of these things."

"Parties with free food and drinks? How could you get tired of that?"

She lifted one elegant shoulder. "I suppose when the drinks are always free, you lose track of why they're special."

"I wouldn't know anything about that."

He'd worked for every damn thing he had.

"Oh. Of course. Sorry. That's an incredibly privileged thing to say."

"Well, if you're who I think you are, you're incredibly privileged. Why wouldn't you feel that way?"

"Just because it's true in my life doesn't mean it's not a tacky thing to say."

"Well, I can think of several tacky things to say right back that might make you feel a little bit better."

She laughed. "Try me."

"If you're not careful, Little Red, wandering through the wilderness like this, a Big Bad Wolf might gobble you up."

It was an incredibly obvious and overtly sexual thing to say. And the little princess, with her engagement ring glittering on her left hand, should have drawn up in full umbrage.

But she didn't. Instead, her body seemed to melt slightly, and she looked away. "Was that supposed to be tacky?"

"It was," he said.

"I guess it didn't feel that way to me."

"You should head back to that party," he said.

"Why? Am I in danger out here?"

"Depends on what you consider danger."

There was nothing wrong—he told himself—with

building a rapport with her. In fact, it would be a damned useful thing in many ways.

"Possibly talking to strange men in vineyards."

"Depends on whether or not you consider me strange."

"I don't know you well enough to have that figured out yet." A crackle of interest moved over his skin, and he didn't know what the hell was wrong with him that the first time he'd felt anything remotely like interest in a hell of a long time was happening now.

With Emerson Maxfield.

But she was the one who took a step back. She was the one whose eyes widened in fear, and he had to wonder if his hatred for the blood that ran through her veins was as evident to her as it was to him.

"I have to go," she said. "I'm… The party."

"Yes, ma'am," he said.

He took a step toward her, almost without thinking.

And then she retreated, as quickly as she could on those impractical stiletto heels.

"You better run, Little Red," he said under his breath.

And then he rocked back on his heels, surveying the grapevines and the house up on the hill. "The Big Bad Wolf is going to gobble all of this up."

Chapter 2

"Emerson," her dad said. "I have a job for you."

Emerson was tired and feeling off balance after last night. She had done something that was so out of character she still couldn't figure out what she'd been thinking.

She had left the party, left her post. She had chased after a strange man out in the grapevines. And then...

He had reminded her of a wolf. She'd gone to a wolf sanctuary once when she was in high school, and she'd been mesmerized by the powerful pack alpha. So beautiful. So much leashed strength.

She'd been afraid. But utterly fascinated all at once. Unable to look away...

He worked on the property.

And that should have been a red light to her all the way down. An absolute *stop, don't go any further*. If the diamond on her finger couldn't serve as that warning, then his status as an employee should have.

But she had felt drawn to him. And then he'd taken a step toward her. And it was like suddenly the correct instincts had woken up inside of her and she had run away.

But she didn't know why it had taken that long for her to run. What was wrong with her?

"A job," she said blankly, in response to her father.

"I've been watching the profits of Grassroots Winery down in town," he said. "They're really building a name for themselves as a destination. Not just a brand that people drink when they're out, but a place people want to visit. We've proved this is an incredibly successful location for weddings and other large events. The party you threw last night was superb."

Emerson basked in the praise. But only for a moment. Because if there was praise, then a request couldn't be far behind.

"One of the things they're offering is rides through the vineyard on horseback. They're also doing sort of a rustic partnership with the neighboring dude ranch, which sounds more like the bastion of Cowboy Wines. Nothing I want to get involved with. We don't want to lower the value of our brand by associating with anything down-market. But horse rides through the vineyards, picnics, things like that—I think those could be profitable."

Emerson had met the owner of Grassroots Winery, Lindy Dodge, on a couple of occasions, and she liked the other woman quite a lot. Emerson had a moment of compunction about stepping on what had clearly been Lindy's idea, but then dismissed it.

It wasn't uncommon at all for similar companies to try comparable ventures. They often borrowed from each other, and given the number of wineries beginning to crop up in the area, it was inevitable there would be crossover.

Plus, to the best of her ability Emerson tried not to look at the others as competition. They were creating a robust wine trail that was a draw in and of itself.

Tourists could visit several wineries when they came to Logan County, traveling from Copper Ridge through Gold Valley and up into the surrounding mountains. That the area was a destination for wine enthusiasts was good for everyone.

The only vineyard that Maxfield Vineyards really viewed as competition was Cowboy Wines. Which Emerson thought was funny in a way, since their brand could not be more disparate from Maxfield's if they tried.

And she suspected they *did* try.

She also suspected there was something darker at the root of the rivalry, but if so, James never said.

And neither had Wren, the middle sister. Wren's role in the company often saw her clashing with Creed Cooper, who worked in the same capacity for his family winery, and Wren hated him with every fiber of her being. Loudly and often.

"So what is the new venture exactly?" Emerson asked.

"I just told you. Trail rides and picnics, but we need a way to make it feel like a Maxfield endeavor. And that, I give over to you."

"That sounds like it would be more Wren's thing." Wren was responsible for events at the winery, while Emerson dealt more globally with brand representation.

"I think ultimately this will be about the way you influence people. I want you to find the best routes, the prime views for the trips, take some photos, put it up on your social media. Use the appropriate pound signs."

"It's a… It's a hashtag."

"I'm not interested in learning what it is, Emerson. That's why I have you."

"Okay. I can do that."

She did have a massive online reach, and she could see how she might position some photos, which would garner media interest, and possibly generate a story in *Sip and Savor* magazine. And really, it would benefit the entire area. The more that Maxfield Vineyards— with its vast reach in the world of wine—brought people into the area, the more the other vineyards benefited too.

"That sounds good to me," she said.

"That's why I hired a manager for the ranching portion of the facility. I need him to oversee some new construction, because if we're going to have guests in the stables, everything needs to be updated. I need for him to oversee the acquisition of a few horses. Plus, the rides, etc."

"Oh," she said. "This…person. This man you hired. He's. tall?"

James shrugged. "I don't know. I didn't consider his height. Did you?"

"No," she said, her face flaming. She felt like a child with her hand caught in the cookie jar. "I just… I think I saw him last night. Down in the vineyard. I left the party to check and see what was happening." Total honesty with her father came as second nature to her.

She tried to be good. She tried to be the daughter he had raised her to be, always.

"You left the party?"

"Everything was well in hand. I left Cricket in charge."

That might be a stretch. But while she was as honest with her father as possible, she tended to leave out some things like…her feelings. And this would be one of those times.

"I met him briefly, then I went back to the house. That's all. He told me he worked on the property."

"You have to be careful," her father said. "You don't want any photographs taken of you alone with a man who's not Donovan. You don't need anything to compromise your engagement."

Sometimes she wondered if her father realized they didn't live in the Victorian era.

"Nothing is going to compromise my engagement to Donovan."

"I'm glad you're certain about it."

She was, in spite of her occasional doubts. Her father might not understand that times had changed, but she did. She felt certain Donovan was carrying on with other women in the absence of a physical relationship with her. Why would she assume anything else? He was a man, after all.

She knew why her father was so invested in her marriage to Donovan. As part of his planned retirement, her father was giving ownership stakes in the winery to each of his daughters' husbands.

He felt Donovan would be an asset to the winery, and Emerson agreed. But she wasn't sure how that fit into a marriage.

Clearly, Donovan didn't much care about how that fit into a marriage either.

And she doubted he would be able to muster up any jealousy over her behavior.

"Image," her father said, bringing her back to the moment. "It isn't what you do that matters, Emerson, it's what the world *thinks* you're doing."

There was something about the way her father said it, so smooth and cold, that made her feel chilled. It shouldn't chill her, because she agreed that image was important in their business.

Still, it *did* chill her.

Emerson shifted. "Right. Well, no worries there. Image is my expertise."

"It's all about the brand," he said.

"I tell you that," she said.

"And you've done it well."

"Thank you," she said, nearly flushed with pleasure. Compliments from James Maxfield were rare, and she clung to them when she got them.

"You should head down to the stables. He'll be waiting for you."

And if that made her stomach tighten, she ignored the sensation. She had a job to do. And that job had nothing to do with how tall the new ranch manager was.

She was as pretty in the ridiculously trendy outfit she was wearing now as she'd been in that red dress.

She was wearing high-cut black pants that went up past her belly button, loose fitted through the leg, with a cuff around the ankle, paired with a matching black top that was cropped to just beneath her breasts and showed a wedge of stomach. Her dark hair was in a high bun, and she was wearing the same red lipstick she'd had on the night before, along with round sunglasses that covered her eyes.

He wished he could see her eyes. And as she approached, she pushed the glasses up to the top of her head.

He hadn't been prepared for how beautiful she was.

He thought he'd seen her beauty in the moonlight,

thought he'd seen it in photographs, but they didn't do her justice. He'd been convinced that the blue of her eyes was accomplished with some kind of a filter. But it was clear to him now, out in the bright sun with the green mountains surrounding them, and her eyes reflecting that particular blue from the center of the sky, that if anything, her eyes had been downplayed in those photographs.

"Good morning," she said.

"Good morning to you too. I take it you spoke with your father?"

It took all of his self-control for that word to come out smoothly.

"Yes," she said. "I did."

"And what do you think of his proposition?"

In Holden's opinion, it was a good one. And when he was through ruining James and sinking his brand, Holden might well buy the entire property and continue making wine himself. He was good at selling things, making money. He could make more money here.

"It's good. I think a few well-placed selfies will drum up interest."

"You're probably right. Though, I can't say I'm real up on selfies."

That was a lie. His younger sister was a pretty powerful influencer. A model, who had met James Maxfield at one of the parties that had brought their type together. He was angry at himself for the part his own money had played in all of this.

Because Soraya had been innocent. A sweet girl from a small town who had been catapulted into a lifestyle she hadn't been prepared to handle.

Holden could relate well enough.

He certainly hadn't known how to handle money in the beginning.

But he'd been helping his family dig out of the hole they'd found themselves in. The first thing he'd done was buy his mother a house. Up on a hill, fancy and safe from the men who had used her all throughout Holden's childhood.

And his sweet, younger half sister... She'd tumbled headfirst into fame. She was beautiful, that much had always been apparent, but she had that lean, hungry kind of beauty, honed by years of poverty, her backstory lending even more interest to her sharp cheekbones and unerring sense of style.

She had millions of people following her, waiting to see her next picture. Waiting to see which party she would attend.

And she attended the wrong one when she met James Maxfield.

He'd pounced on her before Holden could say "daddy issues." And James had left her devastated. Holden would never forget having to admit his sister for a psychiatric hold. Soraya's suicide attempt, the miscarriage... The devastation.

It was burned in him.

Along with the reality that his money hadn't protected her. His money had opened her up to this.

Now all that was left was revenge, because he couldn't make it right. He couldn't take her pain away.

But he could take everything away from the Maxfield family.

And that was what he intended to do.

"I don't think we've officially met," she said. She stuck her hand out—the one that didn't have the ring on it. That one angled at her side, the gem sparkling in the sunlight. "I'm Emerson Maxfield."

"Holden Brown," he said, extending his own hand.

If James Maxfield weren't a raging narcissist, Holden might have worried about using his real first name.

But he doubted the older man would ever connect the younger model he'd used for a couple of months and then discarded with Holden. Why would he? James probably barely remembered Soraya's first name, much less any of her family connections. Holden himself wasn't famous. And that was how he liked it. He'd always thought it would be handy to have anonymity. He hadn't imagined it would be for reasons of revenge.

He closed his hand around hers. It was soft, desperately so. The hand of a woman who had never done hard labor in her life, and something in him suddenly felt desperate to make this little princess do some down and dirty work.

Preferably on his body.

He pulled his hand away.

"It's nice to meet you, Holden," she said.

"Nice to meet you too." He bit the pleasantry off at the end, because anything more and he might make a mistake.

"I have some routes in mind for this new venture. Let's go for a ride."

Chapter 3

Let's go for a ride was not sexual.

Not in the context of the ranch. Not to a woman who was so used to being exposed to horses. As she was.

Except, she kept replaying that line over and over in her head. Kept imagining herself saying it to him.

Let's go for a ride.

And then she would imagine herself saying it to him in bed.

She had never, ever felt like this in her entire life.

Her first time had been fine. Painless, which was nice, she supposed, but not exactly exciting.

It had been with her boyfriend at the time, who she'd known very well, and who had been extraordinarily careful and considerate.

Though, he'd cared more about keeping her comfortable than keeping her impassioned. But they had been young. So that seemed fair enough.

Her boyfriend after that had been smooth, urbane and fascinating to her. A world traveler before she had done any traveling of her own. She had enjoyed conversations with him, but she hadn't been consumed by passion or lust or anything like that.

She had just sort of thought she was that way. And she was fine with it. She had a lot of excitement in her life. She wasn't hurting for lack of passion.

But Holden made her feel like she might actually be missing something.

Like there was a part of herself that had been dormant for a very long time.

Right. You've been in the man's presence for...a combined total of forty minutes.

Well, that made an even stronger case for the idea of exploring the thing between them. Because in that combined forty minutes, she had imagined him naked at least six times.

Had thought about closing the distance between them and kissing him on the mouth no less than seven times.

And that was insane.

He was working on the ranch, working for her father. Working for her, in essence, as she was part of the winery and had a stake in the business.

And somehow, that aroused her even more.

A man like her fiancé, Donovan, knew a whole lot about the world.

He knew advertising, and there was a heck of a lot of human psychology involved in that. And it was interesting.

But she had a feeling that a man like Holden could teach her about her own body, and that was more than interesting. It was a strange and intoxicating thought.

Also, totally unrealistic and nothing you're going to act on.

No, she thought as she mounted her horse, and the two of them began riding along a trail that she wanted to investigate as a route for the new venture. She would never give in to this just for the sake of exploring her sensuality. For a whole list of reasons.

So you're just going to marry Donovan and wonder what this could have been like?

Sink into the mediocre sex life that the lack of attraction between you promises. Never know what you're missing.

Well, the thing about fantasies was they were only fantasies.

And the thing about sex with a stranger—per a great many of her friends who'd had sex with strangers—was that the men involved rarely lived up to the fantasy. Because they had no reason to make anything good for a woman they didn't really know.

They were too focused on making it good for themselves. And men always won in those games. Emerson knew her way around her own body, knew how to find release when she needed it. But she'd yet to find a man who could please her in the same way, and when she was intimate with someone, she couldn't ever quite let go… There were just too many things to think about, and her brain was always consumed.

It wouldn't be different with Holden. No matter how hot he was.

And blowing up all her inhibitions over an experience that was bound to be a letdown was something Emerson simply wasn't going to risk.

So there.

She turned her thoughts away from the illicit and forced them onto the beauty around her.

Her family's estate had been her favorite place in the world since she was a child. But of course, when she was younger, that preference had been a hollow kind of favoritism, because she didn't have a wide array of experiences or places to compare it to.

She did now. She'd been all over the world, had stayed in some of the most amazing hotels, had enjoyed food in the most glamorous locales. And while she loved to travel, she couldn't imagine a time when she wouldn't call Maxfield Vineyards home.

From the elegant spirals of the vines around the wooden trellises, all in neat rows spreading over vast acres, to the manicured green lawns, to the farther reaches where it grew wild, the majestic beauty of the wilderness so big and awe-inspiring, making her feel appropriately small and insignificant when the occasion required.

"Can I ask you a question?" His voice was deep and thick, like honey, and it made Emerson feel like she was on the verge of a sugar high.

She'd never felt anything like this before.

This, she supposed, was chemistry. And she couldn't for the life of her figure out why it would suddenly be *this* man who inspired it. She had met so many men who weren't so far outside the sphere of what she should find attractive. She'd met them at parties all around the world. None of those men—including the one her father wanted her to be engaged to—had managed to elicit this kind of response in her.

And yet... Holden did it effortlessly.

"Ask away," she said, resolutely fixing her focus on

the scene around them. Anything to keep from fixating on him.

"Why the hell did you wear *that* knowing we were going out riding?"

She blinked. Then she turned and looked at him. "What's wrong with my outfit?"

"I have never seen anyone get on a horse in something so impractical."

"Oh, come now. Surely you've seen period pieces where the woman is in a giant dress riding sidesaddle."

"Yes," he said. "But you have other options."

"It has to be photographable," she said.

"And you couldn't do some sexy cowgirl thing?"

Considering he was playing the part of sexy cowboy—in his tight black T-shirt and black cowboy hat—she suddenly wished she were playing the part of sexy cowgirl. Maybe with a plaid top knotted just beneath her breasts, some short shorts and cowgirl boots. Maybe, if she were in an outfit like that, she would feel suitably bold enough to ask him for a literal roll in the hay.

You've lost your mind.

"That isn't exactly my aesthetic."

"Your aesthetic is… *I Dream of Jeannie* in Mourning?"

She laughed. "I hadn't thought about it that way. But sure. *I Dream of Jeannie* in Mourning sounds about right. In fact, I think I might go ahead and label the outfit that when I post pics."

"Whatever works," he said.

His comment was funny. And okay, maybe the fact that he'd been clever a couple of times in her presence was bestowing the label of *funny* on him too early. But it made her feel a little bit better about her wayward hormones that he wasn't just beautiful, that he was fascinating as well.

"So today's ride isn't just a scouting mission for you," he said. "If you're worried about your aesthetic."

"No," she said. "I want to start generating interest in this idea. You know, pictures of me on the horse. In fact, hang on a second." She stopped, maneuvering her mount, turning so she was facing Holden, with the brilliant backdrop of the trail and the mountains behind them. Then she flipped her phone front facing and raised it up in the air, tilting it downward and grinning as she hit the button. She looked at the result, frowned, and then did it again. The second one would be fine once she put some filters on it.

"What was that?"

She maneuvered her horse back around in the other direction, stuffed her phone in her pocket and carried on.

"It was me getting a photograph," she said. "One that I can post. 'Something new and exciting is coming to the Maxfield label.'"

"Are you really going to put it like that?"

"Yes. I mean, eventually we'll do official press releases and other forms of media, but the way you use social media advertisements is a little different. I personally am part of that online brand. And my lifestyle— including my clothes—is part of what makes people interested in the vineyard."

"Right," he said.

"People want to be jealous," she said. "If they didn't, they wouldn't spend hours scrolling through photos of other people's lives. Or of houses they'll never be able to live in. Exotic locations they'll never be able to go. A little envy, that bit of aspiration, it drives some people."

"Do you really believe that?"

"Yes. I think the success of my portion of the family empire suggests I know what I'm talking about."

He didn't say anything for a long moment. "You know, I suppose you're right. People choose to indulge in that feeling, but when you really don't have anything, it's not fun to see all that stuff you'll never have. It cuts deep. It creates a hunger, rather than enjoyment. It can drive some people to the edge of destruction."

There was something about the way he said it that sent a ripple of disquiet through her. Because his words didn't sound hypothetical.

"That's never my goal," she said. "And I can't control who consumes the media I put out there. At a certain point, people have to know themselves, don't they?"

"True enough," he said. "But some people don't. And it's worse when there's another person involved who sees weakness in them even when they don't see it themselves. Someone who exploits that weakness. Plenty of sad, hungry girls have been lost along that envious road, when they took the wrong hand desperate for a hand up into satisfaction."

"Well, I'm not selling wild parties," she said. "I'm selling an afternoon ride at a family winery, and a trip here is not that out of reach for most people. That's the thing. There's all this wild aspirational stuff out there online, and the vineyard is just a little more accessible. That's what makes it advertising and not luxury porn."

"I see. Create a desire so big it can never be filled, and then offer a winery as the consolation prize."

"If the rest of our culture supports that, it's hardly my fault."

"Have you ever had to want for anything in your

entire life, Emerson?" The question was asked innoc-
uously enough, but the way he asked it, in that dark,
rough voice, made it buzz over her skin, crackling like
electricity as it moved through her. "Or have you always
been given everything you could ever desire?"

"I've wanted things," she said, maybe too quickly.
Too defensively.

"What?" he pressed.

She desperately went through the catalog of her life,
trying to come up with a moment when she had been denied something that she had wanted in a material sense.
And there was only one word that burned in her brain.

You.

Yes, that was what she would say. *I want you, and I
can't have you. Because I'm engaged to a man who's not
interested in kissing me, much less getting into bed with
me. And I'm no more interested in doing that with him.*

*But I can't break off the engagement no matter how
much I want to because I so desperately need...*

"Approval," she said. "That's...that's something I
want."

Her stomach twisted, and she kept her eyes fixed
ahead, because she didn't know why she had let the
word escape out loud. She should have said nothing.

He wasn't interested in hearing about her emotional
issues.

"From your father?" he asked.

"No," she said. "I have his approval. My mother, on
the other hand..."

"You're famous, successful, beautiful. And you don't
have your mother's approval?"

"Yeah, shockingly, my mother's goal for me wasn't to
take pictures of myself and put them up on the internet."

"Unless you have a secret stash of pictures, I don't see how your mother could disapprove of these sorts of photographs. Unless, of course, it's your pants. Which I do think are questionable."

"These are *wonderful* pants. And actually deceptively practical. Because they allow me to sit on the horse comfortably. Whatever you might think."

"What doesn't your mother approve of?"

"She wanted me to do something more. Something that was my own. She doesn't want me just running publicity for the family business. But I like it. I enjoy what I do, I enjoy this brand. Representing it is easy for me, because I care about it. I went to school for marketing, close to home. She felt like it was…limiting my potential."

He chuckled. "I'm sorry. Your mother felt like you limited your potential by going to get a degree in marketing and then going on to be an ambassador for a successful brand."

"Yes," she said.

She could still remember the brittle irritation in her mother's voice when she had told her about the engagement to Donovan.

"So you're marrying a man more successful in advertising in the broader world even though you could have done that."

"You're married to a successful man."

"I was never given the opportunities that you were given. You don't have to hide behind a husband's shadow. You could've done more."

"Yeah, that's about the size of it," she said. "Look, my mother is brilliant. And scrappy. And I respect her. But she's never going to be overly impressed with me.

As far as she's concerned, I haven't worked a day in my life for anything, and I took the path of least resistance into this version of success."

"What does she think of your sisters?"

"Well, Wren works for the winery too, but the only thing that annoys my mother more than her daughters taking a free pass is the Cooper family, and since Wren makes it her life's work to go toe-to-toe with them, my mother isn't quite as irritated with everything Wren does. And Cricket… I don't know that anyone knows what Cricket wants."

Poor Cricket was a later addition to the family. Eight years younger than Emerson, and six years younger than Wren. Their parents hadn't planned on having another child, and they especially hadn't planned on one like Cricket, who didn't seem to have inherited the need to please…well, anyone.

Cricket had run wild over the winery, raised more by the staff than by their mother or father.

Sometimes Emerson envied Cricket and the independence she seemed to have found before turning twenty-one, when Emerson couldn't quite capture independence even at twenty-nine.

"Sounds to me like your mother is pretty difficult to please."

"Impossible," she agreed.

But her father wasn't. He was proud of her. She was doing exactly what he wanted her to do. And she would keep on doing it.

The trail ended in a grassy clearing on the side of the mountain, overlooking the valley below. The wineries rolled on for miles, and the little redbrick town of Gold Valley was all the way at the bottom.

"Yes," she said. "This is perfect." She got down off the horse, snapped another few pictures with herself in them and the view in the background. And then a sudden inspiration took hold, and she whipped around quickly, capturing the blurred outline of Holden, on his horse with his cowboy hat, behind her.

He frowned, dismounting the horse, and she looked into the phone screen, keeping her eyes on him, and took another shot. He was mostly a silhouette, but it was clear that he was a good-looking, well-built man in a cowboy hat.

"Now, *there's* an ad," she said.

"What're you doing?"

He sounded angry. Not amused at all.

"I just thought it would be good to get you in the background. A full-on Western fantasy."

"You said that wasn't the aesthetic."

"It's not mine. Just because a girl doesn't want to wear cutoff shorts doesn't mean she's not interested in looking at a cowboy."

"You can't post that," he said, his voice hard like granite.

She turned to face him. "Why not?"

"Because I don't want to be on your bullshit website."

"It's not a website. It's… Never mind. Are you… You're not, like, fleeing from the law or something, are you?"

"No," he said. "I'm not."

"Then why won't you let me post your picture? It's not like you can really see you."

"I'm not interested in that stuff."

"Well, that stuff is my entire life's work." She turned her focus to the scenery around them and pretended to be interested in taking a few random pictures that were not of him.

"Some website that isn't going to exist in a couple of years is not your life's work. Your life's work might be figuring out how to sell things to people, advertising, marketing. Whatever you want to call it. But the *how* of it is going to change, and it's going to keep on changing. What you've done is figure out how to understand the way people discover things right now. But it will change. And you'll figure that out too. These pictures are not your life's work."

It was an impassioned speech, and one she almost felt certain he'd given before, though she couldn't quite figure out why he would have, or to who.

"That's nice," she said. "But I don't need a pep talk. I wasn't belittling myself. I won't post the pictures. Though, I think they would have caused a lot of excitement."

"I'm not going to be anyone's trail guide. So there's no point using me."

"You're not even *my* trail guide, not really." She turned to face him, and found he was much closer than she had thought. All the breath was sucked from her body. He was so big and broad, imposing.

There was an intensity about him that should repel her, but instead it fascinated her.

The air was warm, and she was a little bit sweaty, and that made her wonder if *he* was sweaty, and something about that thought made her want to press her face against his chest and smell his skin.

"Have you ever gone without something?"

She didn't know why she'd asked him that, except that maybe it was the only thing keeping her from actually giving in to her fantasy and pressing her face against his body.

"I don't really think that's any of your business."

"Why not? I just downloaded all of my family issues onto you, and I'm not even sure why. Except that you asked. And I don't think anyone else has ever asked. So… It's just you and me out here."

"And your phone. Which is your link to the outside world on a scale that I can barely understand."

Somehow, that rang false.

"I don't have service," she said. "And anyway, my phone is going back in my pocket." She slipped it into the silky pocket of her black pants.

He looked at her, his dark eyes moving over her body, and she knew he was deliberately taking his time examining her curves. Knew that his gaze was deliberately sexual.

And she didn't feel like she could be trusted with that kind of knowledge, because something deep inside her was dancing around the edge of being bold. That one little piece of her that felt repressed, that had felt bored at the party last night…

That one little piece of her wanted this.

"A few things," he said slowly. And his words were deliberate too.

Without thinking, she sucked her lip between her teeth and bit down on it, then swiped her tongue over the stinging surface to soothe it.

And the intensity in his eyes leaped higher.

She couldn't pretend she didn't know what she'd done. She'd deliberately drawn his focus to her mouth.

Now, she might have done it deliberately, but she didn't know what she wanted out of it.

Well, she did. But she couldn't want *that*. She couldn't. Not when…

Suddenly, he reached out, grabbing her chin between his thumb and forefinger. "I don't know how the boys who run around in your world play, Emerson. But I'm not a man who scrolls through photos and wishes he could touch something. If I want something, I take it. So if I were you… I wouldn't go around teasing."

She stuttered, "I… I… I…" and stumbled backward. She nearly tripped down onto the grass, onto her butt, but he reached out, looping his strong arm around her waist and pulling her upright. The breath whooshed from her lungs, and she found herself pressed hard against his solid body. She put her hand gingerly on his chest. Yeah. He was a little bit sweaty.

And damned if it wasn't sexy.

She racked her brain, trying to come up with something witty to say, something to defuse the situation, but she couldn't think. Her heart was thundering fast, and there was an echoing pulse down in the center of her thighs making it impossible for her to breathe. Impossible for her to think. She felt like she was having an out-of-body experience, or a wild fantasy that was surely happening in her head only, and not in reality.

But his body was hot and hard underneath her hand, and there was a point at which she really couldn't pretend she wasn't touching an actual man.

Because her fingers burned. Because her body burned. Because everything burned.

And she couldn't think of a single word to say, which wasn't like her, but usually she wasn't affected by men.

They liked her. They liked to flirt and talk with her, and since becoming engaged, they'd only liked it even more. Seeing her as a bit of a challenge, and it didn't cost her anything to play into that a little bit. Because she was never tempted to do anything. Because she was never affected. Because it was only ever a conversation and nothing more.

But this felt like more.

The air was thick with *more*, and she couldn't figure out why him, why now.

His lips curved up into a half smile, and suddenly, in a brief flash, she saw it.

Sure, his sculpted face and body were part of it. But he was…an outlaw.

Everything she wasn't.

He was a man who didn't care at all what anyone thought. It was visible in every part of him. In the laconic grace with which he moved, the easy way he smiled, the slow honeyed timbre of his voice.

Yes.

He was a man without a cell phone.

A man who wasn't tied or tethered to anything. Who didn't have comments to respond to at two in the morning that kept him up at night, as he worried about not doing it fast enough, about doing something to damage the very public image she had cultivated—not just for herself—but for her father's entire industry.

A man who didn't care if he fell short of the expectations of a parent, at least he didn't seem like he would.

Looking at him in all his rough glory, the way that he blended into the terrain, she felt like a smooth shiny shell with nothing but a sad, listless urchin curled up inside, who was nothing like the facade that she presented.

He was the real deal.

He was like that mountain behind him. Strong and firm and steady. Unmovable.

It made her want a taste.

A taste of him.

A taste of freedom.

She found herself moving forward, but he took a step back.

"Come on now, princess," he said, grabbing hold of her left hand and raising it up, so that her ring caught the sunlight. "You don't want to be doing that."

Horror rolled over her and she stepped away.

"I don't... Nothing."

He chuckled. "Something."

"I... My fiancé and I have an understanding," she said. And she made a mental note to actually check with Donovan to see if they did. Because she suspected they might, given that they had never touched each other. And she could hardly imagine that Donovan had been celibate for the past two years.

You have been.

Yeah, she needed to check on the Donovan thing.

"Do you now?"

"Yes," she lied.

"Well, I have an understanding with your father that I'm in his employment. And I would sure hate to take advantage of that."

"I'm a grown woman," she said.

"Yeah, what do you suppose your daddy would think if he found that you were fucking the help?"

Heat washed over her, her scalp prickling.

"I don't keep my father much informed about my sex life," she said.

"The problem is, you and me would be his business.

I try to make my sex life no one's business but mine and the lady I'm naked with."

"Me nearly kissing you is not the same as me offering you sex. Your ego betrays you."

"And your blush betrays you, darlin'."

The entire interaction felt fraught and spiky, and Emerson didn't know how to proceed, which was as rare as her feeling at a loss for words. He was right. He worked for her father, and by extension, for the family, for her. But she didn't feel like she had the power here. Didn't feel like she had the control. She was the one with money, with the Maxfield family name, and he was just…a *ranch hand.*

So why did she feel so decidedly at a disadvantage?

"We'd better carry on," she said. "I have things to do."

"Pictures to post."

"But not of you," she said.

He shook his head once. "Not of me."

She got back on her horse, and he did the same. And this time he led the way back down the trail, and she was somewhat relieved. Because she didn't know what she would do if she had to bear the burden of knowing he was watching the back of her the whole way.

She would drive herself crazy thinking about how to hold her shoulders so that she didn't look like she knew that he was staring at her.

But then, maybe he wouldn't stare at her, and that was the thing. She would wonder either way. And she didn't particularly want to wonder.

And when she got back to her office, she tapped her fingers on the desk next to her phone, and did her very best to stop herself from texting Donovan.

Tap. *Don't*. Tap. *Don't*.

And then suddenly she picked up the phone and started a new message.

Are we exclusive?

There were no dots, no movement. She set the phone down and tried to look away. It pinged a few minutes later.

We are engaged.

That's not an answer.

We don't live in the same city.

She took a breath.

Have you slept with someone else?

She wasn't going to wait around with his back-and-forth nonsense. She wasn't interested in him sparing himself repercussions.

We don't live in the same city. So yes, I have.

And if I did?

Whatever you do before the wedding is your business.

She didn't respond, and his next text came in on the heels of the last.

Did you want to talk on the phone?

No.

K.

And that was it. Because they didn't love each other. She hadn't needed to text him, because nothing was going to happen with her and Holden.

And how do you feel about the fact that Donovan had slept with other people?

She wasn't sure.

Except she didn't feel much of anything.

Except now she had a get-out-of-jail-free card, and that was about the only way she could see it. That wasn't normal, was it? It wasn't normal for him to be okay with the fact that she had asked those questions. That she had made it clear she'd thought about sleeping with someone else.

And it wasn't normal for her to not be jealous when Donovan said he *had* slept with someone else.

But she wasn't jealous.

And his admission didn't dredge any deep feelings up to the surface either.

No, her reaction just underlined the fact that something was missing from their arrangement. Which she had known. Neither of them was under the impression they were in a real relationship. They had allowed themselves to be matched, but before this moment she had been sure feelings would grow in time, but they hadn't, and she and Donovan had ignored that.

But she couldn't…

Her father didn't ask much of her. And he gave her endless support. If she disappointed him...

Well, then she would be a failure all around, wouldn't she?

He's not choosing Wren's husband. He isn't choosing Cricket's.

Well, Wren would likely refuse. Emerson couldn't imagine her strong-headed sister giving in to that. And Cricket... Well, nobody could tame Cricket.

Her father hadn't asked them. He'd asked her. And she'd agreed, because that was who she was. She was the one who could be counted on for anything, and it was too late to stop being who she was now.

Texting Donovan had been insane, leaning in toward Holden had been even more insane. And she didn't have time for any of that behavior. She had a campaign to launch and she was going to do it. Because she knew who she was. She was not the kind of person who kissed men she barely knew, not the kind of person who engaged in physical-only flings, not the kind of person who crossed professional boundaries.

The problem was, Holden made her feel very, very *not* like herself. And that was the most concerning thing of all.

Chapter 4

Emerson was proving to be deeply problematic.

What he should do was go down to the local bar and find himself a woman to pick up. Because God knew he didn't need to be running around getting hard over his enemy's daughter. He had expected to be disgusted by everything the Maxfield family was. And indeed, when he had stood across from James Maxfield in the man's office while interviewing for this position, it had taken every ounce of Holden's willpower not to fly across the desk and strangle the man to death.

The thing was, death would be too easy an out for a man like him. Holden would rather give James the full experience of degradation in life before he consigned him to burning in hell for all eternity. Holden wanted to maximize the punishment.

Hell could wait.

And hell was no less than he deserved.

Holden had finally gotten what he'd come for.

It had come in the form of nondisclosure agreements he'd found in James's office. He'd paid attention to the code on the door when James had let him in for the interview, and all he'd had to do was wait for a time when the man was out and get back in there.

It fascinated Holden that everything was left unguarded, but it wasn't really a mystery.

This was James's office in his family home. Not a corporate environment. He trusted his family, and why wouldn't he? It was clear that Emerson had nothing but good feelings about her father. And Holden suspected everyone else in the household felt the same.

Except the women James had coerced into bed. Employees. All young. All dependent on him for a paycheck. But he'd sent them off with gag orders and payoffs.

And once Holden figured out exactly how to approach this, James would be finished.

But now there was the matter of Emerson.

Holden hadn't expected the attraction that had flared up immediately the first time he'd seen her not to let up.

And she was always…around. The problem with taking on a job as an opportunity to commit corporate espionage, and to find proof either of monetary malfeasance or of the relationship between James and Holden's sister, was that he had to actually *work* during the day.

That ate up a hell of a lot of his time. It also meant he was in close proximity to Emerson.

And speak of the devil, right as he finished mucking out a stall, she walked in wearing skintight tan breeches that molded to every dimple of her body.

"That's a different sort of riding getup," he said.

"I'm not taking selfies today," she said, a teasing gleam in her blue eyes that made his gut tight.

"Just going on a ride?"

"I needed to clear my head," she said.

She looked at him, seeming vaguely edgy.

"What is it?"

But he knew what it was. It was that attraction that he felt every time she was near. She felt it too, and that made it a damn sight worse.

"Nothing. I just… What is it that you normally do? Are you always a ranch hand? I mean, you must specialize in something, or my father wouldn't have hired you to help with the horses."

"I'm good with horses."

Most everything he'd said about himself since coming to the winery was a lie. But this, at least, was true. He had grown up working other people's ranches.

Now he happened to own one of his own, a good-sized spread, but he still did a portion of the labor. He liked working his own land. It was a gift, after so many years of working other people's.

If there was work to be given over to others, he preferred to farm out his office work, not the ranch work.

He'd found an affinity with animals early on, and that had continued. It had given him something to do, given him something to *be*.

He had been nothing but a poor boy from a poor family. He'd been a cowboy from birth. That connection with animals had gotten him his first job at a ranch, and that line of work had gotten him where he was today.

When one of his employers had died, he'd gifted Holden with a large plot of land. It wasn't his ranch, but totally dilapidated fields a few miles from the ranch he now owned.

He hadn't known what the hell to do with land so undeveloped at first, until he'd gone down to the county offices and found it could be divided. From there, he'd started working with a developer.

Building a subdivision had been an interesting project, because a part of him had hated the idea of turning a perfectly good stretch of land into houses. But then, another part of him had enjoyed the fact that new houses meant more people would experience the land he loved and the town he called home.

Making homes for families felt satisfying.

As a kid who had grown up without one at times, he didn't take for granted the effect four walls could have on someone's life.

And that had been a bargain he'd struck with the developer. That a couple of the homes were his to do with as he chose. They'd been gifted to homeless families going on ten years ago now. And each of the children had been given college scholarships, funded by his corporation now that he was more successful.

He'd done the same ever since, with every development he'd created. It wouldn't save the whole world, but it changed the lives of the individuals involved. And he knew well enough what kind of effect that change could have on a person.

He'd experienced it himself.

Cataloging everything good you've done in the past won't erase what you're doing now.

Maybe not. But he didn't much care. Yes, destroying the Maxfield empire would sweep Emerson right up in his revenge, which was another reason he'd thought it might be more convenient to hate everyone connected with James Maxfield.

He'd managed to steer clear of the youngest daughter, Cricket, who always seemed to be flitting in and out of the place, and he'd seen Wren on many occasions, marching around purposefully, but he hadn't quite figured out exactly what her purpose was. Nor did he want to.

But Emerson… Emerson he couldn't seem to stay away from. Or maybe she couldn't stay away from him. At the end of it all, he didn't know if it mattered which it was.

They kept colliding either way.

"You must be very good with horses," she said.

"I don't know about that. But I was here, available to do the job, so your father gave it to me."

She tilted her head to the side, appraising him like he was a confusing piece of modern art. "Are you married?"

"Hell no," he said. "No desire for that kind of nonsense."

"You think love is nonsense?" she pressed.

"You didn't ask me about love. You asked me about marriage."

"Don't they usually go together?"

"Does it for you? Because you nearly kissed me yesterday, and you're wearing another man's ring."

Great. He'd gone and brought that up. Not a good idea, all things considered. Though, it might make her angry, and if he could get her good and angry, that might be for the best.

Maybe then she would stay away.

"I told you, we're not living near each other right now, so we…have an arrangement."

"So you said. But what does that mean?"

"We are not exclusive."

"Then what the hell is the point of being engaged? As I understand it, the only reason to put a ring on a woman's finger is to make her yours. Sure and certain. If you were my woman, I certainly wouldn't let another man touch you."

Her cheeks flushed red. "Well, you certainly have a lot of opinions for someone who doesn't see a point to the institution of marriage."

"Isn't the point *possession*?"

"Women aren't seen as cattle anymore. So no."

"I didn't mean a woman being a possession. The husband and wife possess each other. Isn't that the point?"

She snorted. "I think that often the point is dynasty and connections, don't you?"

"Damn, that's cynical, even for me."

She ignored that. "So, you're good with horses, and you don't believe in marriage," she said. "Anything else?"

"Not a thing."

"If you don't believe in marriage, then what do you believe in?"

"Passion," he said. "For as long as it burns hot. But that's it."

She nodded slowly, and then she turned away from him. "Aren't you going to ride?"

"I... Not right now. I need to... I need to go think."

And then without another word, Emerson Maxfield ran away from him.

The cabin was a shit hole. He really wasn't enjoying staying there. He had worked himself out of places like this. Marginal dwellings that had only woodstoves for heat. But this was the situation. Revenge was a dish best served cold, and apparently his ass had to be kind of cold right along with it.

Not that he didn't know how to build a fire. It seemed tonight he'd have to.

He went outside, into the failing light, wearing nothing but his jeans and a pair of boots, and searched around for an ax.

There was no preprepared firewood. That would've been way too convenient, and Holden had the notion that James Maxfield was an asshole in just about every way. It wasn't just Soraya that James didn't care about. It was everyone. Right down to the people who lived and worked on his property. He didn't much care about the convenience of his employees. It was a good reminder. Of why Holden was here.

Though, Emerson seemed to be under the impression that James cared for *her*. An interesting thing. Because when she had spoken about trying to earn the approval of one of her parents, he had been convinced, of course, that she had meant James's.

But apparently, James was proud of his daughter, and supported her.

Maybe James had used up every ounce of his humanity in his parenting. Though, Holden still had questions about that.

And it was also entirely possible that Emerson knew the truth about how her father behaved. And that she was complicit in covering up his actions in order to protect the brand.

Holden didn't know, and he didn't care. He couldn't concern himself with the fate of anyone involved with James Maxfield.

If you drink water from a poison well, whatever happened, happened.

As far as Holden was concerned, each and every grapevine on this property was soaked through with James Maxfield's poison.

He found an ax and swung it up in the air, splitting the log in front of him with ease. That, at least, did something to get his body warmed up, and quell some of the murder in his blood. He chuckled, positioned another log on top of the large stone sitting before him and swung the ax down.

"Well," came the sound of a soft, feminine voice. "I didn't expect to find you out here. Undressed."

He paused, and turned to see Emerson standing there, wearing a belted black coat, her dark hair loose.

She was wearing high heels.

Nothing covered her legs.

It was cold, and she was standing out in the middle of the muddy ground in front of his cabin, and none of it made much sense.

"What the hell are you doing here?" He looked her up and down. "Dressed like that."

"I could ask you the same question. Why didn't you put a shirt on? It's freezing out here."

"Why didn't *you* put pants on?"

She hesitated, but only for a moment, and then her expression went regal, which he was beginning to recognize meant she was digging deep to find all her stubbornness.

"Because I would be burdened by having to take them off again soon. At least, that's what I hope." Only the faint pink color in her cheeks betrayed the fact that she'd embarrassed herself. Otherwise he'd have thought she was nothing more than an ice queen, throwing out the suggestion of a seduction so cold it might give his dick frostbite.

But that wasn't the truth. No, he could see it in that blush. Underneath all that coolness, Emerson was burning.

And damned if he wasn't on fire himself.

But it made no damn sense to him, that this woman, the princess of Maxfield Vineyards, would come all the way out here, dragging her designer heels in the mud, to seduce him.

He looked behind his shoulder at the tiny cabin, then back at her.

"Really," he said.

The color in her cheeks deepened.

Lust and interest fired through him, and damned if he'd do anything to stop it. Dark, tempting images of taking Emerson into that rough cabin and sullying her on the rock-hard mattress… It was satisfying on so many levels, he couldn't even begin to sort through them all.

His enemy's daughter. Naked and begging for him, in a cabin reserved for workers, people James clearly thought so far beneath his own family that he'd not even given a thought to their basic needs.

Knowing Holden could have her in there, in a hundred different ways, fired his blood in a way nothing but rage had for ages.

Damn, he was hungry for her. In this twisted, intense way he had told himself he wasn't going to indulge.

But she was here.

Maybe with nothing on under that coat. Which meant they were both already half undressed, and it begged the question whether or not they should go ahead and get naked the rest of the way.

A look at her hand. He noticed she didn't have her engagement ring on.

"What the hell kind of game are you playing?" he asked.

"You said that whatever happened between you and a woman in bed was between you and that woman. Well, I'm of the same mind. It's nobody's business but ours what happens here." She bit her lip. "I'm going to be really, really honest with you."

There was something about that statement that burned, because if there was one thing he was never going to be with her, it was honest.

"I don't love my fiancé. I haven't slept with him. Why? Because I'm not that interested in sleeping with him. It's the strangest thing. We've been together for a couple of years, but we don't live near each other. And every time we could have, we just didn't. And the fact that we're not even tempted… Well, that tells you something about the chemistry between us. But this…you. I want to do this with you. It's all I can think about, and trust me when I say that's not me. I don't understand it, I didn't ask for it, or want it, but I can't fight it."

"I'm supposed to be flattered that you're deigning to come down from your shining tower because you can't stop thinking about me?"

"I want you," she said, lifting her chin up. "You asked me earlier if there was anything I had ever wanted that I couldn't have. It's you. I shouldn't have you. But I want you. And if my father found out that I was doing this, he would kill us both. Because my engagement to Donovan matters to him."

"You said you had an arrangement," he stated.

"Oh, Donovan wouldn't care. Donovan knows. I mean, in a vague sense. I texted him to make sure I wasn't just making assumptions. And I found out he already has. Been with someone else, I mean. So, it's not a big deal. But my father... He would never want it being made public. Image is everything to him, and my engagement to Donovan is part of the image right now."

And just like that, he sensed that her relationship with her father was a whole lot more complicated than she let on. But her relationship with James wasn't Holden's problem either way. And neither was whether or not Emerson was a good person, or one who covered up her father's transgressions. None of it mattered.

Nothing really mattered right here but the two of them.

The really fascinating thing was, Emerson didn't know who Holden was. And even if she did, she didn't need anything from him. Not monetarily. It had been a long damn time since he'd appealed to a woman in a strictly physical way. Not that women didn't enjoy him physically. But they also enjoyed what he had—a luxury hotel suite, connections, invitations to coveted parties.

He was standing here with none of that, nothing but a very dilapidated cabin that wasn't even his own.

And she wanted him.

And that, he found, was an incredibly compelling aphrodisiac, a turn-on he hadn't even been aware he'd been missing.

Emerson had *no idea* that he was Holden McCall, the

wealthiest developer in the state. All she wanted was a roll in the hay, and why the hell not? Sure, he was supposed to hate her and everything she stood for.

But there was something to be said for a hate screw.

"So let me get this straight," he said. "You haven't even kissed me. You don't even know if I want to kiss you. But you were willing to come down here not even knowing what the payoff would be?"

Her face was frozen, its beauty profound even as she stared at him with blank blue eyes, her red lips pressed into a thin line. And he realized, this was not a woman who knew how to endure being questioned.

She was a woman used to getting what she wanted. A woman used to commanding the show, that much was clear. It was obvious that Emerson was accustomed to bulldozing down doors, a characteristic that seemed to stand in sharp contrast to the fact that she also held deep concerns over what her parents thought of her and her decisions.

"That should tell you, then," she said, the words stiff. "It should tell you how strong I think the connection is. If it's not as strong for you, that's fine. You're not the one on the verge of getting married, and you're just a man, after all. So you'll get yours either way. This might be *it* for me before I go to the land of boring, banal monogamous sex."

"So you intend to be fully faithful to this man you're marrying? The one you've never been naked with?"

"What's the point of marriage otherwise? You said that yourself. I believe in monogamy. It's just in my particular style of engagement I feel a little less…intense about it than I otherwise might."

He could take this moment to tell her that her father certainly didn't seem to look at marriage that way. But that would be stupid. He didn't have enough information yet to come at James, and when he did, he wasn't going to miss.

"So you just expect that I'll fuck you whether I feel a connection to you or not. Even if I don't feel like it."

She lifted her chin, her imperiousness seeming to intensify. "It's my understanding that men always feel like it."

"Fair enough," he said. "But that's an awfully low bar, don't you think?"

"I don't…"

"I'll tell you what," he said. "I'm going to give you a kiss. And if afterward you can walk away, then you should."

She blinked. "I don't want to."

"See how you feel after the kiss."

He dropped the ax, and it hit the frozen ground with a dull thump.

He already knew.

He already knew that he was going to have a hard time getting his hands off her once they'd been on her. The way that she appealed to him hit a primitive part of him he couldn't explain. A part of him that was something other than civilized.

She took a step toward him, those ridiculous high heels somehow skimming over the top of the dirt and rocks. She was soft and elegant, and he was half dressed and sweaty from chopping wood, his breath a cloud in the cold air.

She reached out and put her hand on his chest. And

it took every last ounce of his willpower not to grab her wrist and pin her palm to him. To hold her against him, make her feel the way his heart was beginning to rage out of control.

He couldn't remember the last time he'd wanted a woman like this.

And he didn't know if it was the touch of the forbidden adding to the thrill, or if it was the fact that she wanted his body and nothing else. Because he could do nothing for Emerson Maxfield, not Holden Brown, the man he was pretending to be. The man who had to depend on the good graces of his employer and lived in a cabin on the property. There was nothing he could do for her.

Nothing he could do but make her scream his name, over and over again.

And that was all she wanted.

She was a woman set to marry another man. She didn't even want emotions from him.

She wanted nothing. Nothing but his body.

And he couldn't remember the last time that was the case, if ever. Everyone wanted something from him. Everyone wanted a piece of him.

Even his mother and sister, who he cared for dearly, needed him. They needed his money, they needed his support.

They needed him to engage in a battle to destroy the man who had devastated Soraya.

But this woman standing in front of him truly wanted only this elemental thing, this spark of heat between them to become a blaze. And who was he to deny her?

He let her guide it. He let her be the one to make the

next move. Here she was, all bold in that coat, with her hand on his chest, and yet there was a hesitancy to her as well. She didn't have a whole lot of experience seducing men, that much was obvious. And damned if he didn't enjoy the moment where she had to steel herself and find the courage to lean in.

There was something so very enjoyable about a woman playing the vixen when it was clear it wasn't her natural role. But she was doing it. For him. All for the desire she felt for him.

What man wouldn't respond to that?

She licked her lips, and then she pressed her mouth to his.

And that was the end of his control.

He wrapped his arm around her waist and pressed her against him, angling his head and consuming her.

Because the fire that erupted between them wasn't something that could be tamed. Wasn't something that could be controlled. Couldn't be tested or tasted. This was not a cocktail to be sipped. He wanted to drink it all down, and her right along with it.

Needed to. There was no other option.

He felt like a dying man making a last gasp for breath in the arms of this woman he should never have touched.

He didn't let his hands roam over her curves, no matter how much he wanted to. He simply held her, licking his way into the kiss, his tongue sliding against hers as he tasted the most luscious forbidden fruit that had ever been placed in front of him.

But it wasn't enough to have a bite. He wanted her juices to run down his chin. And he was going to have just that.

"Want to walk away?" he asked, his voice rough, his body hard.

"No," she breathed.

And then he lifted her up and carried her into the cabin.

Chapter 5

If this moment were to be translated into a headline, it would read: Maxfield Heiress Sacrifices All for an Orgasm.

Assuming, of course, that she would have an orgasm. She'd never had one yet with a man. But if she were going to…it would be with him.

If it were possible, it would be now.

When she had come up to the cabin and seen him standing there chopping wood—of all things—his chest bare, his jeans slung low on his hips, she had known that all good sense and morality were lost. Utterly and completely lost. In a fog of lust that showed no sign of lifting.

There was nothing she could do but give in.

Because she knew, she absolutely *knew*, that whatever this was needed to be explored. That she could not marry Donovan wondering what this thing between herself and Holden was.

Not because she thought there might be something lasting between them—no—she was fairly certain this was one of those moments of insanity that had nothing to do with anything like real life or good sense.

But she needed to know what desire was. Needed to know what sex could be.

For all she knew, this was the key to unlocking it with the man she was going to marry. And that was somewhat important. Maybe Holden was her particular key.

The man who was destined to teach her about her own sexuality.

Whatever the excuse, she was in his arms now, being carried into a modest cabin that was a bit more run-down than she had imagined any building on the property might be.

She had never been in any of the workers' quarters before. She had never had occasion to.

She shivered, with cold or fear she didn't know.

This was like some strange, unexpected, delayed rebellion. Sneaking out of her room in the big house to come and fool around with one of the men who worked for her father. He would be furious if he knew.

And so he would never know.

No one would ever know about this. No one but the two of them.

It would be their dirty secret. And at the moment, she was hoping that it would be very, very dirty. Because she had never had these feelings in her life.

This desire to get naked as quickly as possible. To be as close to someone as possible.

She wanted to get this coat off and rub herself all over his body, and she had never, ever felt that before.

She was a woman who was used to being certain. She knew why she made the decisions she did, and she made them without overthinking.

She was *confident*.

But this was a part of herself she had never been terribly confident in.

Oh, it had nothing to do with her looks. Men liked her curves. She knew that. She didn't have insecurities when it came to her body.

It was what her body was capable of. What it could feel.

That gave her all kinds of insecurity. Enough that in her previous relationships she had decided to make her own pleasure a nonissue. If ever her college boyfriend had noticed that she hadn't climaxed, he had never said. But he had been young enough, inexperienced enough, that he might not have realized.

She was sure, however, that her last ex had realized.

Occasionally he'd asked her if she was all right. And she had gotten very good at soothing his ego.

It's nice to be close.

It was good for me.

And one night, when he had expressed frustration at her tepid response to his kisses, she had simply shrugged and said, *I'm not very sexual.*

And she had believed it. She had believed each and every one of those excuses. And had justified the times when she had faked it, because of course her inability to feel something wasn't his fault.

But just looking at Holden made a pulse pound between her thighs that was more powerful than any sensation she'd felt during intercourse with a man before.

And with his hands on her like they were right now, with her body cradled in his strong arms…

She could barely breathe. She could barely think.

All she felt was a blinding, white-hot shock of need, and she had never experienced anything like it before in her life.

He set her down on the uneven wood floor. It was cold.

"I was going to build a fire," he said. "Wait right here, I'll be back."

And then he went back outside, leaving her standing in the middle of the cabin, alone and not in his arms, which gave her a moment to pause.

Was she really about to do this?

She didn't have any experience with casual sex. She had experience with sex only in the context of a relationship. And she had never, ever felt anything this intense.

It was the intensity that scared her. Not so much the fact that it was physical only, but the fact that it was so incredibly physical.

She didn't know how this might change her.

Because she absolutely felt like she was on the cusp of being changed. And maybe that was dramatic, but she couldn't rid herself of the sensation. This was somehow significant. It would somehow alter the fabric of who she was. She felt brittle and thin, on the verge of being shattered. And she wasn't entirely sure what was going to put her back together.

It was frightening, that thought. But not frightening enough to make her leave.

He returned a moment later, a stack of wood in his arms.

And she watched as he knelt down before the wood-stove, his muscles shifting and bunching in his back as he began to work at lighting a fire.

"I didn't realize the cabins were so…rustic."

"They are a bit. Giving you second thoughts?"

"No," she said quickly.

If he changed his mind now, if he sent her away, she would die. She was sure of it.

He was kneeling down half naked, and he looked so damned hot that he chased away the cold.

"It'll take a bit for the fire to warm the place up," he said. "But I can keep you warm in the meantime."

He stood, brushing the dust off his jeans and making his way over to her.

She had meant to—at some point—take stock of the room. To look around and see what furniture it had, get a sense of the layout. But she found it too hard to look away from him. And when he fixed those eyes on her, she was held captive.

Utterly and completely.

His chest was broad, sprinkled with just the right amount of hair, his muscles cut and well-defined. His pants were low, showing those lines that arrow downward, as if pointing toward the most masculine part of him.

She had never been with a man who had a body like this. It was like having only ever eaten store-bought pie, and suddenly being treated to a homemade extravaganza.

"You are… You're beautiful," she said.

He chuckled. "I think that's my line."

"No. It's definitely mine."

One side of his mouth quirked upward into a grin, and even though the man was a stranger to her, suddenly she felt like he might not be.

Because that smile touched her somewhere inside her chest and made her *feel* when she knew it ought not to. Because this should be about just her body. And not in any way about her heart. But it was far too easy to imagine a world where nothing existed beyond this cabin, beyond this man and the intensity in his eyes, the desire etched into every line of his face.

And that body. Hot *damn*, that body.

Yes, it was very easy to imagine she was a different girl who lived in a different world.

Who could slip away to a secluded cabin and find herself swept up in the arms of a rugged cowboy, and it didn't matter whether or not it was *on brand*. Right now, it didn't.

Right now, it didn't.

This was elemental, something deeper than reality. It was fantasy in all of its bright, brilliant glory. Except it was real. Brought to life with stunning visuals, and it didn't matter whether it should be or not.

It was.

It felt suddenly much bigger than her. And because of that, she felt more connected with her body than she ever had before.

Because this wasn't building inside of her, it surrounded her, encompassed her. She could never have contained so much sensation, so much need. And so it became the world around her.

Until she couldn't remember what it was like to draw breath in a space where his scent didn't fill her lungs, where her need didn't dictate the way she stood, the way she moved.

She put her hands on the tie around her waist.

And he watched.

His attention was rapt, his focus unwavering.

The need between her thighs escalated.

She unknotted the belt and then undid the buttons, let her coat fall to her feet.

She was wearing nothing but a red lace bra and panties and her black high heels.

"Oh, Little Red," he growled. "I do like that color on you."

The hunger in his eyes was so intense she could feel it echoing inside of herself. Could feel her own desire answering back.

No man had ever looked at her like this.

They had wanted her, sure. Had desired her.

But they hadn't wanted to consume her, and she had a feeling that her own personal Big Bad Wolf just might.

She expected him to move to her, but instead he moved away, walking over to the bed that sat in the corner of the humble room. He sat on the edge of the mattress, his thighs splayed, his eyes fixed on her.

"I want you to come on over here," he said.

She began to walk toward him, her heels clicking on the floor, and she didn't need to be given detailed instruction, because she somehow knew what he wanted.

It was strange, and it was impossible, that somehow this man she had barely spent any time with felt known to her in a way that men she'd dated for long periods of time never had.

But he did.

And maybe that was something she had overlooked in all of this.

What she wanted to happen between them might be physical, but there was a spiritual element that couldn't be denied. Something that went deeper than just attraction. Something that spoke to a more desperate need.

His body was both deliciously unknown, and somehow right and familiar all at the same time.

And so were his needs.

She crossed the room and draped an arm over his shoulder, lifting her knee to the edge of the mattress, rocking forward so that the center of her pressed against his hardness. "I'm here," she said.

He wrapped his arm around her waist, pushed his fingertips beneath the waistband of her panties and slid his hands down over her ass. Then he squeezed. Hard. And she gasped.

"I'm going to go out on a limb here and guess that part of the attraction you have to all of this is that it's a little bit rough."

She licked her lips, nodded when no words would come.

She hadn't realized that was what she'd wanted, but when he said it, it made sense. When he touched her like this—possessive and commanding—she knew it was what she needed.

"That suits me just fine, princess, because I'm a man who likes it that way. So you have to tell me right now if you can handle it."

"I can handle whatever you give me," she said, her voice coming out with much more certainty than she felt.

Rough.

The word skated over her skin, painted delicious

pictures in her mind and made that place between her legs throb with desire.

Rough. Uncivilized. Untamed.

Right then she wanted that, with a desperation that defied explanation.

She wanted to be marked by this. Changed by it. She wanted to have the evidence of it on her skin as well as on her soul.

Because somehow she felt that tonight, in this bed, it might be the only chance she'd have to find out what she was.

What she wanted.

What she desired apart from anything else, apart from family and social expectations. Tonight, this, had nothing to do with what anyone else might expect of her.

This was about her.

And on some level she felt like if she didn't have this, the rest of her life would be a slow descent into the madness of wondering.

"If anything goes too far for you, you just say it, you understand?"

"Yes," she said.

"I want to make you scream," he said. "But I want it to be the good kind."

She had never in her life screamed during sex.

The promise, the heat in his eyes, made her suspect she was about to.

That was when he tightened his grip on her and reversed their positions.

He pinned her down on her back, grabbing both wrists with one hand and stretching her arms up over her head. He had his thighs on either side of her hips, the denim rough against her skin. He was large and hard and glorious above her, his face filled with the kind of intensity that thrilled her down to her core.

She rocked her hips upward, desperate for fulfillment. Desperate to be touched by him.

He denied her.

He held her pinned down and began a leisurely tour of her body with his free hand.

He traced her collarbone, the edge of her bra, down the valley between her breasts and to her belly button. Before tracing the edge of her panties. But he didn't touch her anywhere that she burned for him. And she could feel the need for his touch, as if those parts of her were lit up bright with their demand for him. And still, he wouldn't do it.

"I thought you said this was going to be rough."

"Rough's not fun if you're not good and wet first," he said. And then he leaned in, his lips right next to her ear. "And I'm going to make sure you get really, really wet first."

Just those words alone did the job. An arrow of need pierced her center, and she could feel it, molten liquid there in her thighs. And that was when he captured her mouth with his, kissing her deep and long, cupping her breast with one hand and teasing her nipple with his thumb.

She whimpered, arching her hips upward, frustrated when there was nothing there for her to make contact with.

He touched her slowly, thoroughly, first through the lace of her bra, before pushing the flimsy fabric down and exposing her breasts. He touched her bare, his thumbs calloused as they moved over her body.

And then he replaced them with his mouth.

He sucked deep, and she worked her hips against nothing, desperate for some kind of relief that she couldn't find as he tormented her.

She would have said that her breasts weren't sensitive.

But he was proving otherwise.

He scraped his teeth across her sensitive skin. And then he bit down.

She cried out, her orgasm shocking her, filling her cheeks with embarrassed heat as wave after wave of desire pulsed through her core.

But she didn't feel satisfied, because he still hadn't touched her there.

She felt aching and raw, empty when she needed to be filled.

"There's a good girl," he said, and her internal muscles pulsed again.

He tugged her panties down her thighs, stopping at her ankles before pushing her knees wide, eyeing her hungrily as he did.

Then he leaned in, inhaling her scent, pressing a kiss to the tender skin on her leg. "The better to eat you with," he said, looking her in the eye as he lowered his head and dragged his tongue through her slick folds.

She gasped. This was the first time he had touched her there, and it was so... So impossibly dirty. So impossibly intimate.

Then he was done teasing. Done talking. He grabbed her hips and pulled her forward, his grip bruising as he set his full focus and attention on consuming her.

She dug her heels into the bed, tried to brace herself, but she couldn't. She had no control over this, over any of it.

He was driving her toward pleasure at his pace, and it was terrifying and exhilarating all at once.

She climaxed again. Impossibly.

It was then she realized he was no longer holding her in place, but she had left her own wrists up above her head, as if she were still pinned there.

She was panting, gasping for breath, when he moved up her body, his lips pressing against hers.

She could taste her own desire there, and it made her shiver.

"Now I want you to turn over," he said.

She didn't even think of disobeying that commanding voice. She did exactly as she was told.

"Up on your knees, princess," he said.

She obeyed, anticipation making the base of her spine tingle as she waited.

She could hear plastic tearing, knew that he must be getting naked. Getting a condom on.

And when he returned to her, he put one hand on her hip, and she felt the head of his arousal pressed against the entrance to her body.

She bit her lip as he pushed forward, filling her.

He was so big, and this was not a position she was used to.

It hurt a bit as he drove his hips forward, a short curse escaping his lips as he sank in to the hilt.

She lowered her head, and he placed his hand between her shoulder blades, drawing it down her spine, then back up. And she wanted to purr like a very contented cat. Then he grabbed hold of both her hips, pulling out slowly, and slamming back home.

She gasped, arching her back as she met him thrust for punishing thrust. She pressed her face down into the mattress as he entered her, over and over again, the only sounds in the room that of skin meeting skin, harsh breaths and the kinds of feral sounds she had never imagined could come from her.

He grabbed hold of her hair, and moved it to one side, and she felt a slight tug, and then with a pull that shocked her with its intensity, he lifted her head as he held her like that, the tug matching his thrust. She gasped, the pain on her scalp somehow adding to the pleasure she felt between her legs.

And he did it over and over again.

Until she was sobbing. Until she was begging for release.

Then he released his hold on her hair, grabbing both her hips again as he raced her to the end, his hold on her bruising, his thrusts pushing her to the point of pain. Then he leaned forward, growling low and biting her neck as he came hard. And she followed him right over the edge into oblivion.

Chapter 6

By the time Emerson went limp in front of him, draped over the mattress like a boneless cat, the fire had begun to warm the space.

Holden was a man who didn't have much in the way of regret in his life—it was impossible when he had been raised with absolutely nothing, and had gotten to a space where he didn't have to worry about his own basic needs, or those of his family. And even now, it was difficult to feel anything but the kind of bone-deep satisfaction that overtook him.

He went into the bathroom and took care of the practicalities, then went back to stoke the fire.

He heard the sound of shifting covers on the bed, and looked over his shoulder to see Emerson lying on her side now, her legs crossed just so, hiding that tempting shadow at the apex of her thighs, her arm draped coquettishly over her breast.

"Enjoying the show?" he asked.

"Yes," she responded, no shame in her voice at all.

"You might return the favor," he said.

She looked down at her own body, as if she only just realized that she was covering a good amount of the tempting bits.

"You're busy," she said. "Making a fire. I would hate to distract."

"You're distracting even as you are."

Maybe even especially as she was, looking timid when he knew how she really was. Wild and uninhibited and the best damn sex he'd ever had in his life.

Hard mattress notwithstanding.

She rolled onto her back then, stretching, raising her arms up above her head, pointing her toes.

He finished with the fire quickly, and returned to the bed.

"I couldn't do it again," she said, her eyes wide.

"Why not?"

"I've never come that many times in a row in my life. Surely it would kill you."

"I'm willing to take the chance," he said.

It surprised him to hear that her response wasn't normal for her. She had seemed more than into it. Though, she had talked about the tepid chemistry between herself and the man she was engaged to.

There was something wrong with that man, because if he couldn't find chemistry with Emerson, Holden doubted he could find it with anyone.

"Well, of course you're willing to take the chance. You're not the one at risk. You only... Once. I already did three times."

"Which means you have the capacity for more," he said. "At least, that's my professional opinion."

"Professional ranch hand opinion? I didn't know that made you an expert on sex."

He chuckled. "I'm an expert on sex because of vast experience in my personal life, not my professional life. Though, I can tell you I've never considered myself a hobbyist when it came to female pleasure. Definitely a professional."

"Well, then I guess I picked a good man to experiment with."

"Is that what this is? An experiment?"

She rolled over so she was halfway on his body, her breast pressed against his chest, her blue eyes suddenly sincere. "I've never had an orgasm with a man before. I have them on my own. But never with… Never with a partner. I've only been with two men. But… They were my boyfriends. So you would think that if it was this easy they would have figured it out. Or I would have figured it out. And I can't for the life of me figure out why we didn't. Myself included."

"Chemistry," he said, brushing her hair back from her face, surprising himself with the tender gesture. But now she was asking him these wide-eyed innocent questions, when she had done things with him only moments ago that were anything but.

"Chemistry," she said. "I thought it might be something like that. Something magical and strange and completely impossible to re-create in a lab setting, sadly."

"We can re-create it right now."

"But what if I can't ever re-create it again? Although,

I suppose now I know that it's possible for me to feel this way, I…"

"I didn't know that I was your one-man sexual revolution."

"Well, I didn't want to put that kind of pressure on you."

"I thrive under pressure."

It was easy to forget, right now, that she was the daughter of his enemy. That he was here to destroy her family. That her engagement and the lack of chemistry between herself and her fiancé would be the least of her worries in the next week.

In fact, maybe he could spare her from the marriage. Because the optics for the family would be pretty damned reduced, probably beyond the point of healing. Her marriage to an ad exec was hardly going to fix that.

And anyway, the man would probably be much less interested in marrying into the Maxfield dynasty when it was reduced to more of a one-horse outfit and they didn't have two coins to rub together.

Holden waited for there to be guilt. But he didn't feel it.

Instead, he felt some kind of indefinable sense of satisfaction. Like in the past few moments he had collected another chess piece that had once belonged to his enemy. And Emerson was so much more than a pawn.

But he didn't know how to play this victory. Not yet.

And anyway, she didn't feel much like a victory or a conquest lying here in bed with him when he was still naked. He felt more than a little bit conquered himself.

"This is terrifying," she whispered. "Because I shouldn't be here. And I shouldn't be with you at all. And I think this is the most relaxed and maybe even the happiest I've ever felt in my life." She looked up at him, and a tear tracked down her cheek, and just like that, the guilt hit him right in the chest. "And I know that it can't go beyond tonight. I know it can't. Because you have your life... And I have mine."

"And there's no chance those two things could ever cross," he said, the words coming out a hell of a lot more hostile than he intended.

"I'm not trying to be snobby or anything," she said. "But there's expectations about the kind of man that I'll end up with. And what he'll bring to the family."

"Princess, I don't know why you're talking about marriage."

"Well, that's another problem in and of itself, isn't it? I'm at that point. Where marriage has to be considered."

"You're at that point? What the hell does that mean? Are we in the 1800s?"

"In a family like mine, it matters. We have to... My father doesn't have sons. His daughters have to marry well, marry men who respect and uphold the winery. His sons-in-law are going to gain a certain amount of ownership of the place, and that means..."

"His sons-in-law are getting ownership of the business?"

"Yes," she said. "I mean, I'll retain my share as well, so don't think it's that kind of draconian nonsense. But when we marry, Donovan is going to get a share of the winery. As large as mine. When Wren marries, it will be the same. Then there's Cricket, and her husband will get a share as well, though not as large. And by the time that's all finished, my father will only have a portion. A very small portion."

"How does that math work? Cricket gets less?"

"Well, so far Cricket doesn't have any interest in running the place, and she never has. So yes."

"No wonder your father is so invested in controlling who you marry."

"It's for my protection as well. It's not like he wants me getting involved with fortune hunters."

"You really are from another world," he said, disdain in his voice, even though he didn't mean it to be there. Because it didn't matter. Because it wasn't true—he had money, he had status. And because he didn't care about her. Or her opinion. He didn't care that she was as shallow as the rest of her family, as her father. It didn't concern him and, in fact, was sort of helpful given the fact that he had taken pretty terrible advantage of her, that he'd lied to her to get her into bed.

"I can tell that you think I'm a snob," she said. "I'm not, I promise. I wouldn't get naked with a man I thought was beneath me."

"Well, that's BS. It's a pretty well-documented fact that people find slumming to be titillating, Emerson."

"Well, I don't. You're different. And yes, I find that sexy. You're forbidden, and maybe I find that sexy too, but it's not about you being less than me, or less than other men that I've been with. Somehow, you're more, and I don't know what to do with that. That's why it hurts. Because I don't know if I will ever feel as contented, ever again, as I do right now lying in this cabin, and this is not supposed to be…"

"It's not supposed to be anything you aspire to. How could it be? When your mother thinks that what you have is beneath you as it is."

She swallowed and looked away. "My life's not mine. It's attached to this thing my father built from scratch.

This legacy that has meant a life that I'm grateful for, whatever you might think. I don't need to have gone without to understand that what I've been given is extraordinary. I do understand that. But it's an incredible responsibility to bear as well, and I have to be…a steward of it. Whether I want to be or not."

And suddenly, he resented it all. Every last bit. The lies that stood between them, the way she saw him, and his perceived lack of power in this moment. He growled, reversing their positions so he was over her.

"None of that matters just now," he said.

She looked up at him, and then she touched his face. "No," she agreed. "I don't suppose it does."

He reached down and found her red lace bra, touching the flimsy fabric and then looking back at her. He took hold of her wrists, like he'd done earlier, and, this time, secured them tightly with the lace.

"Right now, you're here," he said. "And I'm the only thing you need to worry about. You're mine right here, and there's nothing outside this room, off of this bed, do you understand?"

Her breath quickened, her breasts rising and falling with the motion. She nodded slowly.

"Good girl," he said. "You have a lot of responsibilities outside, but when you're here, the only thing you have to worry about is pleasing me."

This burned away the words of the last few minutes, somehow making it all feel okay again, even if it shouldn't. As if securing her wrists now might help him hold on to this moment a little tighter. Before he had to worry about the rest, before he had to deal with the fallout and what it would mean for Emerson.

This thing that she cared about so deeply, this dynasty, which she was willing to marry a man she didn't care about at all to secure.

He would free her from it, and in the end, it might be a blessing.

He looked at the way her wrists were tied, and suddenly he didn't want to free her at all.

What he wanted was to keep her.

He got a condom from his wallet and returned to her, where she lay on the bed, her wrists bound, her thighs spread wide in invitation.

He sheathed himself and gripped her hips, entering her in one smooth stroke. Her climax was instant, and it was hard, squeezing him tight as he pounded into her without mercy.

And he set about proving to her that there was no limit to the number of times she could find her pleasure.

But there was a cost to that game, one that crystallized in his mind after the third time she cried out his name and settled herself against his chest, her wrists still tightly tied.

She was bound to him now.

And she had betrayed a very crucial piece of information.

And the ways it could all come together for him became suddenly clear.

He knew exactly what he was going to do.

Chapter 7

It had been three days since her night in the cabin with Holden. And he was all she could think about. She knew she was being ridiculous. They had another event happening at the winery tonight, and she couldn't afford to be distracted.

There was going to be an engagement party in the large barn, which had been completely and totally made over into an elegant, rustic setting, with vast open windows that made the most of the view, and elegant chandeliers throughout.

Tonight's event wasn't all on her shoulders. Mostly, it was Wren's responsibility, but Emerson was helping, and she had a feeling that in her current state she wasn't helping much.

All she could do was think about Holden. The things he had done to her body. The things he had taught her about her body.

She felt like an idiot. Spinning fantasies about a man, obsessing about him.

She'd never realized she would be into something like bondage, but he had shown her the absolute freedom there could be in giving up control.

She was so used to controlling everything all the time. And for just a few hours in his bed, he had taken the lead. It was like a burden had been lifted from her.

"Are you there, Emerson? It's me, Wren."

Emerson turned to look at her sister, who was fussing with the guest list in front of her.

"I'm here, and I've been here, helping you obsess over details."

"You're here," Wren said. "But you're not *here*."

Emerson looked down at her left hand and cursed. Because there was supposed to be a ring there. She had taken it off before going to Holden's cabin, but she needed to get it back on before tonight. Before she was circulating in a room full of guests.

Tonight's party was different from a brand-related launch. The event was at the heart of the winery itself, and as the manager of the property, Wren was the person taking the lead. When it came to broader brand representation, it was down to Emerson. But Emerson would still be taking discreet photographs of the event to share on social media, as that helped with the broader awareness of the brand.

Their jobs often crossed, as this was a family operation and not a large corporation. But neither of them minded. And in fact, Emerson considered it a good day when she got to spend extra time with her sister. But less so today when Wren was so apparently frazzled.

"What's wrong with you?" Wren asked, and then her

eye fell meaningfully to her left hand. "Did something happen with Donovan?"

"No," Emerson said. "I just forgot to put the ring on."

"That doesn't sound like you. Because you're ever conscious of the fact that a ring like that is a statement."

"I'm well aware of what I'm ever conscious of, *Wren*," she said. "I don't need you to remind me."

"And yet, you forgot something today, so it seems like you need a reminder."

"It's really nothing."

"Except it *is* something. Because if it were nothing, then you wouldn't be acting weird."

"Fine. Don't tell anyone," Emerson said, knowing already that she would regret what she was about to say.

"I like secrets," Wren said, leaning in.

"I had a… I had a one-night stand." Her sister stared at her. Unmoving. "With a man."

Wren huffed a laugh. "Well, I didn't figure you were telling me about the furniture in your bedroom."

"I mean, Donovan and I aren't exclusive, but it didn't feel right to wear his ring while I was…with someone else."

"I had no idea," Wren said, her eyes widening. "I didn't know you were that…"

"Much of a hussy?"

"That *progressive*," she said.

"Well, I'm not. In general. But I was, and am a little thrown off by it. And no one can ever know."

"Solemnly swear."

"You cannot tell Cricket."

"Why would I tell Cricket? She would never be able to look you in the eyes again, and she would absolutely give you away. Not on purpose, mind you."

"No, but it's a secret that she couldn't handle."

"Absolutely."

"Have you met a man that you just...couldn't get out of your head even though he was absolutely unsuitable?"

Wren jolted, her whole body looking like it had been touched by a live wire. "I am very busy with my job."

"Wren."

"Yes. Fine. I do know what it's like to have a sexual obsession with the wrong guy. But I've never...acted on it." The look on her face was so horrified it would have been funny, if Emerson herself hadn't just done the thing that so appalled her sister.

"There's nothing wrong with...being with someone you want, is there? No, I don't really know him, but I knew I wanted him and that seems like a decent reason to sleep with someone, right?"

Wren looked twitchy. "I... Look. Lust and like aren't the same. I get it."

"I like him fine enough," Emerson said. "But we can't ever... *He works for Dad.*"

"Like...in the corporate office?"

"No, like, on the ranch."

"Emersonnnnn."

"What?"

"Are you living out a stable boy fantasy?"

Emerson drew her lip between her teeth and worried it back and forth. "He's not a boy. He's a man. On that you can trust me."

"The question stands."

"Maybe it was sort of that fantasy, I don't know. It was a fantasy, that much I can tell you. But it was supposed to just happen and be done, and I'm obsessing about him instead."

"Who would have ever thought that could happen?" Wren asked in mock surprise.

"In this advanced modern era, I should simply be able to claim my sexuality. Own it! Bring it with me wherever I go. Not…leave it behind in some run-down cabin with the hottest man I've ever seen in my life."

"Those are truly sage words. You should put them on a pretty graphic and post it to your page. Hashtag— girl-boss-of-your-own-sexuality. Put your hair up and screw his brains out!"

Emerson shot her sister a deadly glare. "You know I hate that."

"I also know you never put a toe out of line, and yet here you are, confessing an extremely scandalous transgression."

"This secret goes to your grave with you, or I put you in the ground early, do you understand?"

Wren smirked and seemed to stretch a little taller, as if reminding Emerson she'd outgrown her by two inches when she was thirteen. She and Wren definitely looked like sisters—the same dark hair and blue eyes— but Wren wasn't curvy. She was tall and lean, her hair sleek like her build. She'd honed her more athletic figure with Krav Maga, kickboxing and all other manner of relatively violent exercise.

She claimed it was the only reason she hadn't killed Creed Cooper yet.

She also claimed she liked knowing she *could* kill him if the occasion arose at one of the many different venues where they crossed paths.

Her martial arts skills were yet another reason it was

hilarious for Emerson to threaten her sister. She'd be pinned to the ground in one second flat. Though, as the older sibling, she'd done her part to emotionally scar her sister to the point that, when she'd outgrown her, she still believed on some level Emerson could destroy her.

"In all seriousness," Wren said, "it does concern me. I mean, that you're marrying Donovan, and you're clearly more into whoever this other guy is."

"Right. Because I'm going to marry one of the men that work here. That would go over like... What's heavier than a lead balloon?"

"Does it matter?"

"What kind of ridiculous question is that? Of course it matters."

"Dad has never shown the slightest bit of interest in who I'm dating or not dating."

"You're not the oldest. I think... I think he figures he'll get me out of the way first. And it isn't a matter of him showing interest in who I'm dating. He directly told me that Donovan was the sort of man that I should associate with. He set me up with him."

"You're just going to marry who Dad tells you to marry?"

"Would you do differently, Wren? Honestly, I'm asking you."

"I don't think I could marry a man that I wasn't even attracted to."

"If Dad told you a certain man met with his approval, if he pushed you in that direction...you wouldn't try to make it work?"

Wren looked away. "I don't know. I guess I might have to try, but if after two years I still wasn't interested physically..."

"Marriage is a partnership. Our bodies will change. And sex drives and attraction will all change too. We need to have something in common. I mean, it makes way more sense to marry a man I have a whole host of things in common with than it does to marry one who I just want to be naked with."

"I didn't suggest you marry the ranch hand. But perhaps there's some middle ground. A man you like to talk to, and a man you want to sleep with."

"Well, I have yet to find a middle ground that would be suitable for Dad."

Anyway, Emerson didn't think that Holden could be called a middle ground. Not really. He was something so much more than that. Much too much of an extreme to be called something as neutral as middle ground.

"Maybe you should wait until you do."

"Or maybe I should just do what feels best," Emerson said. "I mean, maybe my marriage won't be the best of the best. Maybe I can't have everything. But we are really lucky, you and I. Look at this life." She gestured around the barn. "We have so much. I can make do with whatever I don't have."

Wren looked sad. "I don't know. That seems…tragic to me."

"What about you? You said you wanted a man and you haven't done anything about it."

"That's different."

"So, there's a man you want, and you can't be with him."

"I don't even like him," she said.

Emerson felt bowled over by that statement. Because there was only one man Emerson knew who Wren hated. And the idea that Wren might want him…

Well, no wonder Wren could barely even speak of it. She hated Creed Cooper more than anything else on earth. If the two of them ever touched…well, they would create an explosion of one kind or another, and Emerson didn't know how she hadn't realized that before.

Possibly because she had never before experienced the kind of intense clash she had experienced just a few nights ago with Holden.

"You do understand, then," Emerson said. "That there is a difference between wanting and having. And having for a limited time." She looked down. "Yes, I'm wildly attracted to this guy, and our chemistry is amazing. But it could never be more than that. Though, as someone who has experienced the temporary fun… You know you could."

Wren affected a full-body shudder.

"I really couldn't. I really, really couldn't."

"Suit yourself. But I'm going to go ahead and say that you're not allowed to give me advice anymore, because you live in a big glass house."

"I do not. It's totally different. I'm not marrying someone I shouldn't."

"Well, I'm marrying someone Dad wants me to. I trust Dad. And at the end of the day, I guess that's it. I'm trusting that it's going to be okay because it's what Dad wants me to do, and he's never… He's never steered me wrong. He's never hurt me. All he's ever done is support me."

Her father wanted the best for her. And she knew it. She was just going to have to trust that in the end, like she trusted him.

"I know," Wren said, putting her arm around Emerson. "At least you have some good memories now."

Emerson smiled. "Really good."

"I don't want details," Wren said, patting Emerson's shoulder.

She flashed back to being tied up in bed with Holden. "I am not giving you details. Those are sacred."

"As long as we're on the same page."

Emerson smiled and went back to the checklist she was supposed to be dealing with. "We are on the same page. Which is currently a checklist. Tonight's party will go off without a hitch."

"Don't jinx it," Wren said, knocking resolutely on one of the wooden tables.

"I'm not going to jinx it. It's one of your parties. So you know it's going to be absolutely perfect."

Chapter 8

The party was going off without a hitch.

Everyone was enjoying themselves, and Emerson was in visual heaven, finding any number of photo opportunities buried in the meticulous decorations that Wren had arranged. With the permission of the couple, she would even share photographs of them, and of the guests. This, at least, served to distract her mildly from the situation with Holden.

Except, there was no *situation*, that was the thing. But it was very difficult for her brain to let go of that truth.

She wanted there to be a situation. But like she had said to Wren earlier, there was really no point in entertaining that idea at all. Marriage was more than just the marriage bed.

And she and Holden might be compatible between the sheets—they were so compatible it made her pulse with desire even thinking about it—but that didn't mean they would be able to make a *relationship*, much less a *marriage*.

They had nothing in common.

You're assuming. You don't actually know that.

Well, it was true. She didn't know, but she could certainly look at the circumstances of his life and make some assumptions.

A passing waiter caught her eye, and she reached out to take hold of a glass of champagne. That was when a couple of things happened all at once. And because they happened so quickly, the reality took her longer to untangle than it might have otherwise.

The first thing she noticed was a man so stunning he took her breath away as he walked into the room.

The second realization was that she knew that man. Even though he looked so different in the sleekly cut black tux he had on his fit body that the name her brain wanted to apply to him couldn't seem to stick.

The third thing that happened was her heart dropping into her feet.

And she didn't even know why.

Because Holden had just walked in wearing a tux.

It might have taken a moment for her brain to link all those details up, but it had now.

She just couldn't figure out what it meant.

That he looked like this. That he was here.

He took a glass of champagne from a tray, and scanned the room. He looked different. But also the same.

Because while he might be clothed in an extremely refined fashion, there was still a ruggedness about him.

Something wild and untamed, even though, on a surface level, he blended in with the people around them.

No, not blended in.

He could never blend in.

He was actually dressed much nicer than anyone else here.

That suit was clearly custom, and it looked horrendously expensive. As did his shoes. As did…everything about him. And could he really be the same man she had happened upon shirtless cutting wood the other day? The same man who had tied her up in his run-down little cabin? The same man who had done desperate, dirty things to her?

And then his eyes collided with hers.

And he smiled.

It made her shiver. It made her ache.

But even so, it was a stranger's smile. It was not the man she knew, and she couldn't make sense of that certainty, even to herself. He walked across the room, acknowledging no one except for her.

And she froze. Like a deer being stalked by a mountain lion. Her heart was pounding in her ears, the sound louder now than the din of chatter going on around her.

"Just the woman I was looking for," he said.

Why did he sound different? He'd been confident in their every interaction. Had never seemed remotely cowed by her position or her money. And maybe that was the real thing she was seeing now.

Not a different man, but one who looked in his element rather than out of it.

"What are you doing here? And where did you get that suit?"

"Would you believe my fairy godmother visited?" The dark humor twisted his lips into a wry smile.

"No," she said, her heart pounding more viciously in her temple.

"Then would you believe that a few of the mice that live in the cabin made the suit for me?"

"Even less likely to believe that. You don't seem like a friend of mice."

"Honey, I'm not really a friend of anyone. And I'm real sorry for what I'm about to do. But if you cooperate with me, things are going to go a whole lot better."

She looked around. As if someone other than him might have answers. Of course, no one offered any if they did. "What do you mean?"

"You see, I haven't been completely honest with you."

"What?"

She couldn't make any sense of this. She looked around the room to see if they were attracting attention, because surely they must be. Because she felt like what was happening between them was shining bright like a beacon on the hill. But somehow they weren't attracting any attention at all.

"Why don't we go outside. I have a meeting with your father in just a few minutes. Unless…unless you are willing to negotiate with me."

"You have a meeting with my father? Negotiate what?"

The thoughts that rolled through her mind sent her into a panic.

He had obviously filmed what had happened between them. He was going to extort money from her family. He was a con man. No *wonder* he didn't want his picture taken.

All those accusations hovered on the edge of her lips, but she couldn't make them. Not here.

"What do you want?" she asked.

He said nothing. The man was a rock in a suit. No more sophisticated than he'd been in jeans. She'd thought he was different, but he wasn't. This was the real man.

And he was harder, darker than the man she'd imagined he'd been.

Funny how dressing up made that clear.

"What do you want?" she asked again.

She refused to move. She felt like the biggest fool on the planet. How had she trusted this man with her body? He was so clearly not who he said, so clearly...

Of course he hadn't actually wanted her. Of course the only man she wanted was actually just playing a game.

"Revenge," he said. "Nothing more. I'm sorry that you're caught in the middle of it."

"Did you film us?" She looked around, trying to see if people had noticed him yet. They still hadn't. "Did you film us together?"

"No," he said. "I'm not posting anything up on the internet, least of all that."

"Are you going to show my father?"

"No," he said, his lip curling. "This isn't about you, Emerson, whether you believe me or not. It isn't. But what I do next is about you. So I need you to come outside with me."

He turned, without waiting to see if she was with

him, and walked back out of the barn. Emerson looked around and then darted after his retreating figure.

When they reached the outdoors, it was dim out, just like the first night they had met. And when he turned to face her, she had the most ridiculous flashback.

He had been in jeans then. With that cowboy hat. And here he was now in a tux. But it was that moment that brought the reality of the situation into focus.

This man was the same man she had been seduced by. Or had she seduced him? It didn't even make sense anymore.

"Tell me what's going on." She looked him up and down. "You clearly aren't actually a ranch hand."

"Your father *did* hire me. Legitimately. So, I guess in total honesty, I do work for your father, and I am a ranch hand."

"What else are you? Are you paparazzi?"

He looked appalled by that. "I'm not a bottom-feeder that makes his living on the misfortunes of others."

"Then what are you? Why are you here?"

"I came here to destroy the winery."

She drew back. The venom in his voice was so intense she could feel the poison sinking down beneath her skin.

He looked her up and down. "But whether or not I do that is up to you now."

"What the hell are you talking about?"

"Your father. Your father had an affair with my sister."

"Your sister? I don't… My father did not have an affair. My father and mother have been married for…more than thirty years. And your sister would have to be…"

"She's younger than you," Holden said. "Younger

than you, and incredibly naive about the ways of the world. And your father took advantage of her. When she got pregnant, he tried to pay her to get an abortion, and when she wouldn't, he left. She miscarried, and she's had nothing but health problems since. She's attempted suicide twice and had to be hospitalized. Your father ruined her. Absolutely ruined her."

"No," Emerson said. "It's a mistake. My father would never do that. He would never hurt…"

"I'm not here to argue semantics with you. You can come with me. I'm about to have a meeting with your father, though he doesn't know why. He'll tell you the whole story."

"What does this have to do with me?"

"It didn't have anything to do with you. Until you came to the cabin the other day. I was happy to leave you alone, but you pursued it, and then… And then you told me something very interesting. About the winery. And who'd own it."

Emerson felt like she might pass out. "The man I marry."

"Exactly." He looked at her, those dark eyes blazing. "So you have two choices, really. Let me have that meeting with your father, and you're welcome to attend, where I'll be explaining to him how I've found stacks of NDAs in his employee files. And it doesn't take a genius to figure out why."

"What?"

"Your father has engaged in many, many affairs with workers here on the property. Once I got ahold of the paperwork in his office, I got in touch with some of the women. Most of them wouldn't talk, but enough did. Coercion. And so much of the money for your vineyard comes through all of your celebrity endorsements. Can you imagine the commercial fallout if your father is found to be yet another man who abuses his power? Manipulates women into bed?"

"I don't believe you."

"It doesn't matter whether you believe me or not, Emerson. What matters is that I know I can make other people believe me. And when this is over, you won't be able to give Maxfield wines away with a car wash."

"I don't understand what that gives you," she said, horror coursing through her veins. She couldn't even entertain the idea of this being true. But the truth of it wasn't the thing, not now. The issue was what he could do.

"Revenge," he said, his voice low and hard.

"Revenge isn't a very lucrative business."

"I don't need the revenge to pay. But... I won't lie to you, I find the idea of revenge and a payout very compelling. The idea of owning a piece of this place instead of simply destroying it. So tell me, how does it work? Your husband getting a stake in the business."

"I get married, and then I just call the lawyers, and they'll do the legal paperwork."

His expression became decisive. "Then you and I are getting married."

"And if I don't?"

"I'll publicize the story. I will make sure to ruin the brand. However, if I marry you, what I'll have is ownership of the brand. And you and I, with our united stakes, will have a hell of a lot of decision-making power."

"But to what end?"

"I want your father to know that I ended up owning part of this. And what I do after that...that will depend on what he's willing to do. But I want to make sure he has to contend with me for as long as I want. Yes, I could ruin the label. But that would destroy everything that you and your sister have worked so hard for, and I'm not necessarily here to hurt you. But gaining a piece of this… Making sure my sister gets something, making sure your father knows that I'm right there… That has value to me."

"What about Donovan?"

"He's not my problem. But it's your call, Emerson. You can marry Donovan. And inherit the smoldering wreckage that I'll leave behind. Or, you marry me."

"How do I know you're telling the truth?"

"Look up Soraya Jane on your favorite social media site."

"I… Wait. I know who she is. She's… She has millions of followers."

"I know," he said.

"She's your sister."

"Yes."

"And…"

"My name is Holden. Holden McCall. I am not famous on the internet, or really anywhere. But I'm one of the wealthiest developers in the state. With my money, my sister gained some connections, got into modeling. Started traveling."

"She's built an empire online," Emerson said.

"I know," he said. "What she's done is nothing short of incredible. But she's lost herself. Your father devastated her. Destroyed her. And I can't let that stand."

"So I… If I don't marry you…you destroy everything. And the reason for me marrying Donovan doesn't even exist anymore."

"That's the size of it."

"And we have to transfer everything before my father realizes what you're doing."

Emerson had no idea what to do. No idea what to think. Holden could be lying to her about all of this, but if he wasn't, then he was going to destroy the winery, and there was really no way for her to be sure about which one was true until it was too late.

"Well, what do we do, then?"

"I told you, that is up to you."

"Okay. So say we get married. Then what?"

"You were already prepared to marry a man you didn't love, might as well be me."

Except… This was worse than marrying a man she didn't love.

She had trusted Holden with something deep and real. Some part of her that she had never shown to anyone else. She had trusted him enough to let him tie her hands.

To let him inside her body.

And now she had to make a decision about marrying him. On the heels of discovering that she didn't know him at all.

"I'll marry you," she said. "I'll marry you."

Chapter 9

The roar of victory in Holden's blood hadn't quieted, not even by the time they boarded his private plane. They'd left the party and were now taking off from the regional airport, bound for Las Vegas, and he was amused by the fact that they both just so happened to be dressed for a wedding, though they hadn't planned it.

"Twenty-four-hour wedding chapels and no waiting period," he said, lifting a glass of champagne, and then extending his hand and offering it to her.

The plane was small, but nicely appointed, and fairly quiet.

He wasn't extraordinarily attached to a great many of the creature comforts that had come with his wealth. But being able to go where he wanted, when he wanted, and without a plane full of people was certainly his favorite.

"You have your own plane," she said, taking the glass

of champagne and downing it quickly. "You are private-plane rich."

She didn't look impressed so much as pissed.

"Yep," he said.

She shook her head, incredulous. "I... I don't even know what to say to that."

"I didn't ask you to say anything."

"No. You asked me to marry you."

"I believe I *demanded* that you marry me or I'd ruin your family."

"My mistake," she said, her tone acerbic. "How could I be so silly?"

"You may not believe me, but I told you, I didn't intend to involve you in this."

"I just conveniently involved myself?"

"If it helps, I found it an inconvenience at first."

"Why? You felt *guilty*? In the middle of your quest to take down my family and our fortune? Yes, that must've been inconvenient for you."

"I didn't want to drag you into it," he said. "Because I'm not your father. And I sure as hell wasn't going to extract revenge by using you for sex. The sex was separate. I only realized the possibilities when you told me about how your husband would be given an ownership stake in the vineyard."

"Right," she said. "Of course. Because I was an idiot who thought that since you had been inside me, I could maybe have a casual conversation with you."

"I'm sorry, but the information was too good for me to let go. And in the end, your family gets off easier."

"Except that you might do something drastic and destroy the winery with your control of the share."

"I was absolutely going to do that, but now I can own

a piece of it instead. And that benefits me. I also have his daughter, right with me."

"Oh, are you going to hold a gun to my head for dramatics?"

"No gun," he said. "In fact, we're on a private plane, and you're drinking champagne. You're not in any danger from me, and I didn't force you to come with me."

"But you did," she said, her voice thick.

"I offered you two choices."

"I didn't like either of them."

"Welcome to life, princess. You not liking your options isn't the same as you not having any."

She ignored that statement. "This is *not* my life."

"It is now." He appraised her for a long moment, the elegant line of her profile. She was staring out the window, doing her very best not to look at him. "The Big Bad Wolf was always going to try and eat you. You know how the fairy tale goes."

"Say whatever you need to say to make yourself feel better," she said. "You're not a wolf. You're just a dick."

"And your father?"

That seemed to kill her desire to banter with him. "I don't know if I believe you."

"But you believe me just enough to be on a plane with me going to Las Vegas to get married, because if I'm right, if I'm telling the truth…"

"It ruins everything. And I don't think I trust anyone quite so much that I would take that chance. Not even my father. I don't trust you at all, but what choice do I have? Because you're right. I was willing to marry a man that I didn't love to support my family. To support the empire. The dynasty. So why the hell wouldn't I do it now?"

"Oh, but you hate me, don't you?"

"I do," she said. "I really do."

He could sense that there was more she wanted to say, but that she wouldn't. And they were silent for the next hour, until the plane touched down in Nevada.

"Did you want an Elvis impersonator?" he asked, when they arrived on the Strip, at the little white wedding chapel he'd reserved before they landed.

"And me without my phone," she said.

"Did you want to take pictures and post them?"

She narrowed her eyes. "I wanted to beat you over the head with it."

"That doesn't answer my question about Elvis."

"Yeah, that would be good. If we don't have an Elvis impersonator, the entire wedding will be ruined."

"Don't tease me, because I will get the Elvis impersonator."

"Get him," she said, making a broad gesture. "Please. Because otherwise this would be *absurd.*"

The edge of hysteria in her voice suggested she felt it was already absurd, but he chose to take what she said as gospel.

And he checked the box on the ridiculous paperwork, requesting Elvis, because she thought he was kidding, and she was going to learn very quickly that he was not a man to be trifled with. Even when it came to things like this.

They waited until their names were called.

And sadly, the only impersonator who was available past ten thirty on a Saturday night seemed to be Elvis from the mid-1970s.

"Do you want me to sing 'Burning Love' or 'Can't

Help Falling in Love' at the end of the ceremony?" he asked in all seriousness.

"Pick your favorite," Emerson replied, her face stony.

And Holden knew she had been certain that this level of farce would extinguish the thing that burned between them. Because she hated him now, and he could see the truth of that in her eyes.

But he was happy to accept her challenge. Happy to stand there exchanging vows with an Elvis imper-sonator as officiant, and a woman in a feathered leo-tard as witness, because it didn't change the fact that he wanted her.

Desperately.

That all he could think about was when this was fin-ished, he was going to take her up to a lavish suite and have her fifty different ways.

And she might not think she wanted it, but she would.

She might think that she could burn it all out with her anger, but she couldn't. He knew it.

He knew it because he was consumed by it.

He should feel only rage. Should feel only the need for revenge.

But he didn't.

And she wouldn't either.

"You may kiss the bride," Elvis said.

She looked at him with a warning in her eyes, but that warning quickly became a challenge.

She would learn pretty quickly that he didn't back down from a challenge.

He cupped her chin with his hand, and kissed her, hard and fast, but just that light, quick brush of their mouths left them both breathing hard.

And as soon as they separated, the music began to

play and Elvis started singing about how he just couldn't help falling in love.

Well, Holden could sure as hell help falling in love. But he couldn't keep himself from wanting Emerson. That was a whole different situation.

They signed the paperwork quickly, and as soon as they were in the car that had been waiting for them, he handed her his phone. "Call your lawyer."

"It's almost midnight," she said.

"He'll take a call from you, you know it. We need to get everything set into motion so we have it all signed tomorrow morning."

"*She* will take a call from me," she said pointedly. But then she did as he asked. "Hi, Julia. It's Emerson. I just got married." He could hear a voice saying indiscriminate words on the other end. "Thank you. I need to make sure that I transfer the shares of the company into my husband's name. As soon as possible." She looked over at him. "Where are we staying?"

She recited all of the necessary information back to Julia at his direction, including the information about him, before getting off the phone.

"She'll have everything faxed to us by morning."

"And she won't tip off your father?"

"No," she said. "She's the family lawyer, but she must know… She's going to realize that I eloped. And she's going to realize that I'm trying to bypass my father. That I want my husband to have the ownership shares he—I—is entitled to. She won't allow my father to interfere."

"She's a friend of yours, then."

"We became friends, yes. People who aren't liars make friends."

"I'm wounded."

"I didn't think you could wound granite."

"Why did you comply with what I asked you to do so easily?"

Suddenly, her voice sounded very small and tired. "Because. It makes no sense to come here, to marry you, if I don't follow through with the rest. You'll ruin my family if you don't get what you asked for. I'm giving it to you. Protesting now is like tying my own self to the railroad tracks, and damsel in distress isn't my style." She looked at him, her blue eyes certain. "I made my bed. I'll lie in it."

They pulled up to the front of a glitzy casino hotel that was far from his taste in anything.

But what he did like about Las Vegas was the sexual excess. Those who created the lavish hotel rooms here understood exactly why a man was willing to pay a lot of money for a hotel room. And it involved elaborate showers, roomy bathtubs and beds that could accommodate all manner of athletics.

The decor didn't matter to him at all with those other things taken into consideration.

They got out of the car, and he tipped the valet.

"Your secretary called ahead, Mr. McCall," the man said. "You're all checked in and ready to go straight upstairs. A code has been texted to your phone."

Holden put his arm around her, and the two of them began to walk to an elevator. "I hope you don't think… I… We're going to a hotel room and…" Emerson said.

"Do you think you're going to share a space with me tonight and keep your hands off me?"

They got inside the elevator, and the doors closed. "I hate you," she said, shoving at his chest.

"And you want me," he said. "And that might make you hate me even more, but it doesn't make it not true."

"I want to…"

"Go ahead," he said. "Whatever you want."

"I'm going to tear that tux right off your body," she said, her voice low and feral. "Absolutely destroy it."

"Only if I can return the favor," he said, arousal coursing through him.

"You might not be all that confident when I have the most fragile part of you in my hand."

He didn't know why, but that turned him on. "I'll take my chances."

"I don't understand what this is," she said. "I should be…disgusted by you."

"It's too late. You already got dirty with me, honey. You might as well just embrace it. Because you know how good it is between us. And you wanted me when I was nothing other than a ranch hand. Why wouldn't you want me when you know that I'm a rich man with a vengeful streak a mile wide?"

"You forced me into this."

"I rescued you from that boring bowl of oatmeal you called a fiancé. At least you hate me. You didn't feel anything for him."

Her hackles were up by the time they got to the suite door, and he entered his code. The door opened and revealed the lavish room that had all the amenities he wanted out of such a place.

"This is tacky," she said, throwing her purse down on the couch.

"And?"

"Warm," she said.

She reached behind her body and grabbed hold of

her zipper, pulling down the tab and letting her dress fall to the floor.

"I figured you were going to make me work for it."

"Your ego doesn't deserve that. Then you'd get to call it a seduction. I want to fuck you, I can't help myself. But I'm not sure you should be particularly flattered by that. I hate myself for it."

"Feel free to indulge your self-loathing, particularly if at some point it involves you getting that pretty lipstick all over me."

"I'm sure it will. Because I'm here with you. And there's not much I can do about my choices now. We're married. And a stake in the vineyard is close to being transferred into your name. I've already had sex with you. I got myself into this. I might as well have an orgasm."

"We can certainly do better than one orgasm," he said.

She looked good enough to eat, standing there in some very bridal underwear, all white and lacy, and unintentionally perfect for the moment, still wearing the red high heels she'd had on with her dress.

He liked her like this.

But he liked her naked even better.

She walked over to where he stood, grabbed hold of his tie and made good on her promise.

She wrenched the knot loose, then tore at his shirt, sending buttons scattering across the floor. "I hope that was expensive," she said, moving her hand over his bare chest.

"It was," he said. "Very, very expensive. But sadly for you, expensive doesn't mean anything to me. I could buy ten more and not notice the expense."

He could see the moment when realization washed over her. About who had the power. She was so very comfortable with her financial status and she'd had an idea about his, and what that meant, and even though she'd seen the plane, seen him in the tux, the reality of who he'd been all along was just now hitting her.

"And to think," she said, "I was very worried about taking advantage of you that night we were together."

"That says more about you and the way you view people without money than it does about me, sweetheart."

"Not because of that. You work for my father. By extension, for me, since I own part of the winery. And I was afraid that I might be taking advantage of you. But here you were, so willing to blackmail me."

"Absolutely. Life's a bastard, and so am I. That's just the way of things."

"Here I thought she was a bitch. Which I've always found handy, I have to say." She pushed his shirt off his shoulders, and he shed it the rest of the way onto the floor, and then she unhooked his belt, pulling it through the loops.

He grinned. "Did you want to use that?"

"What?"

"You know, you could tie me down if you wanted," he said. "If it would make you feel better. Make you feel like you have some control."

Something flared in her eyes, but he couldn't quite read it. "Why would I want that? That wouldn't give me more control. It would just mean I was doing most of the work." She lifted her wrists up in supplication, her eyes never leaving his. "You can tie my wrists, and I'll still have the control."

He put the tip of the leather through the buckle, and looped it over her wrists, pulling the end tight before he looped it through the buckle again, her wrists held fast together. Then, those blue eyes never leaving his, she sank down onto her knees in front of him.

Chapter 10

She had lost her mind, or something. Her heart was pounding so hard, a mixture of arousal, rage and shame pouring over her.

She should have told him no. She should have told him he was never touching her again. But something about her anger only made her want to play these games with him even more, and she didn't know what that said about her.

But he was challenging her, with everything from his marriage proposal to the Elvis at the chapel. This room itself was a challenge, and then the offer to let her tie him up.

All of it was seeing if he could make her or break her, and she refused to break. Because she was Emerson Maxfield, and she excelled at everything she did. And if this was the way she was going to save her family's dynasty, then she was going to save it on her knees in front of Holden McCall.

"You think I'm just going to give you what you want?" he asked, stroking himself through his pants. She could see the aggressive outline of his arousal beneath the dark fabric, and her internal muscles pulsed.

"Yes," she said. "Because I don't think you're strong enough to resist me."

"You might be right about that," he said. "Because I don't do resisting. I spent too much of my life wanting, and that's not something that I allow. I don't want anymore. I have."

He unhooked the closure on his pants, slid the zipper down slowly and then freed himself.

He wrapped his hand around the base, holding himself steady for her. She arched up on her knees and took him into her mouth, keeping her eyes on his the entire time.

With her hands bound as they were, she allowed him to guide her, her hair wrapped around his fist as he dictated her movements.

It was a game.

She could get out of the restraints if she wanted to. Could leave him standing there, hard and aching. But she was submitting to this fiction that she was trapped, because somehow, given the marriage—which she truly was trapped in—this felt like power.

This choice.

Feeling him begin to tremble as she took him in deep, feeling his power fracture as she licked him, tasted him.

She was the one bound, but he couldn't have walked away from her now if he wanted to, and she knew it.

They both did.

He held all the power outside this room, outside this moment. But she'd claimed her own here, and she was going to relish every second.

She teased him. Tormented him.

"Stand up," he said, the words scraping his throat raw.

She looked up at him, keeping her expression serene. "Are you not enjoying yourself?"

"Stand up," he commanded. "I want you to walk to the bed."

She stood slowly, her hands still held in that position of chosen obedience. Then with her eyes never leaving his, she walked slowly toward the bedroom. She didn't turn away from him until she had to, and even then, she could feel his gaze burning into her. Lighting a fire inside of her.

Whatever this was, it was bigger than them both.

Because he hated her father, and whether or not the reasons that he hated James Maxfield were strictly true or not, the fact was he did.

And she didn't get the impression that he was excited to find himself sexually obsessed with her. But he was.

She actually believed that what he wanted from her in terms of the winery was separate from him wanting her body, because this kind of intensity couldn't be faked.

And most important, it wasn't only on his side.

That had humiliated her at first.

The realization that she had been utterly captivated by this man, even while he was engaged in a charade.

But the fact of the matter was, he was just as enthralled with her.

They were both tangled in it.

Whether they wanted to be or not.

She climbed onto the bed, positioning herself on her back, her arms held straight down in front of her, covering her breasts, covering that space between her thighs. And she held that pose when he walked in.

Hunger lit his gaze and affirmed what she already knew to be true in her heart. He wanted her.

He hated it.

There was something so deliciously wicked about the contrast.

About this control she had over him even now.

A spark flamed inside her stomach.

He doesn't approve of this, or of you. But he can't help himself.

She arched her hips upward unconsciously, seeking some kind of satisfaction.

It was so much more arousing than it had any right to be. This moment of triumph.

Because it was private. Because it was secret.

Emerson lived for appearances.

She had been prepared to marry a man for those appearances.

And yet, this moment with Holden was about nothing more than the desire between two people. That he resented their connection? That only made it all feel stronger, hotter.

He removed his clothes completely as he approached the bed.

She looked down at her own body, realizing she was still wearing her bra and panties, her high heels.

"You like me like this," she whispered.

"I like you any way I can get you," he said, his voice low and filled with gravel.

"You like this, don't you? You had so much commentary on me wanting to slum it with a ranch hand. I think you like something about having a rich girl. Though, now I don't know why."

"Is there any man on earth who doesn't fantasize about corrupting the daughter of his enemy?"

"Did you corrupt me? I must've missed the memo."

"If I haven't yet, honey, then it's going to be a long night." He scooted her up the mattress, and lifted her arms, looping them back over her head, around one of the posts on the bed frame. Her hands parted, the leather from the belt stretching tight over the furniture, holding her fast. "At my mercy," he said.

He took his time with her then.

Took her high heels off her feet slowly, kissing her ankle, her calf, the inside of her thigh. Then he teased the edges of her underwear before pulling them down slowly, kissing her more intimately. He traveled upward, to her breasts, teasing her through the lace before removing the bra and casting it to the floor. And then he stood back, as if admiring his hard work.

"As fun as this is," he said, "I want your hands on me."

She could take her own hands out of the belt, but she refused. Refused to break the fiction that had built between the two of them.

So she waited. Waited as he slowly, painstakingly undid the belt and made a show of releasing her wrists. Her entire body pulsed with need for him. And thankfully, it was Vegas, so there were condoms on the bedside table.

He took care of the necessities, quickly, and then joined her on the bed, pinning her down on the mattress.

She smiled up at him, lifting her hand and tracing the line of his jaw with her fingertip. "Let's go for a ride," she whispered.

He growled, gripped her hips and held her steady as he entered her in one smooth stroke.

She gasped at the welcome invasion, arching against his body as he tortured them both mercilessly, drove them both higher than she thought she could stand.

And when she looked into his eyes, she saw the man she had been with that first night, not a rich stranger.

Holden.

His last name didn't matter. It didn't matter where he was from. What was real was *this*.

And she knew it, because their desire hadn't changed, even if their circumstances had. If anything, their desire had sharpened, grown in intensity.

And she believed with her whole soul that what they'd shared in his bed had never been about manipulating her.

Because the intensity was beyond them. Beyond sex in a normal sense, so much deeper. So much more terrifying.

She took advantage of her freedom. In every sense of the word.

The freedom of her hands to explore every ridge of muscle on his back, down his spine, to his sculpted ass.

And the freedom of being in this moment. A moment that had nothing to do with anything except need.

This…this benefited no one. In fact, it was a short road off a cliff, but that hadn't stopped either of them.

They couldn't stop.

He lowered his head, growling again as he thrust

into her one last time, his entire body shaking with his release.

And she followed him over the edge.

She let out a hoarse cry, digging her fingernails into his skin as she crested that wave of desire over and over again.

She didn't think it would end.

She thought she might die.

She thought she might not mind, if this was heaven, between the sheets with him.

And when her orgasm passed, she knew she was going to have to deal with the fact that he was her husband.

With the reality of what her father would think.

With Holden, her father's enemy, owning a share in the winery.

But those realizations made her head pound and her heart ache.

And she would rather focus on the places where her body burned with pleasure.

Tomorrow would come soon enough, and there would be documents to fax and sign, and they would have to fly back to Oregon.

But that was all for later.

And Emerson had no desire to check her phone. No desire to have any contact with the outside world.

No desire to take a picture to document anything.

Because none of this could be contained in a pithy post. None of it could even be summed up in something half so coherent as words.

The only communication they needed was between their bodies.

Tomorrow would require words. Explanations. Probably recriminations.

But tonight, they had this.

And so Emerson shut the world out, and turned to him.

Chapter 11

By the time he and his new wife were on a plane back to Oregon, Emerson was looking sullen.

"It's possible he'll know what happened by the time we get there," she said.

"But you're confident there's nothing he can do to stop it?"

She looked at him, prickles of irritation radiating off her. A sharp contrast to the willing woman who had been in his bed last night.

"Why do you care? It works out for you either way."

"True. But it doesn't work out particularly well for you."

"And you care about that?"

"I married you."

"Yeah, I still don't really get that. What exactly do you think is going to happen now?"

"We'll have a marriage. Why not?"

"You told me you didn't believe in marriage."

"I also told you I was a ranch hand."

"Have you been married before?" She frowned.

"No. Would it matter if I had?"

"In a practical sense, obviously nothing is a deal breaker, since I'm already married to you, for the winery. So no. But yes. Actually, it does."

"Never been married. No kids."

"Dammit," she said. "It didn't even occur to me that you might have children."

"Well, I don't."

"Thank God."

"Do you want to have some?"

The idea should horrify him. But for some reason, the image of Emerson getting round with his baby didn't horrify him at all. In fact, the side effect of bringing her into his plans pleased him in ways he couldn't quite articulate.

The idea of simply ruining James Maxfield had been risky. Because there was every chance that no matter how hard Holden tried there would be no serious blowback for the man who had harmed Holden's sister the way that he had.

Wealthy men tended to be tougher targets than young women. Particularly young women who traded on the image of their beauty.

Not that Holden wasn't up to the task of trying to ruin the man.

Holden was powerful in his own right, and he was ruthless with it.

But there was something deeply satisfying about owning a piece of his enemy's legacy. And not only that, he got James's precious daughter in the bargain.

This felt right.

"I can't believe that you're suggesting we…"

"You wanted children, right?"

"I… Yes."

"So, it's not such an outrageous thought."

"You think we're going to stay married?"

"You didn't sign a prenuptial agreement, Emerson. You leave me, I still get half of your shares of the vineyard."

"You didn't sign one either. I have the impression half of what's yours comes out to an awful lot of money."

"Money is just money. I'll make more. I don't have anything I care about half as much as you care about the vineyard. About the whole label."

"Well, why don't we wait to discuss children until I decide how much I hate you."

"You hate me so much you climbed on me at least five times last night."

"Yes, and in the cold light of day that seems less exciting than it did last night. The chemistry between us doesn't have anything to do with…our marriage."

"It has everything to do with it," he said, his tone far darker and more intense than he'd intended it to be.

"What? You manufactured this chemistry so we could…"

"No. The marriage made sense because of our chemistry. I was hardly going to let you walk away from me and marry another man, Emerson. Let him get his hands on your body when he has had all this time? He's had the last two years and he did nothing? He doesn't deserve you. And your father doesn't get to use you as a pawn."

"My father…"

"He's not a good man. Whether you believe me or not, it's true. But I imagine that when we impart the happy news to him today… You can make that decision for yourself."

"Thanks. But I don't need your permission to make my own decisions about my father or anything else."

But the look on her face was something close to haunted, and if he were a man prone to guilt, he might feel it now. They landed not long after, and his truck was there, still where he'd left it.

When they paused in front of it, she gave it a withering stare. "This thing is quite the performance."

It was a pretty beat-up truck. But it was genuinely his.

"It's mine," he said.

"From when?"

"Well, I got it when I was about…eighteen. So going on fifteen years ago."

"I don't even know how old you are. I mean, I do now, because I can do math. But really, I don't know anything about you, Holden."

"Well, I'll be happy to give you the rundown after we meet with your father."

"Well, looking forward to all that."

She was still wearing her dress from last night. He had found a replacement shirt in the hotel shop before they'd left, and it was too tight on his shoulders and not snug enough in the waist. When they arrived at the winery and entered the family's estate together, he could only imagine the picture they made.

Him in part of a tux, and her in last night's gown.

"Is my father in his study yet?" she questioned one of the first members of the household staff who walked by.

"Yes," the woman said, looking between Emerson and him. "Shall I see if he's receiving visitors?"

"He doesn't really have a choice," Holden said. "He'll make time to see us."

He took Emerson's hand and led her through the house, their footsteps loud on the marble floors. And he realized as they approached the office, what a pretentious show this whole place was.

James Maxfield wasn't that different from Holden. A man from humble beginnings hell-bent on forging a different path. But the difference between James and Holden was that Holden hadn't forgotten where he'd come from. He hadn't forgotten what it was to be powerless, and he would never make anyone else feel that kind of desperation.

James seemed to enjoy his position and all the power that came with it.

You don't enjoy it? Is that why you're standing here getting ready to walk through that door with his daughter and make him squirm? Is that why you forced Emerson to marry you?

He pushed those thoughts aside. And walked into the office without knocking, still holding tightly to Emerson.

Her father looked up, looked at him and then at Emerson. "What the hell is this?" he asked.

"I..."

"A hostile takeover," Holden said. "You ruined my sister's life. And now I'm here to make yours very, very difficult. And only by your daughter's good grace am I leaving you with anything other than a smoldering pile of wreckage. Believe me when I say it's not for your sake. But for the innocent people in your family who don't deserve to lose everything just because of your sins."

"Which sins are those?"

"My sister. Soraya Jane."

The silence in the room was palpable. Finally, James spoke.

"What is it you intend to do?"

"You need to guard your office better. I know you think this house isn't a corporation so you don't need high security, but you're such a damned narcissist you didn't realize you'd hired someone who was after the secrets you keep in your home. And now I have them. And thanks to Emerson, I now have a stake in this winery too. You can contest the marriage and my ownership, but it won't end well for you. It might not be my first choice now, but I'm still willing to detonate everything if it suits me."

James Maxfield's expression remained neutral, and his focus turned to his daughter.

"Emerson," her father said, "you agreed to this? You are allowing him to blackmail us?"

"What choice did I have?" she asked, a thread of desperation in her voice. "I trust you, Dad, I do. But he planned to destroy us. Whether his accusations are true or not, that was his intent. He gave me no time, and he didn't give me a lot of options. This marriage was the only way I could salvage what we've built, because he was ready to wage a campaign against you, against our family, at any cost. He was going to come at us personally and professionally. I couldn't take any chances. I couldn't. I did what I had to do. I did what you would have done, I'm sure. I did what needed doing."

"You were supposed to marry Donovan," James said, his tone icy.

"I know," Emerson said. "But what was I supposed to do when the situation changed? This man…"

"Have you slept with him?"

Emerson drew back, clearly shocked that her father had asked her that question. "I don't understand what that has to do with anything."

"It certainly compromises the purity of your claims," James returned. "You say you've been blackmailed into this arrangement, but if you're in a relationship with him…"

"Did you sleep with his sister?" she asked. "All those… All those other women in the files. Did you… Did you cheat on Mom?"

"Emerson, there are things you don't need to know about, and things you don't understand. My relationship with your mother works, even if it's not traditional."

"You *did*." She lowered her voice to a near whisper. "His sister. She's younger than me."

"Emerson…"

Holden took a step toward James's desk. "Men like you always think it won't come back on you. You think you can take advantage of women who are young, who are desperate, and no one will come for you. But I am here for you. This empire of yours? It serves me now. Your daughter? She's mine too. And if you push me, I swear I will see it all ruined and everyone will know what you are. How many people do you think will come here for a wedding, or parties, then? What of the brand worldwide? Who wants to think about sexual harassment, coercion and the destruction of a woman young enough to be your daughter when they have a sip of your merlot?"

Silence fell, tense and hard between them.

"The brand is everything," James said finally. "I've done everything I can to foster that family brand, as has your mother. What we do in private is between us."

"And the gag order you had my sister sign, and all those other women? Soraya has been institutionalized because of all of this. Because of the fallout. And she might have signed papers, but I did not. And now I don't need to tell the world about your transgressions to have control over what you've built. And believe me, in the years to come, I will make your life hell." Holden leaned forward, placing his palms on the desk. "Emerson was your pawn. You were going to use her as a wife to the man you wanted as part of this empire. But Emerson is with me now. She's no longer yours."

"*Emerson* is right here," Emerson said, her voice vibrating with emotion. "And frankly, I'm disgusted by the both of you. I don't belong to either of you. Dad, I did what I had to do to save the vineyard. I did it because I trusted you. I trusted that Holden's accusations were false. But you did all of this, didn't you?"

"It was an affair," James said. "It looks to me like you are having one of your own, so it's a bit rich for you to stand in judgment of me."

"I hadn't made vows to Donovan. And I never claimed to love him. He also knows…"

"Your mother knows," James said. "The terms of a marriage are not things you discuss with your children. You clearly have the same view of relationships that I do, and here you are lecturing me."

"It's not the same," she said. "And as for you," she

said, turning to Holden. "I married you because it was the lesser of two evils. But that doesn't make me yours. You lied to me. You made me believe you were someone you weren't. You're no different from him."

Emerson stormed out of the room, and left Holden standing there with James.

"She makes your victory ring hollow," James said.

"Even if she divorces me, part of the winery is still mine. We didn't have a prenuptial agreement drafted between us, something I'm sure you were intending to take care of when she married that soft boy from the East Coast."

"What exactly are you going to do now?"

"I haven't decided yet. And the beauty of this is I have time. You can consider me the sword of Damocles hanging over your head. And one day, you know the thread will break. The question is when."

"And what do you intend to do to Emerson?"

"I've done it already. She's married to me. She's mine."

Those words burned with conviction, no matter her protests before storming out. And he didn't know why he felt the truth of those words deeper than anything else.

He had married her. It was done as far as he was concerned.

He went out of the office, and saw Emerson standing there, her hands planted firmly on the balustrade, overlooking the entry below.

"Let's talk," he said.

She turned to face him. "I don't want to talk. You should go talk with my father some more. The two of you seemed to be enjoying that dialogue."

"*Enjoy* is a strong word."

"You betrayed me," she said.

"I don't know you, Emerson. You don't know me. We hadn't ever made promises to each other. I didn't betray you. Your *father* betrayed you."

She looked stricken by that, and she said nothing.

"I want you to come live with me."

"Why would I do that?"

"Because we're married. Because it's not fake."

"Does that mean you love me?" she asked, her tone scathing.

"No. But there's a lot of mileage between love and fake. And you know it."

"I live here. I work here. I can't leave."

"Handily, I have bought a property on the adjacent mountain. You won't have to leave. I do have another ranch in Jackson Creek, and I'd like to visit there from time to time. I do a bit of traveling. But there's no reason we can't be based here, in Gold Valley."

"You'll have to forgive me. I'm not understanding the part of your maniacal plan where we try to pretend we're a happy family."

"The vineyard is more yours now than it was before. I have no issue deferring to you on a great many things."

"You're not just going to…let it get run into the ground?"

"If I wanted to do that, I wouldn't have to own a piece. I own part of your father's legacy. And that appeases me.

"So," he concluded, "shall we go?"

Chapter 12

Emerson looked around the marble halls of the Maxfield estate, and for the very first time in all her life, she didn't feel like she was home.

The man in the office behind her was a stranger.

The man in front of her was her husband, whether or not he was a stranger.

And his words kept echoing in her head.

I didn't betray you. Your father betrayed you.

"Let's go," she said. Before she could think the words through.

She found herself bundled back up into his truck, still wearing the dress she had been wearing at yesterday's party. His house was a quick drive away from the estate, a modern feat of design built into the hillside, all windows to make the most of the view.

"Tell me about your sister," she said, standing in the

drive with him, feeling decidedly flat and more than a bit defeated.

"She's my half sister," Holden said, taking long strides toward the front entry. He entered a code, opened the door and ushered her into a fully furnished living area.

"I had everything taken care of already," he said. "It's ready for us."

Ready for us.

She didn't know why she found that comforting. She shouldn't. She was unaccountably wounded by his betrayal, had been forced into this marriage. And yet, she wanted him. She couldn't explain it.

And her old life didn't feel right anymore, because it was even more of a lie than this one.

"My mother never had much luck with love," Holden said, his voice rough. "I had to take care of her. Because the men she was with didn't. They would either abuse her outright or manipulate her, and she wasn't very strong. Soraya came along when I was eight. About the cutest thing I'd ever seen. And a hell of a lot of trouble. I had to get her ready, had to make sure her hair was brushed for school. All of that. But I did it. I worked, and I took care of them, and once I got money, I made sure they had whatever they wanted." He looked away from her, a muscle jumping in his jaw. "It was after Soraya had money that she met your father. I don't think it takes a genius to realize she's got daddy issues. And he played each and every one of them. She got pregnant. He tried to get her to terminate. She wouldn't. She lost the baby anyway. And she lost her mind right along with it."

Hearing those words again, now knowing that they were true...they hit her differently.

She sat down on the couch, her stomach cramping with horror.

"You must love her a lot," she said. "To do all of this for her."

She thought about her father, and how she had been willing to marry a stranger for him. And then how she had married Holden to protect the winery, to protect her family, her father. And now she wasn't entirely convinced she shouldn't have just let Holden do what he wanted.

He frowned. "I did what had to be done. Like I always do. I take care of them."

"Because you love them," she said.

"Because no one else takes care of them." He shook his head. "My family wasn't loving. They still aren't. My mother is one of the most cantankerous people on the face of the planet, but you do what you do. You keep people going. When they're your responsibility, there's no other choice."

"Oh," she said. She took a deep, shuddering breath. "You see, I love my father. I love my mother. That's why her disapproval hurts. That's why his betrayal... I didn't know that he was like this. That he could have done those things to someone like your sister. It hurts me to know it. You're right. He is the one who betrayed me. And I will never be able to go into the estate again and look at it, at him, the same way. I'll never be able to look at him the same. It's just all broken, and I don't think it can ever be put back together."

"We'll see," he said. "I never came here to put anything back together. Because I knew it was all broken beyond the fixing of it. I came here to break *him*, because he broke Soraya. And I don't think she's going to be fixed either." He came to stand in front of Emerson, his hands shoved into his pockets, his expression grim. "And I'm sorry that you're caught up in the middle of this, because I don't have any stake in breaking you. But here's what I know about broken things. They can't be put back together exactly as they were. I think you can make something new out of them, though."

"Are you giving me life advice? Really? The man who blackmailed me into marriage?" He was still so absurdly beautiful, so ridiculously gorgeous and compelling to her. It was wrong. But she didn't know how to fix it. How to change it. Like anything else in her life. And really, right at the moment, it was only one of the deeply messed up things in her reality.

That she felt bonded to him even as the bonds that connected her to her family were shattered.

"You can take it or not," he said. "That doesn't change the fact that it's true. Whether or not I exposed him, your father is a predator. This is who he is. You could have lived your life without knowing the truth, but I don't see how that's comforting."

It wasn't. It made a shiver race down her spine, made her feel cold all over. "I just… I trusted him. I trusted him so much that I was willing to marry a man he chose for me. I would have done anything he asked me to do. He built a life for me, and he gave me a wonderful childhood, and he made me the woman that I am. For better or for worse. He did a whole host of wonderful things for me, and I don't know how to reconcile that with what else I now know about him."

"All *I* know is your father is a fool. Because the way

you believe in him... I've never believed in anyone that way. Anyone or anything. And the way my sister believed in him... He didn't deserve that, from either of you. And if just one person believed in me the way that either of you believed in him, the way that I think your mother believes in him, your sisters... I wouldn't have done anything to mess that up."

Something quiet and sad bloomed inside of her. And she realized that the sadness wasn't for losing her faith in her father. Not even a little.

"I did," she said.

"What?"

"I did. Believe in you like that. Holden Brown. That ranch hand I met not so long ago. I don't know what you think about me, or women like me. But it mattered to me that I slept with you. That I let you into my body. I've only been with two other men. For me, sex is an intimate thing. And I've never shared it with someone outside of a relationship. But there was something about you. I trusted you. I believed what you told me about who you were. And I believed in what my body told me about what was between us. And now what we shared has kind of turned into this weird and awful thing, and I just... I don't think I'll ever trust myself again. Between my father and you..."

"I didn't lie to you." His voice was almost furious in its harshness. "Not about wanting you. Nothing that happened between you and me in bed was a lie. Not last night, and not the first night. I swear to you, I did not seduce you to get revenge on your father. Quite the opposite. I told myself when I came here that I would never touch you. You were forbidden to me, Emerson, because I didn't want to do the same thing your father had done. Because I didn't want to lie to you or take advantage of you in any way. When I first met you in that vineyard, I told myself I was disgusted by you. Because you had his blood in your veins. But no matter how much I told myself that, I couldn't make it true. You're not your father. And that's how I feel. This thing between us is separate, and real."

"But the marriage is for revenge."

"Yes. But I wouldn't have taken the wedding *night* if I didn't want you."

"Can I believe in you?"

She didn't know where that question came from, all vulnerable and sad, and she wasn't entirely sure that she liked the fact that she'd asked it. But she needed to grab on to something. In this world where nothing made sense, in this moment when she felt rootless, because not even her father was who she thought he was, and she didn't know how she was going to face having that conversation with Wren, or with Cricket. Didn't know what she was going to say to her mother, because no matter how difficult their own relationship was, this gave Emerson intense sympathy for her mother.

Not to mention her sympathy for the young woman her father had harmed. And the other women who were like her. How many had there been just like Soraya? It made Emerson hurt to wonder.

She had no solid ground to stand on, and she was desperate to find purchase.

If Holden was telling the truth, if the chemistry between them was as real to him as it was to her, then she could believe in that if nothing else. And she needed to believe in it. Desperately.

"If I… If I go all in on this marriage, Holden, on this

thing between us, if we work together to make the vineyard…ours—Wren and Cricket included—promise me
that you'll be honest with me. That you will be faithful
to me. Because right now, I'll pledge myself to you, because I don't know what the hell else to believe in. I'm
angry with you, but if you're telling me the truth about
wanting me, and you also told me the truth about my
father, then you are the most real and honest thing in
my life right now, and I will… I'll bet on that. But only
if you promise me right now that you won't lie to me."

"I promise," he said, his eyes like two chips of ob-
sidian, dark and fathomless. Hard.

And in her world that had proven to be built on a
shifting sand foundation, his hardness was something
steady. Something real.

She needed something real.

She stood up from her position on the couch, her legs
wobbling when she closed the distance between them.
"Then take me to bed. Because the only thing that feels
good right now is you and me."

"I notice you didn't say it's the only thing that makes
sense," he said, his voice rough. He cupped her cheek,
rubbing his thumb over her cheekbone.

"Because it doesn't make sense. I should hate you.
But I can't. Maybe it's just because I don't have the energy right now. Because I'm too sad. But this…whatever
we have, it feels *real*. And I'm not sure what else is."

"This *is* real," he said, taking her hand and putting
it on his chest. His heart was raging out of control, and
she felt a surge of power roll through her.

It was real. Whatever else wasn't, the attraction between them couldn't be denied.

He carried her to the bed, and they said vows to each

other's bodies. And somehow, it felt right. Somehow, in the midst of all that she had lost, her desire for Holden felt like the one right thing she had done.

Marrying him. Making this real.

Tonight, there were no restraints, no verbal demands. Just their bodies. Unspoken promises that she was going to hold in her heart forever.

And as the hours passed, a feeling welled up in her chest that terrified her more than anything else.

It wasn't hate. Not even close.

But she refused to give it a name. Not yet. Not now.

She would have a whole lot of time to sort out what she felt for this man.

She'd have the rest of her life.

Chapter 13

The day he put Maxfield Vineyards as one of the assets on his corporate holdings was sadistically satisfying. He was going to make a special new label of wine as well. Soraya deserved to be indelibly part of the Maxfield legacy.

Because James Maxfield was indelibly part of Soraya's. And Holden's entire philosophy on the situation was that James didn't deserve to walk away from her without being marked by the experience.

Holden was now a man in possession of a very powerful method through which to dole out if not traditional revenge, then a steady dose of justice.

He was also a man in possession of a wife.

That was very strange indeed. But he counted his marriage to Emerson among the benefits of this arrangement.

Her words kept coming back to him. Echoing inside of him. All day, and every night when he reached for her.

Can I believe in you?

He found that he wanted her to believe in him, and he couldn't quite figure out why. Why should it matter that he not sweep Emerson into a web of destruction?

Why had he decided to go about marrying her in the first place when he could have simply wiped James Maxfield off the map?

But no. He didn't want to question himself.

Marrying her was a more sophisticated power play. And at the end of the day, he liked it better.

He had possession of the man's daughter. He had a stake in the man's company.

The sword of Damocles.

After all, ruination could be accomplished only once, but this was a method of torture that could continue on for a very long time.

His sense of satisfaction wasn't just because of Emerson.

He wasn't so soft that he would change direction because of a woman he'd slept with a few times.

Though, every night that he had her, he felt more and more connected to her.

He had taken great pleasure a few days ago when she broke the news to her fiancé.

The other man had been upset, but not about Emerson being with another man, rather about the fact that he was losing his stake in the Maxfield dynasty. In Holden's estimation that meant the man didn't deserve Emerson at all. Of course, he didn't care what anyone deserved, not in this scenario. *He* didn't deserve Emerson either, but he wanted her. That was all that mattered to him.

It was more than her ex-fiancé felt for her.

There was one person he had yet to call, though. Soraya. She deserved to know everything that had happened.

He was one of her very few approved contacts. She was allowed to speak to him over the phone.

They had done some very careful and clever things to protect Soraya from contact with the outside world. He, his mother and Soraya's therapists were careful not to cut her off completely, but her social media use was monitored.

They had learned that with people like her, who had built an empire and a web of connections in the digital world, they had to be very careful about cutting them off entirely, or they felt like they had been cast into darkness.

But then, a good amount of their depression often came from that public world.

It was a balance. She was actually on her accounts less now than she had been when she'd first been hospitalized.

He called, and it didn't take long for someone to answer.

"This is Holden McCall. I'm calling for Soraya."

"Your sister is just finishing an art class. She should be with you in a moment."

In art class. He would have never picked something like that for her, but then, her sense of fashion was art in and of itself, he supposed. The way she framed her life and the scenes she found herself in. It was why she was so popular online. That she made her life into art. It pleased him to know she had found another way to express that. One that was maybe about her more than it was about the broader world.

"Holden?" Her voice sounded less frantic, more relaxed than he was used to.

"Yes," he said. "It's me."

"I haven't heard from you in a while." She sounded a bit petulant, childlike and accusing. Which, frankly, was the closest to her old self he'd heard her sound in quite some time.

"I know. I'm sorry. I've been busy. But I have something to tell you. And I hope this won't upset you. I think it might make you happy."

"What is happy?" She said it a bit sharply, and he wondered if she was being funny. It was almost impossible to tell with her anymore.

He ignored that question, and the way it landed inside of him. The way that it hollowed him out.

"I got married," he said.

"Holden," she said, sounding genuinely pleased. "I'm so glad. Did you fall in love? Love is wonderful. When it isn't terrible."

He swallowed hard. "No. I've married James Maxfield's daughter."

She gasped, the sound sharp in his ear, stabbing him with regret. "Why?"

"Well, that's the interesting part," he said. "I now own some of Maxfield Vineyards. And, Soraya, I'm going to make a wine and name it after you. Because he shouldn't be able to forget you, or what he did to you."

There was silence. For a long moment. "And I'm the one that's locked up because I'm crazy."

"What?"

"Did you hear yourself? You sound… You married somebody you don't love."

"It's not about love. It's about justice. He didn't deserve to get away with what he did to you."

"But he has," she said. "He has because he doesn't care."

"And I've made him care. His daughter knows what kind of man he is now. He's lost a controlling share in his own winery. He's also lost an alliance that he was hoping to build by marrying Emerson off to someone else."

"And the cost of those victories is your happiness. Because you aren't with a woman you love."

"I was never going to fall in love," he said. "It's not in me."

"Yeah, that's what I said too. Money was the only thing I loved. Until it wasn't." There was another long stretch of silence.

"I thought you would be happy. I'm getting a piece of this for you."

"I don't… I don't want it."

"You don't…"

"You have to do what you have to do," she said.

"I guess so." He didn't know what to say to that, and for the first time since he'd set out on this course, he questioned himself.

"Holden, where is my baby? They won't answer me."

Rage and grief seized up in his chest. She had sounded better, but she wasn't. "Sweetheart," he said. "You lost the baby. Remember?"

The silence was shattering. "I guess I did. I'm sorry. That's silly. It doesn't seem real. I don't seem real sometimes."

And he knew then, that no matter what she said, whether or not she accepted this gift he'd won for her, he didn't regret it. Didn't regret doing this for his sister, who slid in and out of terrible grief so often, and then had to relive her loss over and over again. At least this time she had accepted his response without having a breakdown. But talking about Maxfield cut her every time, he knew.

"Take care of yourself," he said.

"I will," she said.

And he was just thankful that there was someone there to take care of her, because whatever she said, he worried she wouldn't do it for herself.

And he was resolved then that what he'd done was right.

It had nothing to do with Emerson, or his feelings for her.

James deserved everything that he got and more.

Holden refused to feel guilt about any of it.

Very little had been said between herself and Wren about her elopement. And Emerson knew she needed to talk to her sister. Both of her sisters. But it was difficult to work up the courage to do it.

Because explaining it to them required sharing secrets about their father, secrets she knew would devastate them. She also knew devastating them would further her husband's goals.

Because she and Holden currently had the majority ownership in the vineyard. And with her sisters, they could take absolute control, which she knew was what Holden wanted ultimately.

Frankly, it all made her very anxious.

But anxious or not, talking with her sisters was why she had invited them to have lunch with her down in Gold Valley.

She walked into Bellissima, and the hostess greeted her, recognizing her instantly, and offering her the usual table.

There wasn't much in the way of incredibly fancy dining in Gold Valley, but her family had a good relationship with the restaurants, since they often supplied wine to them, and while they weren't places that required reservations or anything like that, a Maxfield could always count on having the best table in the house.

She sat at her table with a view, morosely perusing the menu while her mouth felt like it was full of sawdust. That was when Cricket and Wren arrived.

"You're actually taking a lunch break," Wren said. "Something must be wrong."

"We need to talk," Emerson said. "I thought it might be best to do it over a basket of bread."

She pushed the basket to the center of the table, like a very tasty peace offering.

Wren eyeballed it. "Things must be terrible if you're suggesting we eat carbs in the middle of the day."

"I eat carbs whenever I want," Cricket said, sitting down first, Wren following her younger sister's lead.

"I haven't really talked to you guys since—"

"Since you defied father and eloped with some guy that none of us even know?" Wren asked.

"Yeah, since that."

"Is he the guy?" Wren asked.

"*What* guy?" Cricket asked.

"She cheated on Donovan, had a one-night stand with some guy that I now assume is the guy she married. And the reason she disappeared from my party the other night."

"You did *what*?" Cricket asked.

"I'm sorry, now you're going to be more shocked about my one-night stand and about my random marriage?"

Cricket blinked. "Well. Yes."

"Yes. It is the same guy."

"Wow," Wren said. "I didn't take you for a romantic, Emerson. But I guess I was wrong."

"No," Emerson said. "I'm not a romantic."

But somehow, the words seemed wrong. Especially with the way her feelings were jumbled up inside of her.

"Then what happened?"

"That's what I need to talk to you about," she said. "It is not a good story. And I didn't want to talk to either of you about it at the winery. But I'm not sure bringing you into a public space to discuss it was the best choice either."

"You do have your own house now," Cricket pointed out.

"Yes. And Holden is there. And… Anyway. It'll all become clear in a second."

Before the waitress could even bring menus to her sisters, Emerson spilled out everything. About their father. About Holden's sister. And about the ultimatum that had led to her marriage.

"You just went along with it?" Wren asked.

"There was no *just* about it," Emerson responded. "I didn't know what he would do to the winery if I didn't comply. And I wasn't sure about Dad's piece in it until… until I talked to him. Holden and I. Dad didn't deny any of it. He says that him and Mom have an understanding, and of course it's something he wouldn't talk about with any of us. But I don't even know if that's true. And my only option is going to Mom and potentially hurting her if I want to find out that truth. So here's what I know so far. That Dad hurt someone. Someone younger than me, someone my new husband loves very much."

"But he's only your husband because he wants to get revenge," Cricket pointed out.

"I... I think that's complicated too. I hope it is."

"You're not in love with him, are you?" Wren asked.

She decided to dodge that question and continue on with the discussion. "I love Dad. And I don't want to believe any of this, but I have to because...it's true."

Cricket looked down. "I wish that I could say I'm surprised. But it's different, being me. I mean, I feel like I see the outside of things. You're both so deep on the inside. Dad loves you, and he pays all kinds of attention to you. I'm kind of forgotten. Along with Mom. And when you're looking at him from a greater distance, I think the cracks show a lot more clearly."

"*I'm* shocked," Wren said sadly. "I've thrown my whole life into this vineyard. Into supporting him. And I... I can't believe that the man who encouraged me, treated me the way he did, could do that to someone else. To many women, it sounds like."

"People and feelings are very complicated," Emerson said slowly. "Nothing has shown me that more than my relationship with Holden."

"You do love him," Wren said.

Did she? Did she love a man who wanted to ruin her family?

"I don't know," Emerson said. "I feel something for him. Because you know what, you're right. I would never have just let him blackmail me into marriage if on some level I didn't... I... It's a real marriage." She felt her face getting hot, which was silly, because she didn't have any hang-ups about that sort of thing normally. "But I'm a little afraid that I'm confusing…well, that part of our relationship being good with actual love."

"I am not the person to consult about that kind of thing," Cricket said, taking a piece of bread out of the basket at the center of the table and biting into it fiercely.

"Don't look at me," Wren said. "We've already had the discussion about my own shameful issues."

Cricket looked at Wren questioningly, but didn't say anything.

"Well, the entire point of this lunch wasn't just to talk about me. Or my feelings. Or Dad. It's to discuss what we are going to do. Because the three of us can band together, and we can make all the controlling decisions for the winery. We supersede my husband even. We can protect the label, keep his actions in check and make our own mark. You're right, Cricket," Emerson said. "You have been on the outside looking in for too long. And you deserve better."

"I don't actually want to do anything at the winery," Cricket said. "I got a job."

"You did?"

"Yes. At Sugar Cup."

"Making coffee?"

"Yes," Cricket said proudly. "I want to do something different. Different from the whole Maxfield thing. But I'm with you, in terms of banding together for decision-making. I'll be a silent partner, and I'll support you."

"I'm in," Wren said. "Although, you realize that your

husband has the ace up his sleeve. He could just decide to ruin us anyway."

"Yes, he could," Emerson said. "But now he owns a piece of the winery, and I think ownership means more to him than that."

"And he has you," Wren pointed out.

"I know," Emerson said. "But what can I do about it?"

"You do love him," Cricket said, her eyes getting wide. "I never thought you were sentimental enough."

"To fall in love? I have a heart, Cricket."

"Yes, but you were going to marry when you didn't love your fiancé. It's so patently obvious that you don't have any feelings for Donovan at all, and you were just going to marry him anyway. So, I assumed it didn't matter to you. Not really, and now you've gone and fallen in love with this guy… Someone who puts in danger the very thing you care about most. The thing you were willing to marry that bowl of oatmeal for."

"He wasn't a bowl of oatmeal," Emerson said.

"You're right," Wren said. "He wasn't. Because at least a person might want to eat a bowl of oatmeal, even if it's plain. You'd never want to eat him."

"Oh, for God's sake."

"Well," Wren said. "It's true."

"What matters is that the three of us are on the same page. No matter what happens. We are stronger together."

"Right," Wren and Cricket agreed.

"I felt like the rug was pulled out from under me when I found out about Dad. The winery didn't feel like it would ever seem like home again. I felt rootless, drifting. But we are a team. *We* are the Maxfield label. We are the Maxfield name. Just as much as he is."

"Agreed," Wren said.

"Agreed," said Cricket.

And their agreement made Emerson feel some sense of affirmation. Some sense of who she was.

She didn't have the relationship with her father she'd thought she had. She didn't have the father she'd thought she had.

Her relationship with Holden was…

Well, she was still trying to figure it out. But her relationship with Wren and Cricket was real. And it was strong. Strong enough to weather this, any of it.

And eventually she would have to talk to her mother. And maybe she would find something there that surprised her too. Because if there was one thing she was learning, it was that it didn't matter how things appeared. What mattered was the truth.

Really, as the person who controlled the brand of an entire label using pictures on the internet, she should have known better from the start. But somehow, she had thought that because she was so good at manipulating those images, that she might be immune to falling for them.

Right at this moment she believed in two things: her sisters, and the sexual heat between herself and Holden. Those seemed to be the only things that made any sense. The only things that had any kind of authenticity to them.

And maybe how you feel about him.

Well. Maybe.

But the problem was she couldn't be sure if he felt the same. And just at the moment she was too afraid to take a chance at being hurt. Because she was already raw and wounded, and she didn't know if she could stand anything more.

But she had her sisters. And she would rest in that for now.

Chapter 14

The weeks that followed were strange. They were serene in some ways, which Emerson really hadn't expected. Her life had changed, and she was surprised how positive she found the change.

Oh, losing her respect for her father wasn't overly positive. But working more closely with her sisters was. She and Wren had always been close, but both of them had always found it a bit of a challenge to connect with Cricket, but it seemed easier now.

The three of them were a team. It wasn't Wren and Emerson on Team Maxfield, with Cricket hanging out on the sidelines.

It was a feat to launch a new sort of wine on the heels of the select label, which they had only just released. But the only demand Holden had made of the company so far was that they release a line of wines under his sister's name.

Actually, Emerson thought it was brilliant. Soraya had such a presence online—even if she wasn't in the public at the moment—and her image was synonymous with youth. Soraya's reputation gave Emerson several ideas for how to market wines geared toward the youthful jet-set crowd who loved to post photographs of their every move.

One of the first things Emerson had done was consult a graphic designer about making labels that were eminently postable, along with coming up with a few snappy names for the unique blends they would use. And of course, they would need for the price point to be right. They would start with three—Tempranillo Tantrum, Chardonyay and No Way Rosé.

Cricket rolled her eyes at the whole thing, feeling out of step with other people her age, as she had no desire to post on any kind of social media site, and found those puns ridiculous. Wren, while not a big enthusiast herself, at least understood the branding campaign. Emerson was ridiculously pleased. And together the three of them had enjoyed doing the work.

Cricket, true to her word, had not overly involved herself, given that she was in training down at the coffee shop. Emerson couldn't quite understand why her sister wanted to work there, but she could understand why Cricket felt the need to gain some independence.

Being a Maxfield was difficult.

But it was also interesting, building something that wasn't for her father's approval. Sure, Holden's approval was involved on some level, but…this was different from any other work she'd done.

She was doing this as much for herself as for him, and he trusted that she would do a good job. She knew she would.

It felt…good.

The prototype labels, along with the charms she had chosen to drape elegantly over the narrow neck of each bottle, came back from production relatively quickly, and she was so excited to show Holden she could hardly contain herself.

She wasn't sure why she was so excited to show him, only that she was.

It wasn't as if she wanted his approval, the way she had with her father. It was more that she wanted to share what she had created. The way she felt she needed to please him. This was more of an excitement sort of feeling.

She wanted to please Holden in a totally different way. Wanted to make him… Happy.

She wondered what would make a man like him happy. If he *could* be happy.

And suddenly, she was beset by the burning desire to try.

He was a strange man, her husband, filled with dark intensity, but she knew that part of that intensity was an intense capacity to love.

The things that he had done for his sister…

All of her life, really. And for his mother.

It wasn't just this, though it was a large gesture, but everything.

He had protected his mother from her endless array of boyfriends. He had made sure Soraya had gotten off to school okay every day. He had bought his mother and sister houses the moment he had begun making money.

She had done research on him, somewhat covertly, in the past weeks. And she had seen that he had donated large amounts of money, homes, to a great many people in need.

He hid all of that generosity underneath a gruff, hard exterior. Knowing what she knew now, she continually came back to that moment when he had refused to say his plan for revenge was born out of love for his sister. As if admitting to something like love would be disastrous for him.

She saw the top of his cowboy hat through the window of the tasting room, where she was waiting with the Soraya-branded wines.

He walked in, and her heart squeezed tight.

"I have three complete products to show you. And I hope you're going to like them."

She held up the first bottle—the Tempranillo Tantrum—with a little silver porcupine charm dangling from the top. "Because porcupines are grumpy," she said.

"Are they?"

"Well, do you want to hassle one and find out how grumpy they are? Because I don't."

"Very nice," he said, brushing his fingers over the gold foil on the label.

"People will want to take pictures of it. Even if they don't buy it, they're going to post and share it."

He looked at the others, one with a rose-gold unicorn charm, the next with a platinum fox. And above each of the names was *Soraya.*

"She'll love this," he said, his voice suddenly soft.

"How is she doing?"

"Last I spoke to her? I don't know. A little bit better. She didn't seem as confused."

"Do they know why she misremembers sometimes?" He had told her about how his sister often didn't remember she'd had a fairly late-term miscarriage. That sometimes she would call him scared, looking for a baby that she didn't have.

It broke Emerson's heart. Knowing everything Soraya had gone through. And she supposed there were plenty of young women who could have gone through something like that and not ended up in such a difficult position, but Soraya wasn't one of them. And the fact that Emerson's father had chosen someone so vulnerable, and upon learning how vulnerable she was, had ignored the distress she was in…

If Emerson had been on the fence about whether or not her father was redeemable…the more she knew about the state Holden's sister had been left in, the less she thought so.

"Her brain is protecting her from the trauma. Though, it's doing a pretty bad job," he said. "Every time she has to hear the truth again…it hurts her all over."

"Well, I hope this makes her happy," she said, gesturing to the wine. "And that it makes her feel like… she is part of this. Because she's part of the family now. Because of you. My sisters and I… We care about what happens to her. People do care."

"You've done an amazing job with this," he said, the sincerity in his voice shocking her. "I could never have figured out how to make this wine something she specifically would like so much, but this… She's going to love it." He touched one of the little charms. "She'll think those are just perfect."

"I'm glad. I'd like to meet her. Someday. When she is feeling well enough for something like that."

"I'm sure we can arrange it."

After that encounter, she kept turning her feelings over and over inside of her.

She was changing. What she wanted was changing.

She was beginning to like her life with Holden. More than like it. There was no denying the chemistry they shared. That what happened between them at night was singular. Like nothing else she had ever experienced. But it was moments like that one—the little moments that happened during the day—that surprised her.

She liked him.

And if she were really honest with herself, she more than liked him.

She needed…

She needed to somehow show him that she wanted more.

Of course, she didn't know what more there was, considering the fact that they were already married.

She was still thinking about what she wanted, what she could do, when she saw Wren later that day.

"Have you ever been in love?"

Wren looked at her, jerking her head abruptly to the side. "No," she said. "Don't you think you would have known if I'd ever been in love?"

"I don't know. We don't really talk about that kind of stuff. We talk about work. You don't know if I've ever been in love."

"Well, other than Holden? You haven't been. You've had boyfriends, but you haven't been in love."

"I didn't tell you I was in love with Holden."

"But you are," Wren said. "Which is why I assume you're asking me about love now."

"Yes," Emerson said. "Okay. I am. I'm in love with

Holden, and I need to figure out a way to tell him. Because how do you tell a man that you want more than marriage?"

"You tell him that you love him."

"It doesn't feel like enough. Anyone can say anything anytime they want. That doesn't make it real. But I want him to see that the way I feel has changed."

"Well, I don't know. Except… Men don't really use words so much as…"

"Sex. Well, our sex life has been good. Very good."

"Glad to hear it," Wren said. "But what might be missing from that?"

Emerson thought about that. "Our wedding night was a bit unconventional." Tearing tuxedos and getting tied up with leather belts might not be everyone's idea of a honeymoon. Though, Emerson didn't really have any complaints.

There had been anger between them that night. Anger that had burned into passion. And since then, they'd had sex in all manner of different ways, because she couldn't be bored when she shared a bed with someone she was so compatible with, and for whatever reason she felt no inhibition when she was with him. But they hadn't had a real wedding night.

Not really.

One where they gave themselves to each other after saying their vows.

That was it. She needed to make a vow to him. With her body, and then with her words.

"I might need to make a trip to town," she said.

"For?"

"Very bridal lingerie."

"I would be happy to knock off work early and help you in your pursuit."

"We really do make a great team."

When she and Wren returned that evening, Emerson was triumphant in her purchases, and more than ready to greet her husband.

Now she just had to hope he would understand what she was saying to him.

And she had to hope he would want the same thing she did.

When Holden got back to the house that night, it was dark.

That was strange, because Emerson usually got home before he did. He was discovering his new work at the winery to be fulfilling, but he also spent a good amount of time dealing with work for his own company, and that made for long days.

He looked down at the floor, and saw a few crimson spots, and for a moment, he knew panic. His throat tightened.

Except… It wasn't blood. It was rose petals.

There was a trail of them, leading from the living room to the stairwell, and up the stairs. He followed the path, down the dimly lit hall, and into the master bedroom that he shared with Emerson.

The rose petals led up to the bed, and there, perched on the mattress, was his wife.

His throat went dry, all the blood in his body rushing south. She was wearing… It was like a bridal gown, but made entirely of see-through lace that gave peeks at her glorious body underneath. The straps were thin, the neckline plunging down between her breasts, which were spilling out over the top of the diaphanous fabric.

She looked like temptation in the most glorious form he'd ever seen.

"What's all this?"

"I… I went to town for a few things today."

"I see that."

"It's kind of a belated wedding gift," she said. "A belated wedding night."

"We had a wedding night. I remember it very clearly."

"Not like this. Not…" She reached next to her, and pulled out a large velvet box. "And we're missing something."

She opened it up, and inside was a thick band of metal next to a slimmer one.

"They're wedding bands," she said. "One for you and one for me."

"What brought this on?"

He didn't really know what to say. He didn't know what to think about this at all.

The past few weeks had been good between the two of them, that couldn't be denied. But he felt like she was proposing to him, and that was an idea he could barely wrap his mind around.

"I want to wear your ring," she said. "And I guess… I bought the rings. But this ring is mine," she said, pulling out the man's ring. "And I want you to wear it. This ring is yours. I want to wear it." She took out the slim band and placed it on her finger, and then held the thicker one out for him.

"I've never been one for jewelry."

"You've never been one for marriage either, but here

we are. I know we had a strange start, but this has... It's been a good partnership so far, hasn't it?"

The work she had done on his sister's wine had been incredible, it was true. The care she had put into it had surprised him. It hadn't simply been a generic nod to Soraya. Emerson had made something that somehow managed to capture his sister's whole personality, and he knew Emerson well enough to know that she had done it by researching who Soraya was. And when Emerson asked him about his sister, he knew that she cared. Their own mother didn't even care that much.

But she seemed to bleed with her caring, with her regret that Soraya had been hurt. And now Emerson wanted rings. Wanted to join herself to him in a serious way.

And why not? She's your wife. She should be wearing your ring.

"Thanks," he said, taking the ring and putting it on quickly.

Her shoulders sagged a little, and he wondered if she had wanted this to go differently, but he was wearing the ring, so it must be okay. She let out a shaking breath. "Holden, with this ring, I take you as my husband. To have and to hold. For better or for worse. For richer or poorer. Until death separates us."

Those vows sent a shiver down his spine.

"We took those vows already."

"I took those vows with you because I had to. Because I felt like I didn't have another choice. I'm saying them now because I choose to. Because I want to. And because I mean them. If all of this, the winery, everything, goes away, I still want to be partners with you. In our lives. Not just in business. I want this to be about more than my father, more than your sister. I want it to be about us. And so that's my promise to you with my words. And I want to make that official with my body."

There were little ties at the center of the dress she was wearing, and she began to undo the first one, the fabric parting between her breasts. Then she undid the next one, and the next, until it opened, revealing the tiny pair of panties she had on underneath. She slipped the dress from her shoulders and then she began to undress him.

It was slow, unhurried. She'd torn the clothes from his body before. She had allowed him to tie her hands. She had surrendered herself to him in challenging and intense ways that had twisted the idea of submission on its head, because when her hands were tied, he was the one that was powerless.

But this was different. And he felt...

Owned.

By that soft, sweet touch, by the brush of her fingertips against him as she pushed his shirt up over his head. By the way her nimble fingers attacked his belt buckle, removing his jeans.

And somehow, *he* was the naked one then, and she was still wearing those panties. There was something generous about what she was doing now. And he didn't know why that word came to the front of his mind.

But she was giving.

Giving from a deep place inside of her that was more than just a physical gift. Without asking for anything in return. She lay back on the bed, lifting her hips slightly and pushing her panties down, revealing that tempting triangle at the apex of her thighs, revealing her whole body to him.

He growled, covering her, covering her mouth with his own, kissing her deep and hard.

And she opened to him. Pliant and willing.

Giving.

Had anyone ever given to him before?

He'd had nothing like this ever. That was the truth.

Everyone in his life had taken from him from the very beginning. But not her. And she had no reason to give to him. And if this were the same as all their other sexual encounters, he could have put it off to chemistry.

Because everybody was a little bit wild when there was sexual attraction involved, but this was more.

Sex didn't require vows.

It didn't require rings.

And it didn't feel like this.

This was more.

It touched him deeper, in so many places deep inside, all the way to his soul.

And he didn't know what to say, or feel, so he just kissed her. Because he knew how to do that. Knew how to touch her and make her wet. Knew how to make her come.

He knew how to find his pleasure in her.

But he didn't know how to find the bottom of this deep, aching need that existed inside of him.

He settled himself between her thighs, thrust into her, and she cried out against his mouth. Then her gaze met his, and she touched him, her fingertips skimming over his cheekbone.

"I love you." The words were like an arrow straight through his chest.

"Emerson…"

She clung to him, grasping his face, her legs wrapped

around his. "I love you," she said, rocking up into him, taking him deeper.

And he would have pulled away, done something to escape the clawing panic, but his desire for her was too intense.

Love.

Had anyone ever said those words to him? He didn't think so. He should let go of her, he should stop. But he was powerless against the driving need to stay joined to her. It wasn't even about release. It was about something else, something he couldn't name or define.

Can't you?

He ignored that voice. He ignored that burning sensation in his chest, and he tried to block out the words she'd said. But she said them over and over again, and something in him was so hungry for them, he didn't know how to deny himself.

He looked down, and his eyes met hers, and he was sure she could see straight inside of him, and that what she saw there would be woefully empty compared to what he saw in hers.

He growled, lowering his head and chasing the pleasure building inside of him, thrusting harder, faster, trying to build up a pace that would make him forget.

Who he was.

What she'd said.

What he wanted.

What he couldn't have.

But when her pleasure crested, his own followed close behind, and he made the mistake of looking at her again. Of watching as pleasure overtook her.

He had wanted her from the beginning.

It had never mattered what he could get by marrying her.

It had always been about her. Always.

Because he had seen her, and he could not have her, from the very first.

He had told himself he should hate her because she had Maxfield blood in her veins. Then he had told himself that he needed her, and that was why it had to be marriage.

But he was selfish, down to his core.

And he had manipulated, used and blackmailed her. He was no different than her father, and now here she was, professing her love. And he was a man who didn't even know what that was.

All this giving. All this generosity from her. And he didn't deserve it. Couldn't begin to.

And he deserved it from her least of all.

Because he had nothing to give back.

He shuddered, his release taking him, stealing his thoughts, making it impossible for him to feel anything but pleasure. No regrets. No guilt. Just the bliss of being joined to her. And when it was over, she looked at him, and she whispered one more time, "I love you."

And that was when he pulled away.

Chapter 15

She had known it was a mistake, but she hadn't been able to hold it back. The declaration of love. Because she did love him. It was true. With all of herself. And while she had been determined to show him, with her body, with the vows she had made and with the rings she had bought, it wasn't enough.

She had thought the words by themselves wouldn't be enough, but the actions without the words didn't mean anything either. Not to her. Not when there was this big shift inside her, as real and deep as anything ever had been. She had wanted for so long to do enough that she would be worthy. And she felt like some things had crystallized inside of her. Because all of those things she craved, that approval, it was surface. It was like a brand. The way that her father saw brand. That as long as the outside looked good, as long as all the external things were getting done, that was all that mattered.

But it wasn't.

Because what she felt, who she was in her deepest parts, those were the things that mattered. And she didn't have to perform or be good to be loved. She, as a person, was enough all on her own. And that was what Holden had become to her. And that was what she wanted. For her life, for her marriage. Not something as shallow as approval for a performance. A brand was meaningless if there was no substance behind it. A beautiful bottle of wine didn't matter if what was inside was nothing more than grape juice.

A marriage was useless if love and commitment weren't at the center.

It was those deep things, those deep connections, and she hadn't had them, not in all her life. Not really. She was beginning to forge them with her sisters, and she needed them from Holden.

And if that meant risking disapproval, risking everything, then she would. She had. And she could see that her declaration definitely hadn't been the most welcome.

Since she'd told him she loved him, everything about him was shut down, shut off. She knew him well enough to recognize that.

"I don't know what you expect me to say."

"Traditionally, people like to hear 'I love you too.' But I'm suspecting I'm not going to get that. So, here's the deal. You don't have to say anything. I just… I wanted you to know how I felt. How serious I am. How much my feelings have changed since I first met you."

"Why?"

"Because," she said. "Because you…you came into my life and you turned it upside down. You uncovered so many things that were hidden in the dark for so long.

And yes, some of that uncovering has been painful. But more than that, you made me realize what I really wanted from life. I thought that as long as everything looked okay, it would be okay. But you destroyed that. You destroyed the illusions all around me, including the ones I had built for myself. Meeting you, feeling that attraction for you, it cut through all this…bullshit. I thought I could marry a man I didn't even feel a temptation to sleep with. And then I met you. I felt more for you in those few minutes in the vineyard that night we met than I had felt for Donovan in the two years we'd been together. I couldn't imagine not being with you. It was like an obsession, and then we were together, and you made me want things, made me do things that I never would have thought I would do. But *those* were all the real parts of me. All that I am.

"I thought that if I put enough makeup on, and smiled wide enough, and put enough filters on the pictures, that I could be the person I needed to be, but it's not who I am. Who I am is the woman I am when I'm with you. In your arms. In your bed. The things you make me feel, the things you make me want. That's real. And it's amazing, because none of this is about optics, it's not about pleasing anyone, it's just about me and you. It's so wonderful. To have found this. To have found you."

"You didn't find me, honey. I found you. I came here to get revenge on your father. This isn't fate. It was calculated through and through."

"It started that way," she said. "I know it did. And I would never call it fate. Because I don't believe that it was divine design that your sister was injured the way that she was. But what I do believe is that there has to be a way to make something good out of something broken, because if there isn't, then I don't know what future you and I could possibly have."

"There are things that make sense in this world," he said. "Emotion isn't one of them. Money is. What we can do with the vineyard, that makes sense. We can build that together. We don't need any of the other stuff."

"The other stuff," she said, "is only everything. It's only love. It took me until right now to realize that. It's the missing piece. It's what I've been looking for all this time. It really is. And I… I love you. I love you down to my bones. It's real. It's not about a hashtag or a brand. It's about what I feel. And how it goes beyond rational and reasonable. How it goes beyond what should be possible. I love you. I love you and it's changed the way that I see myself."

"Are you sure you're not just looking for approval from somewhere else? You lost the relationship with your father, and now…"

"You're not my father. And I'm not confused. Don't try to tell me that I am."

"I don't do love," he said, his voice hard as stone.

"Somehow I knew you would say that. You're so desperate to make me believe that, aren't you? Mostly because I think you're so desperate to make yourself believe it. You won't even admit that you did all of this because you love your sister."

"Because you are thinking about happy families, and you're thinking about people who share their lives. That's never been what I've had with my mother and sister. I take care of them. And when I say that, I'm telling you the truth. It's not… It's not give-and-take."

"You loving them," she said, "and them being selfish

with that love has nothing to do with who you are. Or what you're capable of. Why can't we have something other than that? Something other than me trying to earn approval and you trying to rescue? Can't we love each other? Give to each other? That's what I want. I think our bodies knew what was right all along. I know why you were here, and what you weren't supposed to want. And I know what I was supposed to do. But I think we were always supposed to be with each other. I do. From the deepest part of my body. I believe that."

"Bodies don't know anything," he said. "They just know they want sex. That's not love. And it's not anything worth tearing yourself apart over."

"But I... I don't have another choice. I'm torn apart by this. By us. By what we could be."

"There isn't an us. There is you and me. And we're married, and I'm willing to make that work. But you have to be realistic about what that means to a man like me."

"No," Emerson said. "I refuse to be realistic. Nothing in my life has ever been better because I was realistic. The things that have been good happened because I stepped out of my comfort zone. I don't want to be trapped in a one-sided relationship. To always be trying to earn my place. I've done that. I've lived it. I don't want to do it anymore."

"Fair enough," he said. "Then we don't have to do this."

"No," she said. "I want our marriage. I want..."

"You want me to love you, and I can't. I'm sorry. But I can't, I won't. And I..." He reached out, his callused fingertips skimming her cheek. "Honey, I appreciate you saying I'm not like your father, but it's pretty clear that I am. I'm not going to make you sign a nondisclosure agreement or anything like that. I'm going to ask one thing of you. Keep the Soraya wine going for my sister. But otherwise, my share of the winery goes to you."

"What?"

"I'm giving it back. I'm giving it to you. Because it's yours, it's not mine."

"You would rather…do all of that than try to love me?"

"I never meant to hurt you," he said. "That was never my goal, whether you believe it or not. I don't have strong enough feelings about you to want to hurt you."

And those words were like an arrow through her heart, piercing deeper than any other cruelty that could have come out of his mouth.

It would've been better, in fact, if he had said that he hated her. If he had threatened to destroy the winery again. If her ultimatum had made him fly into a rage. But it didn't. Instead, he was cold, closed off and utterly impassive. Instead, he looked like a man who truly didn't care, and she would've taken hatred over that any day, because it would have meant that at least he felt something. But she didn't get that. Instead, she got a blank wall of nothing.

She couldn't fight this. Couldn't push back against nothing. If he didn't want to fight, then there was nothing for her to do.

"So that's it," she said. "You came in here like a thunderstorm, ready to destroy everything in your path, and now you're just…letting me go?"

"Your father is handled. The control of the winery is with you and your sisters. I don't have any reason to destroy you."

"I don't think that you're being chivalrous. I think you're being a coward."

"Cowards don't change their lives, don't make something of themselves the way I did. Cowards don't go out seeking justice for their sisters."

"Cowards *do* run when someone demands something that scares them, though. And that's what you're doing. Make no mistake. You can pretend you're a man without fear. You're hard in some ways, and I know it. But all that hardness is just to protect yourself. I wish I knew why. I wish I knew what I could do."

"It won't last," he said. "Whatever you think you want to give me, it won't last."

"Why do you think that?"

"I've never actually seen anyone want to do something that wasn't ultimately about serving themselves. Why would you be any different?"

"It's not me that's different. It's the feelings."

"But you have to be able to put your trust in feelings in order to believe in something like that, and I don't. I believe in the things you can see, in the things you can buy."

"I believe in us," she said, pressing her hand against her chest.

"You believe wrong, darlin'."

Pain welled up inside of her. "You're not the Big Bad Wolf after all," she said. "At least he had the courage to eat Red Riding Hood all up. You don't even have the courage to do that."

"You should be grateful."

"You don't get to break my heart and tell me I should be grateful because you didn't do it a certain way. The end result is the same. And I hope that someday you realize you broke your own heart too. I hope that someday you look back on this and realize we had love, and you were afraid to take it. And I hope you ask yourself why it was so much easier for you to cross a state because of rage than it was for you to cross a room and tell someone you love them."

She started to collect her clothes, doing her very best to move with dignity, to keep her shoulders from shaking, to keep herself from dissolving. And she waited. As she collected her clothes. Waited for her big, gruff cowboy to sweep her up in his arms and stop her from leaving. But he didn't. He let her gather her clothes. And he let her walk out the bedroom door. Let her walk out of the house. Let her walk out of his life. And as Emerson stood out in front of the place she had called home with a man she had come to love, she found herself yet again unsure of what her life was.

Except… Unlike when the revelations about her father had upended everything, this time she had a clear idea of who *she* was.

Holden had changed her. Had made her realize the depth of her capacity for pleasure. For desire. For love. Had given her an appreciation of depth.

An understanding of what she could feel if she dug deep, instead of clinging to the perfection of the surface.

And whatever happened, she would walk away from this experience changed. Would walk away from this wanting more, wanting better.

He wouldn't, though.

And of all the things that broke her heart in this moment, that truth was the one that cut deepest.

Emerson knew she couldn't avoid having a conversation with her mother any longer. There were several reasons for that. The first being that she'd had to move back home. The second being that she had an offer to make her father. But she needed to talk to her mom about it first.

Emerson took a deep breath, and walked into the sitting room, where she knew she would find her mother at this time of day.

She always took tea in the sitting room with a book in the afternoon.

"Hi," she said. "Can we talk?"

"Of course," her mom said, straightening and setting her book down. "I didn't expect to see you here today."

"Well. I'm kind of…back here. Because I hit a rough patch in my marriage. You know, by which I mean my husband doesn't want to be married to me anymore."

"That is a surprise."

"Is it? I married him quickly, and really not for the best reasons."

"It seemed like you cared for him quite a bit."

"I did. But the feeling wasn't mutual. So there's not much I can do about that in any case."

"We all make choices. Although, I thought you had finally found your spine with this one."

Emerson frowned. "My spine?"

"Emerson, you have to understand, the reason I've always resisted your involvement in the winery is because I didn't want your father to own you."

"What are you talking about?"

"I know you know. The way that he is. It's not a surprise to me, I've known it for years. He's never been faithful to me. But that's beside the point. The real issue is the way that he uses people."

"You've known. All along?"

"Yes. And when I had you girls the biggest issue was

that if I left, he would make sure that I never saw you again. That wasn't a risk I could take. And I won't lie to you, I feared poverty more than I should have. I didn't want to go back to it. And so I made some decisions that I regret now. Especially as I watched you grow up. And I watched the way he was able to find closeness with you and with Wren. When I wasn't able to."

"I just... No matter what I did, you never seemed like you thought I did enough. Or like I had done it right."

"And I'm sorry about that. I made mistakes. In pushing you, I pushed you away, and I think I pushed you toward your father. Which I didn't mean to do. I was afraid, always, and I wanted you to be able to stand on your own feet because I had ended up hobbling myself. I was dependent on his money. I didn't know how to do anything separate from this place, separate from him that could keep me from sinking back into the poverty that I was raised in. I was trapped in many ways by my own greed. I gave up so much for this. For him." Her eyes clouded over. "That's another part of the problem. When I chose your father over... When I chose your father, it was such a deep, controversial thing, it caused so much pain, to myself included, in many ways, and I'm too stubborn and stiff-necked to take back that kind of thing."

"I don't understand."

She ran a hand over her lined brow, pushing her dark hair off her face. "I was in love with someone else. There was a misunderstanding between us, and we broke up. Then your father began to show an interest, because of a rivalry he had with my former beau. I figured that I would use that. And it all went too far. This is the life I made for myself. And what I really wanted, to try and atone for my sins, was to make sure you girls had it different. But then he was pushing you to marry… So when you came back from Las Vegas married to Holden, what I hoped was that you had found something more."

Emerson was silent for a long moment, trying to process all this information. And suddenly, she saw everything so clearly through her mother's eyes. Her fears, the reason she had pushed Emerson the way she had. The way she had disapproved of Emerson pouring everything into the winery.

"I do love Holden," Emerson said. "But he…he says he doesn't love me."

"That's what happened with the man I loved. And I got angry, and I went off on my own. Then I went to someone else. I've always regretted it. Because I've never loved your father the way that I loved him. Then it was too late. I held on to pride, I didn't want to lower myself to beg him to be with me, but now I wish I had. I wish I had exhausted everything in the name of love. Rather than giving so much to stubbornness and spite. To financial security. Without love, these sorts of places just feel like a mausoleum. A crypt for dead dreams." She smiled sadly, looking around the vast, beautiful room that seemed suddenly so much darker. "I have you girls. And I've never regretted that. I have regretted our lack of closeness, Emerson, and I know that it's my fault."

"It's mine too," Emerson said. "We've never really talked before, not like this."

"There wasn't much I could tell you. Not with the way you felt about your father. And… You have to understand, while I wanted to protect you, I also didn't want to shatter your love for him. Because no matter what else he has done, he does love his daughters. He's a flawed man, make no mistake. But what he feels for you is real."

"I don't know that I'm in a place where that can matter much to me."

"No, I don't suppose you are. And I don't blame you."

"I want to buy Dad out of the winery," Emerson said. "When Holden left, he returned his stake to me. I want to buy Dad out. I want to run the winery with Wren and Cricket. And there will be a place here for you, Mom. But not for him."

"He's never going to agree to that."

"If he doesn't, I'll expose him myself. Because I won't sit by and allow the abuse of women and of his power to continue. He has two choices. He can leave of his own accord, or I'll burn this place to the ground around me, but I won't let injustice go on."

"I didn't have to worry about you after all," her mother said. "You have more of a spine than I've ever had."

"Well, now I do. For this. But when it comes to Holden…"

"Your pride won't keep you warm at night. And you can't trade one man for another, believe me, I've tried. If you don't put it all on the line, you'll regret it. You'll have to sit by while he marries someone else, has children with her. And everything will fester inside of you until it turns into something dark and ugly. Don't let that be you. Don't make the mistakes that I did."

"Mom… Who…"

"It doesn't matter now. It's been so long. He probably doesn't remember me anyway."

"I doubt that."

"All right, he remembers me," she said. "But not fondly."

"I love him," Emerson said. "I love him, and I don't know what I'm going to do without him. Which is silly, because I've lived twenty-nine years without him. You would think that I would be just fine."

"When you fall in love like that, you give away a piece of yourself," her mom said. "And that person always has it. It doesn't matter how long you had them for. When it's real, that's how it is."

"Well, I don't know what I'm supposed to do."

"Hope that he gave you a piece of him. Hope that whatever he says, he loves you just the way you love him. And then do more than hope. You're strong enough to come in here and stand up to your father. To do what's right for other people. Do what's right for you too."

Emerson nodded slowly. "Okay." She looked around, and suddenly laughter bubbled up inside of her.

"What?"

"It's just… A few weeks ago, at the launch for the select label, I was thinking how bored I was. Looking forward to my boring future. My boring marriage. I would almost pay to be bored again, because at least I wasn't heartbroken."

"Oh, trust me," her mom said. "As painful as it is, love is what gets you through the years. Even if you don't have it anymore. You once did. Your heart remembers that it exists in the world, and then suddenly the world looks a whole lot more hopeful. Because when you can believe that two people from completely different places can come together and find something that goes beyond explanation, something that goes beyond what you can see with your eyes…that's the thing that gives you hope in your darkest hour. Whatever happens with him…"

"Yeah," Emerson said softly. "I know."

She did. Because he was the reason she was standing here connecting with her mother now. He was the reason she was deciding to take this action against her father.

And she wouldn't be the reason they didn't end up together. She wouldn't give up too soon.

She didn't care how it looked. She would go down swinging.

Optics be damned.

Chapter 16

Holden wasn't a man given to questioning himself. He acted with decisiveness, and he did what had to be done. But his last conversation with Emerson kept replaying itself in his head over and over again. And worse, it echoed in his chest, made a terrible, painful tearing sensation around his heart every time he tried to breathe. It felt like... He didn't the hell know. Because he had never felt anything like it before. He felt like he had cut off an essential part of himself and left it behind and it had nothing to do with revenge.

He was at the facility where his sister lived, visiting her today, because it seemed like an important thing to do. He owed her an apology.

He walked through the manicured grounds and up to the front desk. "I'm here to see Soraya Jane."

The facility was more like high-end apartments, and

his sister had her rooms on the second floor, overlooking the ocean. When he walked in, she was sitting there on the end of the bed, her hair loose.

"Good to see you," he said.

"Holden."

She smiled, but she didn't hug him.

They weren't like that.

"I came to see you because I owe you an apology."

"An apology? That doesn't sound like you."

"I know. It doesn't."

"What happened?"

"I did some thinking and I realized that what I did might have hurt you more than it helped you. And I'm sorry."

"You've never hurt me," she said. "Everything you do is just trying to take care of me. And nobody else does that."

He looked at his sister, so brittle and raw, and he realized that her issues went back further than James Maxfield. She was wounded in a thousand ways, by a life that had been more hard knocks than not. And she was right. No one had taken care of her but him. And he had been the oldest, so no one had taken care of him at all.

And the one time that Soraya had tried to reach out, the one time she had tried to love, she had been punished for it.

No wonder it had broken her the way it had.

"I abandoned my revenge plot. Emerson and I are going to divorce."

"You don't look happy," she said.

"I'm not," he said. "I hurt someone I didn't mean to hurt."

"Are you talking about me or her?"

He was quiet for a moment. "I didn't mean to hurt either of you."

"Did you really just marry her to get back at her father?"

"No. Not only that. I mean, that's not why I married her."

"You look miserable."

"I am, but I'm not sure what that has to do with anything."

"It has to do with love. This is how love is. It's miserable. It makes you crazy. And I can say that."

"You're not crazy," he said, fiercely. "Don't say that about yourself, don't think it."

"Look where I am."

"It's not a failure. And it doesn't… Soraya, there's no shame in having a problem. There's no shame in getting help."

"Fine. Well, what's your excuse then? I got help and you ruined your life."

"I'm not in love."

"You're not? Because you have that horrible look about you. You know, like someone who just had their heart utterly ripped out of their chest."

He was quiet for a moment, and he took a breath. He listened to his heart beat steadily in his ears. "My heart is still there," he said.

"Sure. But not your *heart* heart. The one that feels things. Do you love her?"

"I don't know how to love people. How would we know what real, healthy love looks like? I believe that you loved James Maxfield, but look where it got you. Weird… We are busted up and broken from the past, how are we supposed to figure out what's real?"

"If it feels real, it is real. I don't think there's anything all that difficult to understand about love. When you feel like everything good about you lives inside another person, and they're wandering around with the best of you in their chest, you just want to be with them all the time. And you're so afraid of losing them, because if you do, you're going to lose everything interesting and bright about you too."

He thought of Emerson, of the way she looked at him. And he didn't know if what Soraya said was true. If he felt like the best of him was anywhere at all. But what he knew for sure was that Emerson made him want to be better. She made him want something other than money or success. Something deep and indefinable that he couldn't quite grasp.

"She said she loved me," he said, his voice scraped raw, the admission unexpected.

"And you left her?"

"I forced her to marry me. I couldn't…"

"She loves you. She's obviously not being forced into anything."

"I took advantage…"

"You know, if you're going to go worrying about taking advantage of women, it might be helpful if you believe them when they tell you what they want. You deciding that you know better than she does what's in her heart is not enlightened. It's just more of some man telling a woman what she ought to be. And what's acceptable for her to like and want."

"I…" He hadn't quite expected that from his sister.

"She loves you. If she loves you, why won't you be with her?"

"I…"

He thought about what Emerson had said. When she called him a coward.

"Because I'm afraid I don't know how to be in love," he said finally.

It was the one true thing he'd said on the matter. He hadn't meant to lie, he hadn't known that he had. But it was clear as day to him now.

"Look at how we were raised. I don't know a damn thing about love."

"You're the only one who ever did," Soraya said. "Look what you've done for me. Look at where I am. It's not because of me."

"No," he said. "It's because of me. I got you started on all the modeling stuff, and you went to the party where you met James…"

"That's not what I meant. I meant the reason that I'm taken care of now, the reason that I've always been taken care of, is because of you. The reason Mom has been taken care of… That's you. All those families you gave money to, houses to. And I know I've been selfish. Being here, I've had a lot of time to think. And I know that sometimes I'm not…lucid. But sometimes I am, and when I am, I think a lot about how much you gave. And no one gave it back to you. And I don't think it's that you don't know how to love, Holden. I think it's that you don't know what it's like when someone loves you back. And you don't know what to do with it."

He just sat and stared, because he had never thought of himself the way that his sister seemed to. But she made him sound…well, kind of like not a bad guy. Maybe even like someone who cared quite a bit.

"I don't blame you for protecting yourself. But this isn't protecting yourself. It's hurting yourself."

"You might be right," he said, his voice rough. "You know, you might be right."

"Do you love her?"

He thought about the way Emerson had looked in the moments before he had rejected her. Beautiful and bare. His wife in every way.

"Yes," he said, his voice rough. "I do."

"Then none of it matters. Not who her father is, not being afraid. Just that you love her."

"Look what it did to you to be in love," he said. "Don't you think I'm right to be afraid of it?"

"Oh," she said. "You're definitely right to be afraid of it. It's terrifying. And it has the power to destroy everything in its path. But the alternative is this. This kind of gray existence. The one that I'm in. The one that you're in. So maybe it won't work out. But what if it did?"

And suddenly, he was filled with a sense of determination. With a sense of absolute certainty. There was no what-if. Because he could make it turn out with his actions. He was a man who had—as Emerson had pointed out—crossed the state for revenge.

He could sure as hell do the work required to make love last. It was a risk. A damn sight bigger risk than being angry.

But he was willing to take it.

"Thank you," he said to his sister.

"Thank you too," she said. "For everything. Even the revenge."

"Emerson is making a wine label for you," he said. "It's pretty brilliant."

Soraya smiled. "She is?"

"Yes."

"Well, I can't wait until I can come and celebrate with the both of you."

"Neither can I."

And now all that was left was for him to go and make sure he had Emerson, so the two of them could be together for the launch of the wine label, and for the rest of forever.

Emerson was standing on the balcony to her bedroom, looking out over the vineyard.

It was hers now, she supposed. Hers and Wren's and Cricket's. The deal with her father had been struck, and her mother had made the decision to stay there at the winery, and let James go off into retirement. The move would cause waves; there was no avoiding it. Her parents' separation, and her father removing himself from the label.

But Emerson had been the public face of Maxfield for so long that it would be a smooth enough transition.

The moonlight was casting a glow across the great fields, and Emerson sighed, taking in the simple beauty of it.

Everything still hurt, the loss of Holden still hurt. But she could already see that her mother was right. Love was miraculous, and believing in the miraculous, having experienced it, enhanced the beauty in the world, even as it hurt.

And then, out in the rows, she was sure that she saw movement.

She held her breath, and there in the moonlight she saw the silhouette of a cowboy.

Not just a cowboy. *Her* cowboy.

For a moment, she thought about not going down.

She thought about staying up in her room. But she couldn't. She had to go to him.

Even if it was foolish.

She stole out and padded down the stairs, out the front door of the estate and straight out to the vines.

"What are you doing here?"

"I know I'm not on the guest list," he said.

"No," she said. "You're not. In fact, you were supposed to have ridden off into the sunset."

"Sorry about that. But the sun has set."

"Holden..."

"I was wondering if you needed a ranch hand."

"What?"

"The winery is yours. I want it to stay yours. Yours and your sisters'. I certainly don't deserve a piece of it. And I just thought... The one time I had it right with you was when I worked here. When it was you and me, and not all this manipulation. So I thought maybe I would just offer me."

"Just you?"

"Yeah," he said. "Just me."

"I mean, you still have your property development money, I assume."

"Yeah," he said. "But... I also love you. And I was sort of hoping that you still love me."

She blinked hard, her heart about to race out of her chest. "Yes," she said. "I love you still. I do. And all I need is you. Not anything else."

"I feel the same way," he said. "You. Just the way you are. It quit being about revenge, and when it quit being about revenge, I didn't have an excuse to stay anymore, and it scared the hell out of me. Because I never thought that I would be the kind of man that wanted forever. And wanting it scared me. And I don't like being scared."

"None of us do. But I'm so glad that you came here, though," she said. "Because if you hadn't... I thought as long as everything looked good, then it was close enough to being good. I had no idea that it could be like this."

"And if I had never met you, then I would never have had anything but money and anger. And believe me, compared to this, compared to you, that's nothing."

"You showed me my heart," she said. "You showed me what I really wanted."

"And you showed me mine. I was wrong," he said. "When I said things couldn't be fixed. They can be. When I told my sister that I came here to get revenge, she wasn't happy. It's not what she needed from me. She needed love. Support. Revenge just destroys, love is what builds. I want to love you and build a life with you. Forever."

"So do I." She threw herself into his arms, wrapped her own around his neck and kissed him. "So do I."

Emerson Maxfield knew without a shadow of a doubt, as her strong, handsome husband held her in his arms, that she was never going to be bored with her life again.

Because she knew now that it wasn't a party, a launch, a successful campaign that was going to bring happiness or decide who she was.

No, that came from inside of her.

And it was enough.

Who she was loved Holden McCall. And whatever came their way, it didn't scare her. Because they would face it together.

She remembered that feeling she'd had, adrift, like she had nowhere to go, like her whole life had been untethered.

But she had found who she was, she had found her heart, in him.

And she knew that she would never have to question where she belonged again. Because it was wherever he was.

Forever.

* * * * *

Read more from
New York Times *bestselling author Maisey Yates*
and Harlequin Desire!

Take Me, Cowboy
Seduce Me, Cowboy
Claim Me, Cowboy
Want Me, Cowboy
Need Me, Cowboy

*No one gets under Jackson Cooper's skin like
Cricket Maxfield. When he goes all in at a charity
poker match, Jackson loses their bet and becomes her
reluctant ranch hand. In close quarters, tempers
flare—and the fire between them ignites into a
passion that won't be ignored...*

Read on for a sneak peek at
The Rancher's Wager
by New York Times *bestselling author Maisey Yates!*

Cricket Maxfield had a hell of a hand. And her confidence made
that clear. Poor little thing didn't think she needed a poker face if
she had a hand that could win.

But he knew better.

She was sitting there with his hat, oversize and over her eyes, on
her head and an unlit cigar in her mouth.

A mouth that was disconcertingly red tonight, as she had clearly
conceded to allowing her sister Emerson to make her up for the
occasion. That bulky, fringed leather jacket should have looked
ridiculous, but over that red dress, cut scandalously low, giving a
tantalizing wedge of scarlet along with pale, creamy cleavage, she
was looking not ridiculous at all.

And right now, she was looking like far too much of a winner.

Lucky for him, around the time he'd escalated the betting, he'd
been sure she would win.

He'd wanted her to win.

"I guess that makes you my ranch hand," she said. "Don't worry.
I'm a very good boss."

Now, Jackson did not want a boss. Not at his job, and not in his
bedroom. But her words sent a streak of fire through his blood. Not
because he wanted her in charge. But because he wanted to show
her what a boss looked like.

Cricket was…

A nuisance. If anything.

That he had any awareness of her at all was problematic enough. Much less that he had any awareness of her as a woman. But that was just because of what she was wearing. The truth of the matter was, Cricket would turn back into the little pumpkin she usually was once this evening was over and he could forget all about the fact that he had ever been tempted to look down her dress during a game of cards.

"Oh, I'm sure you are, sugar."

"I'm your boss. Not your sugar."

"I wasn't aware that you winning me in a game of cards gave you the right to tell me how to talk."

"If I'm your boss, then I definitely have the right to tell you how to talk."

"Seems like a gray area to me." He waited for a moment, let the word roll around on his tongue, savoring it so he could really, really give himself all the anticipation he was due. "Sugar."

"We're going to have to work on your attitude. You're insubordinate."

"Again," he said, offering her a smile, "I don't recall promising a specific attitude."

There was activity going on around him. The small crowd watching the game was cheering, enjoying the way this rivalry was playing out in front of them. He couldn't blame them. If the situation wasn't at his expense, then he would have probably been smirking and enjoying himself along with the rest of the audience, watching the idiot who had lost to the little girl with the cigar.

He might have lost the hand, but he had a feeling he'd win the game.

Don't miss what happens next in…
The Rancher's Wager
by New York Times *bestselling author Maisey Yates!*

Available January 2021 wherever
Harlequin Desire books and ebooks are sold.

Harlequin.com

HARLEQUIN
DESIRE

Luxury, scandal, desire—welcome to the lives of the American elite.

Save **$1.00**

on the purchase of ANY

Harlequin Desire book.

Available wherever books are sold, including most bookstores, supermarkets, drugstores and discount stores.

Save $1.00

on the purchase of ANY Harlequin Desire book.

Coupon valid until January 31, 2021.
Redeemable at participating outlets in the US and Canada only.
Not redeemable at Barnes & Noble stores. Limit one coupon per customer.

52616929

Canadian Retailers: Harlequin Enterprises ULC will pay the face value of this coupon plus 10.25¢ if submitted by customer for this product only. Any other use constitutes fraud. Coupon is nonassignable. Void if taxed, prohibited or restricted by law. Consumer must pay any government taxes. Void if copied. Inmar Promotional Services ("IPS") customers submit coupons and proof of sales to Harlequin Enterprises ULC, P.O. Box 31000, Scarborough, ON M1R 0E7, Canada. Non-IPS retailer—for reimbursement submit coupons and proof of sales directly to Harlequin Enterprises ULC, Retail Marketing Department, Bay Adelaide Centre, East Tower, 22 Adelaide Street West, 40th Floor, Toronto, Ontario M5H 4E3, Canada.

5 65373 00076 2   (8100)0 12479

U.S. Retailers: Harlequin Enterprises ULC will pay the face value of this coupon plus 8¢ if submitted by customer for this product only. Any other use constitutes fraud. Coupon is nonassignable. Void if taxed, prohibited or restricted by law. Consumer must pay any government taxes. Void if copied. For reimbursement submit coupons and proof of sales directly to Harlequin Enterprises ULC 482, NCH Marketing Services, P.O. Box 880001, El Paso, TX 88588-0001, U.S.A. Cash value 1/100 cents.

HDCOUP15400

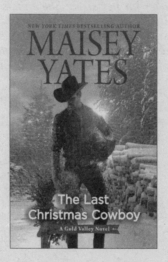

SPECIAL EXCERPT FROM

HQN

This Christmas, cowgirl Rose Daniels is determined to play matchmaker for her sister. She enlists the reluctant help of family friend Logan Heath, but his insistence that she doesn't understand chemistry is exasperating. Until they share one electrifying moment that shows her exactly what chemistry is all about…

Read on for a sneak preview of
The Last Christmas Cowboy
by New York Times *and* USA TODAY
bestselling author Maisey Yates.

There was a breath where Logan stopped. Just one. Rose's eyes went wide. Her chest hitched upward, and her lips parted.

And then he closed the distance between them.

The taste of her exploded through him, shrapnel from the impact embedding in his chest. He didn't know what he had imagined. That it might be gentle or easy because she was young. That he would have control over it because she was inexperienced and he knew it.

It wasn't gentle. It wasn't easy.

And he did not have control.

Her mouth was so damn soft, and it was the softness that he thought might bring him down to his knees.

He would brawl with any man at a bar, even if he was twice Logan's size. He would be confident in his ability to win. Strength didn't scare him.

He would test himself against a sheer rock face, and he wouldn't be intimidated. He was a man who had survived so much there wasn't a whole lot that scared him. Wasn't a whole lot he thought might be able to bring him to his knees.

But this softness could.

This softness very nearly did.

It wasn't an avalanche. Wasn't an explosion. It was like the sun. Warming him through, melting ice in his veins he hadn't even realized was there. And it hurt. Like when your hands froze solid out working without gloves and you came inside and pressed them up against a heater.

It always hurt. When feeling returned to parts of your body that had lost it.

That was this kiss.

It wasn't what he intended. The bet had been to teach her a lesson, and hell…he'd had to follow it through. And part of him wanted to punish her for torturing him, for refusing to listen. He thought to crush her mouth beneath his and make her take the desire that rioted through his chest, whether he wanted it to or not.

Instead, he found himself just holding her there, her mouth against his, immersed in that softness, damn near devastated by it.

Then she moved.

A whimper beginning in the back of her throat, her hands coming up and taking handfuls of his T-shirt. He didn't know if she was planning on pushing him away or pulling him more firmly against her. He didn't give her a chance to make the choice.

He wrapped his arm around her waist and pulled her more firmly against his body, fitting her petite curves to his chest.

He could feel her fingers tightening on his shirt, could feel the way that she tugged him to her, even just slightly.

She wasn't pushing him away.

No, she wasn't pushing him away at all.

He angled his head, slipping his tongue between her lips, and she gasped, reeling backward and stumbling away from him. Her eyes were wide, her lips flushed pink and swollen looking.

It was the most intoxicating aphrodisiac he'd ever come into contact with.

Rose. Rose Daniels, looking like a woman aroused, flushed and turned on because of him.

Don't miss The Last Christmas Cowboy
by New York Times *and* USA TODAY *bestselling
author Maisey Yates, available October 2020,
wherever HQN Books and ebooks are sold.*

HQNBooks.com

PHMYEXP0920